Peter Hilditch is a 30-year-old tea⌐ ⌐. From an early age, he used to spend man⌐ ⌐ratives with his toys, and he used to love building the ⌐t older, he enjoyed many other types of storytelling, from books, ⌐ms, or videogames. Always trying to find the best story. Eventually, he decided to write his own and there is nothing he loves more than disappearing into one of the worlds he has created.

For all the children I have worked with over the years.

Peter Hilditch

LIEUTENANT: TALES FROM THE SUPER CONTINENT

AUSTIN MACAULEY PUBLISHERS™

LONDON * CAMBRIDGE * NEW YORK * SHARJAH

A CIP catalogue record for this title is available from the British Library.

ISBN 9781528973014 (Paperback)
ISBN 9781528989619 (ePub e-book)

www.austinmacauley.com

First Published 2023
Austin Macauley Publishers Ltd®
1 Canada Square
Canary Wharf
London
E14 5AA

Thank you to my brothers, David, Andrew and Joshua, who had the unfortunate displeasure of reading my first drafts.

Prologue

In the far-flung future, the continents have continued their endlessly slow dance across the planet; once again concluding in a smashing together of the massive landmasses. Whole civilisations rose and fell as the continents meandered; they had no interest when they caused mountain ranges to ebb and flow. Forests grew and died in seconds for them. The resulting conclusion of the never-ending waltz was the creation of a super continent named Pangaea Ultima. The final landmass was the largest the world had ever experienced. The continent was so vast that rain clouds struggled to reach the centre, resulting in a sprawling desert forming in the middle. Rising out of the southern part of the continent, rich and fertile jungle grew around the equatorial line. Mountain ranges were formed on the right and left flanks of the vast kingdom. The individual continents forcing together pushed up the monoliths of stone higher than ever seen before. Life as ever endured, knowing no difference in their everyday lives.

Humanity had survived the millions of years but had become a shell of its once glorious past. Little fiefdoms and kingdoms rose and fell as the individual warlords and emperors fought each other desperate to gain dominance.

Then came the rule of King Jeroboam, the foremost fighter and general. He conquered the entire continent in a single lifetime. This was a glorious chapter in humanities' book of time. Jeroboam used his considerable influence to establish many new concepts; one economy, doing away with the confusion of multiple cultures using multiple currencies. He introduced one universal language, through the culling of several inferior dialects. But his greatest invention was the creation of the Guild. The Guild was in charge of all the knowledge of the empire; the only technology that had been passed down over the years; the knowledge of forging iron.

Unfortunately, everything has its time and the king died leaving his rule behind to his squabbling children; resulting in the immediate creation of many new kingdoms and the loss of control of the entire continent. The people were back to an era of open war between squabbling states and tribalism. Within in a hundred years the continent was back to what it once was; a seething mass of squabbling warlords and murderous despots.

Chapter 1

The super continent of Pangaea Ultima spread out onto the planet previously called Earth. At the core of the landmass was a vast and empty desert, bereft of any substantial life. Some experienced scavengers dipped in and out to find crucial resources and sell what little they could find, keeping their meagre existence going. To the west of the desert sat the King mountain range, with some of the highest mountains on Earth. The tallest points never being explored as the lack of breathable air made the trek impossible for humans to conquer. South of the huge desert was a colossal natural harbour formed by the continent stretching out to protect a large body of water. Two large rainforests sat either side of the coastline reinforced by the heat of the equator. To the west of the continent, the climate and the terrain came together to form vast areas of grasslands and large unconquered forests. It was here that one of the most important people in unrecorded history began his story.

Jesse had little interest in the rest of the world; he had not yet experienced many of these natural wonders. He was too busy trying to survive in one of the smaller fiefdoms that were dotted across the continent.

The town of Rugged sat beside a large forest to the west of the continent. The town's main supply of commerce was the forest and they were known for supplying good quality lumber to many other towns and settlements in the west, including the metropolis of Pretoria, the home of the Baron Jackson.

Jesse's morning began early; he awoke before the rise of the sun. Leaving the dilapidated dojo behind, he took off down the hill. The town was yet to awake and the sun was starting to throw its rays onto the empty canvas of black sky. Jesse passed two other competing dojos as he headed to the main gate. The large training complexes were starting to wake and Jesse saw a few trainees arriving early to impress their superiors. Each of these dojos towered over the smaller buildings sitting on either side of them. Mainly they were constructed from lumber and large wooden beams. Lady Emma ruled over one of the dojos and

Master Manish over the other, each mighty warrior educating their pupils in their style of combat.

Jesse tore past the blacksmiths' quarters situated slightly further down the road. Some of the apprentices were up, starting the fires of the forges, and he caught sight of his friend stooping over a few small embers. Jesse would catch up with him later but for now he had to be somewhere else. A defensive wall surrounded the entirety of the upper town; this too was constructed from large wooden beams sourced from the nearby lumber yard.

The stationed guards saw Jesse approaching at speed; and with the well-executed skill of completing the same action every day; they opened the small gate within the larger door quickly. Jesse flew through the opening to burst into the market district. The guards were used to seeing this figure on his morning routine so did not question why he was moving at such a speed.

There was never anyone around in the lower town at this time. As the customers didn't appear for a few hours, the shopkeepers took their time, slowly presenting their wares for maximum engagement. Small two-storey houses lined the well-trodden road each one built with a store front. The quality of the buildings' lumber was slightly worse than the higher town but regardless the houses stood tall and strong. The high street went on for another half a mile like this.

Further on, the shops thinned out to reveal residential houses for the townspeople who worked in the fields and the forest. These houses were too constructed lumber but from the off cuttings. All the timbers used were different sizes yet they had been skilfully arranged to form solid living quarters. The handiwork of the lumber smiths was on full display. The buildings too eventually gave way.

Jesse passed the cavalry barracks containing the messenger stallions, just before he entered the cultivated fields. He turned slightly at pace and made for the river where the granary mill was. The fields lay still, soaking in the early morning sunshine. He saw large crops of vegetables beginning to emerge from the cultivated soil. A straight muddy road ran through the fields and Jesse followed the highway to his destination.

The river emerged ahead through the morning mist and revealed a large building sitting on the side of the waterway. The granary had a water wheel attached which was currently turning with the slow-moving river. Jesse stopped to hammer on the ruggedly carved door; being careful to not pick up a splinter. Something he had managed to do repeatedly in the past.

The door swung open and the miller's wife appeared into view. She recognised him and smiled. The young man had slightly tanned skin from the continuous sunshine, the area received in the summertime. His black hair stood out amongst the brown and blonde hair of the average townsperson making his appearance unusual for the people living in this region. It had been suggested to Jesse in the past that his ancestry might have hailed from the south lands. For the young man who had spent his early years on the streets, this information had very little interest to him. With a quick movement the strong woman grabbed the two heavy sacks by the door and passed them over to the young man.

"Mind how you go," she said with a calm smile.

Jesse smiled back and then set his face for the feat of strength he was about to perform. Grabbing both sacks he hauled them onto his shoulders. Then he turned to make his way back into town. The young trainee was tall for his age and he still had time to grow further still. At just over six foot, Jesse was already the height of most of the men in the village. His broad shoulders aided him with the transportation of the delivery.

The journey back was significantly slower and as Jesse made his way, the town was starting to wake up. The forest workers were beginning to leave their houses steadying themselves to head towards the forest. The foresters were stony-faced, bulky men capable of felling trees several metres across. The occupation was notoriously dangerous work as accidents were prevalent. The foremen were milling around to make sure that everyone was accounted for. Several of them goaded the slower members of their teams quicker up the road. The over laden trainee was a common sight and they weaved around Jesse as he trudged closer to his goal.

The young man picked up the pace as he sensed his destination approaching. One of the first shops on the high street was the baker. Jesse headed around the back and knocked on the wooden door. It swung forward and almost took Jesse out.

"Excellent, we have just finished using the morning flour!" shouted the baker over the hustle and bustle going on in the kitchen.

He grabbed the sacks on Jesse's shoulder and hauled them across the floor. The large figure of the baker was a fearsome sight. He was dressed in his baker's whites puffing and bellowing. Evidently in the middle of his busy morning schedule, the pastry man was red in the face from the effort or the heat.

"Sloth, come and get these!" the large man shouted into the bakery.

A dishevelled scraggily boy appeared and started trying to drag the bags across the floor. The baker kicked him to hurry him up. He was about to close the door in Jesse's face but the delivery boy stood in the doorway. Jesse was a foot taller than him and much harder to push around than his usual stooge.

"Yes?" asked the baker impatiently, shooting Jesse a filthy look.

"My usual fee, please," asked Jesse, irritated he had to go through this charade every morning.

A common tactic of the baker was to 'forget' to pay his workers and Jesse had been caught out by this too many times.

The baker grabbed a lumpy bag that was sitting on the side and passed it to Jesse hurriedly, not looking the young man in the eyes. Jesse took it with a cursory nod and disappeared through the back door. He entered the main high street once again catching a sight of the baker's daughter putting out this morning's wares. They were nicely glossed and ready to enjoy for the passing customers. Not surprisingly, the baker used his daughter to sell the wares as she was far more effective than he was.

Jesse looked ahead and saw an oncoming troop of cadets. They were from the Dao dojo, experts with the finely balanced Dao sword. Only the leaders of the troop carried Dao swords; this signified their place in the warrior unit. The warriors in the dojos were allowed to carry weapons around the town. In return for this privilege, they were expected to train new recruits and to serve the lord at his pleasure. Weapons were scarce and closely monitored not only in Rugged but also across the mega continent. The construction process of such weapons was also closely guarded, the blacksmiths being the only ones with the means, knowledge and the resources. It was common law that anyone carrying a forged weapon had to be branded.

The lead warrior halted the march to talk to a passing townsperson and the trainees spread out waiting for the conversation to end. Jesse passed around them taking a wide berth to avoid any additional complications. They had a reputation for bullying outsiders of their dojo. Jesse did catch a glimpse of the lead warrior who was conversing with a passer-by. The experienced fighter's blade hung at his side and on his arm burned the brand authorising the use of such a weapon.

'A street dweller and should be treated as such.' A familiar statement Jesse had often heard hurled at him over the years. He had grown up initially on the street and had never forgotten the hostile treatment he had experienced whilst doing so. It did teach him though to keep his eyes open and to trust people's actions rather than their words.

As Jesse approached the main gate that protected the higher town from the squalor and bustle of the lower town, he gestured towards the guards on duty. The sentries perked up at his arrival. Jesse drove his hand into the bag and produced two bread cakes, misshapen but still fresh from the oven. He passed one to each of the guards on his way past, both muttered their thanks. The young man slowed as the road steepened ahead.

He approached the blacksmith area while trudging up the steeping hill. The forge apprentices had been busy while he had been gone. The fires were all blazing away and the students were feeding the wood in carefully. One of the smiths was out and about monitoring the situation.

The overseer stood close to the forges watching in silence. The hulk of a man was shaven bald allowing everyone to see his proudest feature. His face was tattooed with the Sigil of the Blacksmith guild. A hammer crossed with a scythe.

The tattoo identified him as an expert in his craft and thus untouchable. To kill anyone bearing that tattoo carried the sentence of death for the crime of losing technology. The guild was quick to exact out punishment, placing kill contracts on anyone who harmed their members. As one of the few organisations that had members all over the continent, they had the reach to mete out justice wherever they needed to.

The blacksmith had his arms folded and was watching Jesse as he wound his way through the forges. Jesse approached and offered the blacksmith the bag; he took it and tossed Jesse a pouch of small coins.

"Thanks," he muttered.

Before turning and entering the building behind him, Jesse waved to his friend Aman who was busy laying out the forge tools. The forge apprentice gave him a little smile before gesturing Jesse forward. Aman had been Jesse's friend for several years; they had met each other growing up in the back alleys of the town.

"The blacksmith you asked about before is visiting next week. Do you have the money?" Aman whispered to Jesse.

Jesse nodded before saying, "I think I do; I need to double check. Sensei needed medicine last week."

Aman nodded and then bustled away sorting out more equipment, anxious to look busy for the blacksmiths. Jesse carried on back home. *Sensei should be awake by now,* he thought to himself.

Luckily, he remembered to save one of the bread cakes to split with him. Jesse pulled the reward out and put it in the money pouch. As he passed the three other dojos, he slipped into a side street. Behind a large-looking silk shop was a much smaller, shabbier looking building. Jesse paced over to the door and walked through.

"Sensei, I've got breakfast," he called out.

Chapter 2

As Jesse entered the threshold of the old building, he felt immediate pain, a heavy blow caught him in the stomach. Jesse collapsed to his knees, the surprise attack winding him. A shadowy figure was standing next to him. The attacker swung again and Jesse reacted. Swinging his foot low and around he attempted to upset the attacker's balance. His leg swung around but it passed through thin air as the figure read the move and stepped over the desperate attack. Subsequently, the attacker was now wrong footed and Jesse made his move. He rolled to the side and aimed for the weapons rack. The rack stood dusty and in a solid state of disrepair. Laying on it were rows and rows of wooden quarter staves. Jesse reached out and grasped one. Spinning around he brought the quarterstaff into a defensive position blocking the next swinging attack.

"Sensei, I've brought breakfast," said Jesse.

His sensei appeared from the shadows that were masking his face. The old warrior was in his late fifties but the wrinkles on his face accentuated his age harshly. The fighter's piercing green eyes penetrated through the shadows being cast across the room. His hair was in dire need of a cut, as it lay thick on his shoulders, mangy and unkempt. Running down through his chin the old fighter had a scar that followed on through to his neck, a souvenir from bygone battles. Regularly the Sensei would stroke the permanent groove when considering his options or just debating a thought in his mind.

In spite of his ragged appearance, the old warrior was a patient man, who was only too happy to repeat himself frequently to his only student. Jesse also found that his Sensei had a quick mind and usually had a witty comment for any situation.

"Breakfast will have to wait; I am feeling much better this morning," said Sensei Thatcher. "It has been too long since you had a proper training session," he announced.

Jesse resigned himself to go hungry a little longer; there was no stopping the master when he was in this mood. He took up the defensive form. His right arm gripping the butt of the weapon and his left arm halfway up. Jesse steadied himself ready for the oncoming attack. However, Thatcher assumed the same position mirroring his student's form.

"You have plenty of practice at the defensive techniques, today we start on the attack," Thatcher informed Jesse. "You are capable of defending yourself against many foes. Eventually however, you will need to attack back in order to finish the fight. Come at me, cadet!"

He finished with a command and stood ready for the attack.

Jesse was taken aback momentarily. He had been taught defensive technique for the last twelve years and now suddenly the lesson was attack. Thinking back, he tried to picture Sensei's form and technique when he attacked. He had practised the attacking form on his own but never against an opponent; countless hours of him striking at shadows on walls and lifeless training dummies. Sensei had always stated that defence was the epitome of combat. So much so that other students had quit because of it, leaving Jesse the only pupil. Jesse had seen it as an opportunity to have one-on-one training regardless of the nature of the training. For many hours, over many years, he had toiled away at improving his defensive technique. Thatcher constantly critiqued his grip; his footwork; the placement of his hands; his agility; his aggressiveness and many other attributes. Now the very same master who had emphasised the importance of defence was switching up the lesson.

He must have stood too long doing nothing as the Sensei stepped forward as quickly as a striking viper. Thatcher jabbed at Jesse. Jesse blocked the blow to the side nonchalantly.

"Let's go, boy!" complained the veteran fighter impatiently.

The old fighter was now switching his body weight between each of his legs, anxiously waiting for the incoming attack.

Jesse copied the previous attack launching himself forward with one foot. His attack was slightly faster than Sensei aided by Jesse's speed and youthful strength. As quick as a whippet, Sensei blocked the incoming attack and then struck Jesse cold in the face with the end of the quarterstaff. Jesse collapsed to the floor but was soon up on his feet. He was about to complain, arguing that his master had cheated him, when he stopped himself. His teacher had little patience for excuses.

Sensei Thatcher had a small smile on his face watching his pupil wrestle with his emotions. He knew his pupil was capable of it; all the years of the same training over and over prepared him for this. The sensei stood as tall as he could; still a foot shorter than his pupil.

"Remember, the problem with attempting to finish a fight is that it can leave you open for your opponent. Now, again!"

The teacher stood back in the defensive position, both hands gripping the wooden staff ready for the incoming attack. Jesse struck again this time from the side swinging high. His opponent ducked beneath the blow and jabbed forward to counter. Jesse was prepared for it though spinning his body to the left. He used the bottom of the wooden stave to block the incoming threat.

"Excellent," announced Sensei Thatcher. "You are combining both forms. Now let us continue."

Jesse attacked again swinging low, aiming for the legs. Legs are the anchor of the fighter, Sensei had always taught. The blow was well-aimed. As it was too high to step over, the teacher was forced to block the attack. The effort of blocking a full-on blow from his student dulled the teacher's edge over his pupil. This gave Jesse another chance at attack. Bringing the back end through, Jesse attempted to catch his master in an uppercut attack. His experienced master smirked slightly before sidestepping and catching Jesse in the stomach again, winding him.

The two fighters continued for the next few hours winding away the morning. The sun rose into the sky forcing the shadows on the windowsill to shorten. The two fighters were left alone to persevere with their training. Jesse continued to be hit in various places as his wily old Sensei began to turn the screws on him. The old warrior seemed to move faster as the fight continued. Every now and then, Thatcher would offer little pieces of advice like when Jesse was telegraphing his attacks too much. The teacher was patient and impatient at the same time. He would be anxious to keep on fighting as quickly as possible, but would explain carefully how to improve Jesse's technique, with the care of an experienced teacher.

By the time the sun had reached its peak, Jesse was finished. He was totally spent. He needed to lean on the quarterstaff to help him catch his breath. Sensei Thatcher looked quite eager and fresh; Jesse was yet to land a blow.

"Don't worry," he consoled. "Attacking takes more out of you than defending. That's why I prefer to stay on the defence."

Thatcher placed his weapon back in the rack at the side of the room; the stave joining the hundred or so spare staffs that lined the room. Jesse collapsed; thankful the training was over. He swallowed large gulps of air. The muscles in his arms were screaming out for more oxygen. He lay on his back looking up at the tattered roof. He really needed to have another look at it before they had a major leak.

"Now, where is that breakfast?" asked Thatcher, flashing a smile in Jesse's direction, looking blissfully unaware he had just spent the last three hours sparring.

Chapter 3

"Now," said Sensei Thatcher, "we have somewhere we need to be this afternoon."

Jesse perked up; it was rare for Sensei to leave the dojo these days, preferring to stay inside, away from the bustle of the day-to-day. However, he did have some responsibilities as he was one of the four Lieutenants. Being a lieutenant entitled him to a seat on the town council and it also allowed him to open a dojo in his name, permitting new pupils to be trained. Thatcher had sworn an oath to Lord Faircastle promising to stay loyal to the charismatic leader till death released either one of them. All lieutenants across the continent made similar oaths before receiving the title.

Thatcher moved to the back of the dojo and selected his favourite quarterstaff; it was an intricately worked piece. Designs spiralled around the finely tuned piece of wood; some depicting famous long battles and others of long dead rulers. Apparently, the wood was from one of the rainforests from the far flung south. The wood was strong and yet had a little bit of spring, giving the fighter an edge against metal forged weapons.

Thatcher flung on a cloak making sure the tattoo on his arm was fully visible. The Sigil of Lord Faircastle was sitting fairly low down on his arm, a cutlass crossed with a quarterstaff. Further up the Sensei's arm were other sigils that had been marked out indicating the veteran fighter's past allegiances.

Jesse caught hold of his Sensei as they left the dojo. While his master was very confident moving around in his dojo, navigating around outside was much trickier on account of his weak eyes. Thatcher would describe his lack of eyesight as being hardly a hindrance as it enabled him to practice his other senses. However, Jesse was always acutely aware of how limited the range of his vision was. The old veteran was fine navigating the world in his immediate vicinity but anything that was a decent distance away was blurry to him.

Thatcher emerged onto the main street and headed up the hill towards the palace of Lord Faircastle. He had been the reigning lord for a good twenty years, expelling the previous lord by trial of combat. Most of the current lieutenants had been brought in to replace older veterans over the years.

"Theoretically, making them more loyal to him," had been what Sensei had said once.

Sensei Thatcher was the only lieutenant left from the old regime and with his failing eyesight was becoming less of an influential figure in the town.

The route up to the palace was starting to get busier as the wealthy of the town and other dojo students were also en route. Jesse and Thatcher looked quite shabby compared to the brightly dressed people of the upper town. Merchants and officials passed by them busily eager to get to the next place they were needed. Many of them chose to go around the two warriors instead of waiting for them to move faster. Amongst them were dojo trainees from other clans. They too ignored the two dishevelled fighters.

"Are we going to the trials?" asked Jesse.

"We are," replied his Sensei, sharing a smile anticipating his student's response.

Jesse's face broke into a broad smile, he had always wished to go but Thatcher had always said that he was not ready. Today was really a day of firsts, the different training and now this.

Jesse felt an increasing sense of excitement, the crowds of people were building up around them and there was a lingering tension in the air. Thatcher had always neglected to bring him to other trials before, preferring to go alone and allowing Jesse to go off and wander around the town finding food for the next meal. Jesse wondered what fighting styles he would see. Maybe he would catch a glimpse of the famous swashbuckling style touted by Lord Faircastle and his dojo or maybe the famous sword skills of the Dao sword, a much thinner blade but way more agile. The wielder of one of these weapons was capable of thrusting quickly and reacting quickly to many various situations. Thatcher could sense his apprentice's building anticipation.

"Calm yourself," he said, "and observe everything around you. Not just the fighters but the people watching. Remember, to be a great warrior is to be strong on the battlefield but also off it."

Jesse nodded, taking a deep breath and calming his heart rate. This would be a good opportunity to spot and analyse potential rivals for the future. He had become Thatcher's pupil so he had a chance to not join the ranks of the forest and field serfs but to become a mighty warrior, in his own right.

Ever since Jesse had remembered, he had looked out of the backstreets at warriors marching past, their shiny weapons glinting in the mesmerising light of the sun. They had seemed a world away for the small child begging for food in the streets. He had fallen asleep back then, on a squalid floor, with only the dreams of wielding such a weapon to warm him.

The days back then were full of desperation and trepidation. So much of the day was spent finding food or money to buy food. Due to the constant turning over of the various regimes around the continent war orphans were often created. Children separated from their parents due to death or indebted servitude, many choosing to send their children away because they did not have the resources to feed them or to help them escape their life of poverty. Workers were a resource like any other to be used and abused for many rulers. The isolated children survived by forming gangs and working together to survive.

The crowd slowed as they approached the ceremonial gates of the palace. The guards were checking the visitors making sure the entry fees were being paid. Thatcher strode around the line, Jesse following in tow. He approached the front of the queue with confidence.

One of the guards saw them approaching and looked inquisitively, wondering who this person was. Thatcher did not give the usual impressive impression of a lieutenant. The guard was clearly young; his weapon hung at his side and it looked like it had never left its scabbard. The blade clearly marked the young fighter as a fully-fledged warrior in his own right. Jesse eyed the newly forged weapon greedily. It was a Dao blade, indicating he was a pupil of Master Manish, Lieutenant of the Dao dojo.

Sensei Thatcher flashed his tattoo indicating his rank. The guard seemed surprised to see it but quickly ushered the superior officer in. Jesse followed; the students of the various dojos were invited as it was considered good experience for them.

The two quarterstaff fighters strode through the open gate into a large vacant training area. This was where Lord Faircastle's warriors trained. All the qualified fighters from the dojos gathered here to train when not on assignment.

The general crowd seeped into the seats furthest from the palace near the gate. Thatcher strode forward into the centre of the training area. On the right the students of the Dao dojo were all sitting. The senior members, proudly bearing their own forged weapons, sat towards the back. The more junior members sat on the floor eager to watch the coming action.

On the left sat the members of the Khopesh dojo. They had fewer members than the other dojos. They were experts with a peculiar curved blade or sickle-sword as other people called it. The sword started off straight from the hilt as you would expect; however, the blade curved around in a semicircle at the end. This gave them an advantage when moving at speed. Often, Lady Emma would recruit from the children of the woodcutters. They were typically giant figures capable of mighty feats of strength. Jesse noticed there were far fewer senior members sitting at the back; Lady Emma was apparently very picky who she chose to train in her fighting style.

Making up the final side of the training square was a large number of empty chairs, including four large ones and a much grander ornately carved seat. Presumably, this had been left for the reigning lord. Thatcher approached one of the large chairs and laid his cloak on it.

"Stay here," he ordered.

He gestured for Jesse to sit on the floor in front of his claimed seat. Jesse sat down, still grateful to have this opportunity to see all these wonderful fighters.

Thatcher carried on wandering up the flagstones and entered the palace. Jesse uncomfortably realised everyone was looking at him and discussing with their neighbour who this mysterious student was. The crowd of townspeople and the watching warriors conversed over who this unknown individual was. In case wandering through the middle of the training pitch wasn't enough to draw attention to him; he was the only one sitting at one end and he was sitting very close to the lord's throne.

Chapter 4

After a few minutes, the crowd went back to talking amongst themselves, ignoring the lone warrior sat on his own. The conversation turned to the fighters that they were expecting to see make an appearance. Merchants were also taking the opportunity to make future trade deals. All the big players for the town were here ready to take advantage of this monthly event.

After a lengthy period the entire crowd took to their feet. Jesse scrambled up as well turning to see a large crowd of warriors coming out of the palace. The cadets from the Falchion dojo headed for the empty fighting area and arranged themselves in neat rows. Each fighter had their own space because they were formulaically placed. Not one person was out of position. The branded warriors from the dojo, each proudly displaying their own cutlass, took their chairs. A few of them spotted Jesse standing behind them and fewer still scowled in confusion at the intruder.

A proud, hawkish man strode past the trainees and stood in front of the massing crowds of people. This experienced warrior wore thick leather armour and paced to the front of the lines. The gates to the palace court closed and everyone fell silent.

One of the trainees sitting to the side of the arena started beating a drum. The students stood to attention in a defensive pose, their wooden duelling swords poised in their hands, ready to strike out. The man at the front started weaving a strange dance, his arms swirling around him. He alone carried a forged steel weapon; his pupils all carried wooden replicas. Then as the drum beat increased, he started accelerating his moves. The beat came to a crescendo and the leader froze. As the drumbeat began again, his students started copying the movements together, this time accelerating slower.

Jesse was impressed to begin with. However, the longer it went on he realised that the students were telegraphing their moves obviously. It was entirely clear what attacks they were about to make. Jesse did not need to memorise the pattern of the actions; he could tell what attack was following after seeing each prior one. Each sweep of the arm or leg indicated where the fighter was moving next. Jesse hoped they did not fight like this when it came to actual duels as this style of practice could lead to the fighters inheriting some bad habits. The hawkish man strode around the court and joined the rest of his dojo who were now sitting down in front of Jesse. The lieutenant had bold blue eyes that stood out clearly as his long hair was tied up behind his head. The cascade of brown hair lay down the fighter's back all the way to his waist. He also wore a roughly shaved goatee.

The crowd were watching the captivating performance in silent rapture; clearly impressed with what they were witnessing. The drum beat increased and the crowd started to anticipate the crescendo. Jesse turned to realise that Sensei Thatcher was sitting behind him. Jesse fell to the floor allowing his master an unobstructed view. The lieutenant was wearing a smile and was watching the dancing fighters in front of him. The other major seats had been filled. Jesse's eyes automatically travelled to Lord Faircastle. Jesse had only caught glimpses of the ruling lord when he passed through the lower parts of the town, so he took the opportunity to examine and admire the large fighter. He was a large man with the scars of past victories on his arms. His thick brown beard tried but failed to hide a broad smile which he was wearing as he stood for the climax. The lead fighter who started the performance sat on the seat to the right. Jesse assumed that this must be Lieutenant Raúl. The beat finally ended and the fighters in the middle of the forecourt posed identically.

"Welcome!" boomed Lord Faircastle. "To the trials!"

The public crowd cheered at the announcement from the other side of the plaza. The ruler of Rugged raised his arms in response to the crowd's cheering. Jesse caught a glimpse of Master Manish sitting on his lord's left side. The master sat poised in a thinking position, he seemed to be analysing his own students, looking for weaknesses. The lieutenant had a shaved head but a long thin beard sprouting from underneath his contracted mouth. His treasured weapon was lying against his chair and Jesse noticed it was on the right-hand side, suggesting the fighter was left-handed. Jesse could not really see Mistress Emma. She sat to Manish's left on the end. She led the Khopesh dojo and rumour had it that she was one of the strongest women alive. Jesse cast a glance at the next smallest dojo to his own; all of the fighters were towering hulking specimens of humanity. While there were only thirty fighters sat on the side line, Jesse did not fancy fighting any of them in a one-on-one. A few of them were fiddling with their weapons clearly bored at the display in front of them. They had sat up straight when Faircastle spoke showing their respect for the chain of command.

"Potential recruits step forward!" announced Lord Faircastle.

Several fighters appeared from the dojo in front of him whereas only one marched over from the Khopesh dojo. Four came from the Dao clan; each one looked young and self-conscious. They lined up on the edge of the fighting area facing their liege lord.

"Congratulations for being chosen to bless this sacred pitch. Unfortunately, there can be only one winner but that winner will become a fully-fledged warrior."

With that Lord Faircastle sat down, ready for the show to begin. The draw had apparently already been decided as two of the fighters entered the arena ready to battle. Each one clutched freshly forged weapons; smelted for just this occasion. There was an uneasy pause as the fighters faced each other; one from the Falchion Dojo and the other from the Dao Dojo.

"Jesse, get up here," grumbled Thatcher.

Jesse got up and stood next to his master.

"Describe," Thatcher instructed; his aged eyes unable to make out the combat about to unfurl in front of him.

"Yes, Sensei," Jesse replied. "The two warriors are facing each other poised to attack," narrated Jesse.

"Proceed," ordered Faircastle.

The two fighters started the duel. The Dao swordsman made the first move attacking from the right. His opponent spun to deflect the effort and launch his own attack.

"They keep launching attacks at each other, Sensei," continued Jesse, "but none of them seem very fruitful."

Master Raúl, who was sat next to Thatcher, stirred in his seat.

"The brawl continues," said Jesse. "The Dao swordsman has gone for a low sweep, his opponent steps over the attack. But he's not spotted the next move."

Sure enough, the Dao swordsman was neglectful with his guard. The cutlass wielding swordsman broke through with the stronger blade and caught his opponent drawing blood in the torso. This signalled the end of the fight. Lord Faircastle stood and loudly clapped his pupil. The crowd yelled their approval at the victor.

"What did you think was the mistake?" asked Thatcher quickly.

"He wanted to finish the duel quickly but was left exposed," replied Jesse, without pausing to think.

Then he added, "The other fighter was on the verge of losing as well."

"Sounds like it," agreed Thatcher.

"A pointless observation," interrupted Master Raúl. "My swordsman clearly won."

"Yes, but his footwork was so poor, it was only a matter of time until he lost against the faster fighter," argued back Jesse.

He said it before he thought who he was talking to. While Sensei Thatcher was interested in constructive criticism the other Sensei may not have been quite so impressed. Master Raúl was about to answer before he was interrupted.

"Ha, he's got you there, Raúl!" laughed Lord Faircastle.

He leaned over and smirked at Jesse.

"But I'd watch that sharp tongue if I were you," he warned the young fighter. Jesse nodded immediately, clamping his mouth shut.

"I apologise, Master Raúl, if any offence was caused," said Sensei Thatcher. "I need to have my student narrate on account of my aging eyesight."

Jesse spotted the tiniest of smirks on his master's face.

Raúl turned away and snorted in disgust. The other preliminary fighters duelled and before Jesse knew it the first round of matches were over. Most of the fighters had seemed to be rushing themselves and were making huge errors while doing so, although there were two interesting candidates. Jesse made sure to watch them more closely over the next few rounds.

One of them was a very young fighter from the cutlass clan who seemed relaxed when he fought. He sat back and allowed his opponent to come to him. The fights were short as the youngster left his older opponents with a painful souvenir to remember him by.

The other fighter, from the Khopesh clan, was very intriguing. The tall young man launched himself forward at speed to attack. His opponents had no idea how to handle it and panicked. The Khopesh clan sang his name from the side-lines, after every victory by their man.

"Tareq, Tareq."

The crowd also loved him for his flashy style. Jesse continued to commentate making sure to keep his opinions to a minimum. He found Tareq good but could clearly see openings in his technique. Eventually, the final round came. It was between Tareq and the young fighter from the Falchion dojo, apparently called Rodrigo.

There was a break before the final. Lord Faircastle had been enjoying himself immensely. After every duel his booming clap could be heard first, echoing around the plaza.

"Mistress Emma, that Tareq of yours seems like a real beast. Good job there." Faircastle praised him. Jesse saw the lieutenant lean forward and nod to acknowledge the compliment. The female warrior was wearing her leather armour buckled up tightly. She seemed ready for a battle at any moment; attached to her side was her mighty curved blade.

"Thatcher, it's great to see you bring a student here at last," continued Faircastle. "It's been a while since I have seen you train anyone."

"It's hard to find the potential," replied Sensei Thatcher, smiling with his green eyes.

"Indeed."

Lord Faircastle smirked.

"This younger generation have never had it so good. When will we see your student fight? He is old enough."

"Oh, I don't know maybe next month," replied Thatcher.

Jesse was listening intently and then felt his stomach collapse. Was he ready for this? But before he had time to dwell on it, Lord Faircastle beckoned him forward. Jesse got to his feet, dusted himself off and approached the large inebriated man. As he got there, he caught sight of Master Raúl leaving his chair to go speak to his victorious student.

Lord Faircastle looked Jesse up and down.

"He looks like a well-built individual!" Faircastle bellowed, to anyone who was listening. "What do you think of the fights today, now that our friend Raúl has disappeared?" The last comment he directed towards Jesse.

"I'm sure my analysis will not be as astute as yours," replied Jesse.

Lord Faircastle laughed loudly.

"Well said, maybe not. Here's what I think. These fighters are very impulsive and while Tareq looks impressive he has some flaws that need patching up."

As he spoke his beady eyes pored straight into Jesse's. Jesse felt like his very soul was being excavated.

Mistress Emma bristled at the comment off to the right.

"Who are you taking for the winner?" asked Lord Faircastle.

29

Jesse thought for a moment.

"I think your dojo will win," he replied.

"That small scrap of a fighter? I don't think he's got it in him," said the lord. "I'm taking Tareq. Which reminds me…"

Lord Faircastle stood up and announced to the whole plaza.

"Let's get on with it already!" he bellowed.

There was a ripple of laughing from the civilian spectators at this.

Jesse slunk away and took his place next to his Sensei.

"Well handled," praised Thatcher.

Tareq and Rodrigo took their places in the centre before bowing to their respective lieutenants. A terse nod from Lord Faircastle indicated the start of the fight.

Tareq took off running straight at his opponent. Rodrigo blocked the strike of the Khopesh. His blade deflected off at a weird angle on account of the strange shape of the opposing weapon. The younger fighter spun to avoid being hit by Tareq as he sped past. It was at this moment that Jesse spotted something. Rodrigo was smiling confidently; he was holding something back.

Tareq turned to initiate the next attack. Digging his heels in he launched himself forward again. Rodrigo paused and then also leapt forward. Ducking under the enemy attack he sliced towards his unfortunate opponent. Tareq had nowhere to go. He could see the attack but was unable to stop himself. The attack hit home and Rodrigo was victorious. The other recruits from his dojo ran forward to congratulate one of their own.

"Hey, kid!" shouted a loud voice.

Jesse turned and caught a large coin tossed to him by Lord Faircastle.

"Good call on the win, see you next month."

The lord's voice echoed through the bustling crowd. Thatcher pulled him towards the gate forcing his way through the seething crowd.

Chapter 5

Jesse neglected to check on his winnings until he got back to the dojo. The coin had been clutched tightly all the way back within the palm of his hand. Sensei Thatcher had dragged him by the scruff of his sleeve through the milling crowd. The old man's eyesight seemed to improve whenever he wanted to get somewhere urgently.

Once they had entered the battered dojo, the old warrior went through a sliding door and fell asleep fully clothed on his bed. Jesse took the opportunity to look at the coin safely stowed away in his hand. It was a gold sovereign. On one side was the Sigil of Jeroboam; two long poles crossed in the middle. On the reverse side was the face of the last ruler to control the mega continent. The golden token was worth at least a few weeks work for Jesse.

He rushed to his quarters feeling elated at his winnings. Jesse headed to one of the beds in the room. The others stood vacant waiting for occupants that would never come. A ring of dust lay around the room and spiders spun away to themselves in the darker corners. Under the musty bed was a box. Jesse ignored it and opened up the floor underneath it. A few loose planks within the floor moved aside to reveal a dusty pouch hidden underneath.

Jesse opened it and started counting the coins on the floor, stacking them in piles till they made a single gold sovereign; for ease of counting. Jesse was left with ten piles of teetering small denominations, the one gold sovereign and a handful of smaller coins. This surely had to be enough. He packed all the money he had away and carefully slid it back under the floor. He put the handful of smaller coins in the box, as a diversion, for any snooping individuals.

Tired after the long day, Jesse fell asleep dreaming of the possibilities in the future. The cold night air swirled around him. How would he fare at the trials? Did he have enough money to be able to buy his own weapon?

The next day he woke with fervour and he headed out aiming for the granary mill again as part of his usual morning routine. He made it as far as the outer gate with the town guard posted on it.

"Hey, you are early for practice," said one of the soldiers on the gate.

Jesse stopped. The mill was not working today and neither was the bakery. One day a week the occupants of the town trained for the local militia. This was a tactical decision made by several smaller towns; it gave the people a day off work to relax but also ensured everyone could be used to defend the town if attacked. The only people who were obligated to not go were the warriors initiated by the lord. Even the town guards were instructed to go as well and lead the training.

Oh, I completely forgot, Jesse thought to himself. There would be no opportunities to earn money today. On the other hand, he would have a chance to speak to the blacksmiths about the possible price for the weapon he wanted.

Jesse left the town guards and headed back up the hill. His feet squelched through the wet mud drying in the early morning sun. He approached the blacksmith but there was no one around save some apprentices starting the fires. Jesse could smell the fumes of burning lumber wafting throughout the artisan yard. The flames of the warming smelters were slowly licking the air as they were exposed to the oxygen.

Jesse sat down and watched them work. None of these workers had the blacksmith mark yet, they were not afforded the same rights as their masters. The blacksmiths did not have to turn up to the militia training. Every now and again a few of them would take part; their great strength aiding to launch arrows across the training area and beyond.

The apprentices fed the fires stoking them to the required temperature for their masters. The flames were eager for more attention and as soon as the wood was fed in the forges fire grew in stature. After about ten minutes, Aman appeared from inside the blacksmith's quarters. Jesse got up and approached him. Aman spotted him and gave a broad smile. The two old friends shook hands as they greeted one another.

"I need to speak to your master," said Jesse. "Is it possible?"

"Good morning to you too," commented Aman.

He could see Jesse was serious so he kept the smart comments to a minimum.

"Follow me, they are having breakfast. I just finished cooking it for them." Aman stated.

He beckoned him into the large building he had just emerged from.

He turned and Jesse followed inside. The large wooden building was similar in construction to a barn. The front doors stood tall and large, each one carved from the centre of a monumentally large tree. The rafters hung in the air above Jesse's head, they crisscrossed all over the canopy of the ceiling. The open building plan meant there were no walls inside the structure. Sleeping quarters lay off to the side but Jesse's attention was on the long rows of tables and benches in the middle of the room. In the centre column of tables sat several blacksmiths, each with identical face tattoos identifying them as experts in their field. The men were broad and muscular from decades of work at the forge. They sat around talking to each other in hushed voices paying no heed to the intruder in their building.

Aman approached and Jesse stood back, waiting patiently. He felt nerves run through his body; could this be the start of his journey to becoming a mighty warrior in his own right?

"Masters, I have a potential customer," reported Aman.

The young smithy assistant stood to attention, paying undeniable respect to his masters.

Jesse could not understand the rest of the conversation. The blacksmiths started muttering to each other in a different language; forge-talk some people called it. Even Aman did not understand. He just stood there, not joining in but waiting and listening. Eventually after three or four minutes of debate, one of the blacksmiths beckoned Jesse over.

"You wish us to forge a weapon?" queried one of them using the common tongue.

The blacksmith had roughly cut thin hair and a large burn mark on his left cheek.

"Yes sir," answered Jesse.

He then stood there, not speaking and trying not to look at the blacksmith's face mark. It seemed to be shaped like the head of one of the hammers that were sitting by the forges outside.

The blacksmiths sat there waiting for more information. There was an awkward pause as no one spoke.

One of the blacksmiths interjected, "I assume it is a quarter-stave."

Jesse nodded, unsure of what to say. He was surprised they knew who he was and where he trained but they clearly did if they knew his desired weapon. Jesse had presumed that they had no idea who he was.

The first blacksmith who had spoken seemed to guess his thoughts.

"We know you train with Master Thatcher. We also are aware that you need a metal weapon to be able to compete in the trials. So, we assume that is why you are here?" the blacksmith continued.

"Yes," replied Jesse, thankful that the conversation was going in the right direction.

"Right, here's the problem," the blacksmith explained. "The skills for forging a weapon like that, we don't have. However, we can send out for an individual who does."

"I know that he is coming here in a few weeks!" blurted out Jesse suddenly.

"Do you now?" queried the blacksmith.

He looked directly at Aman when he said this, apparently guessing where the information had come from. Aman turned a shade of red and looked away.

"Regardless, we will not beat around the bush. This weapon is going to be expensive. It will contain a lot more metal than we are used to using," the blacksmith warned.

"Just at an estimate, it will cost at least thirteen gold sovereigns minimum. And that's before I know what the construction costs are going to be."

Jesse was taken aback by the cost; he would have to scramble to find the rest of the money. It was a good thing he had his winnings from yesterday which would be a great help towards the target goal.

Jesse realised the conversation was over; the blacksmiths started eating again. They turned away and started conversing to each other again in forge-talk. Jesse left the building with Aman.

"I might have got you into trouble then."

Jesse was worried, concerned if there would be any repercussions for his friend.

"It's fine," replied Aman. "They knew I was talking to you. They encourage us to have connections to the different dojos as it's good for business."

After a few moments Aman spoke again.

"Isn't it time to go to the militia anyway?"

The young worker gave Jesse an encouraging smile. Jesse nodded. Since Aman wasn't a fully-fledged blacksmith yet, he had to go as well as him.

The two friends chatted as they headed down the hill towards the giant forest nearby. Jesse talked about the trials. Aman was extremely jealous as he had never had the opportunity to go. He made Jesse describe all the match ups. Jesse showed Aman the gold sovereign he had won; for some reason he must have put it in his pocket last night. Aman was less impressed than Jesse. Apparently, he had seen several already at the forges.

"Do you think you will be able to get all the money you need together?" asked Aman.

"I guess I don't have a choice but to find a way," replied Jesse.

Aman nodded, looking away. He caught sight of one of the side streets they were passing.

"Do you remember when Bulk caught you down there?" asked Aman, flashing Jesse a smile.

"I remember rescuing you, before you were beaten to a pulp," Jesse replied, returning the smile.

"That's not how I remember it," replied Aman, arguing his case as to why he had saved Jesse.

The two old friends jibed back and forth as they made their way through the town. Jesse had met Aman on the streets and they had watched each other's backs for years. As they had grown up, each of them had fought to realise their own dreams.

As long as he could remember Jesse had always dreamed of being a warrior and protecting people. As an orphan on the streets Jesse had always tried to protect others, often to no avail. Many times, Jesse came off worse for ware, after intervening into the wrong fights with other gangs. He had even met Thatcher because of it.

As they approached the edge of the forest several guards were setting up training areas. There was a long shooting range and also a stave fighting arena. Thirty or forty wooden quarterstaffs lay unused on the floor ready for combat. A few hundred metres away were many training targets lined up in rows. Bundles of bows and countless arrows lay facing them.

Jesse always favoured the archery course; he liked the change of pace. Sensei always made him spend hours training so he enjoyed the break from the familiar routine.

"They're here early." Aman gestured.

Jesse turned and saw recruits from the Falchion guild approaching. A motley crew of warrior recruits were making their way forward towards the stave training area. Many of them Jesse recognised from living on the street.

Another reason Jesse did not train with wooden staves here was because many young recruits took the opportunity to take out their frustrations on the other members of the town. The stave training was barely monitored unlike the archery training which was quite formal and well taught by the town guards. The guards did not have the courage or the rank to go and control the troublemakers.

As potential recruits for the reigning lord's army, the troublemakers were protected from many of the crimes they committed. A blind eye was turned from them allowing the budding warriors to have free reign on the inhabitants of the town. As long as they did not go over the top, they were left mostly alone. Therefore, the normal townspeople were wary of the possible troublemakers; particularly the Falchion dojo. It had a bad reputation for breeding bullies. The Dao Dojo had a better reputation. Lady Emma's dojo though, had a spotless reputation as she made sure to keep her warriors in line.

The young recruits went straight to the wooden staves like usual. Jesse could feel some of them casting looks over their shoulders catching glimpses of him. Soon the other townspeople arrived and the training began.

The town guard started organising the general populace into groups. The first row of people moved forward and clutched their weapons. One of the guards gave a short tutorial on how to handle the bows before moving out of the way to allow the students an opportunity to open fire. A flurry of arrows flew forward; a handful of the arrows hit the target. The guard teaching moved between the archers instructing form and technique. A second wave of arrows were loosed and a few more then penetrated the straw targets. One minute later a third wave was released. A few guards retrieved the fallen arrows that had not met their target and passed them through the crowd back to the firing line. The next townsperson took over and the whole process repeated itself.

Eventually it was Jesse's turn; he had been working on his bow skills for a while and they were much improved. He could hit the target far more regularly. Now he was focusing on being more precise, the trick was to remember to take the wind and his breathing into account. Jesse loosened the first arrow and it found the edge of the target at the end of the shooting range.

"Lock another arrow!" shouted one of the guards to the entire group of archers.

Jesse complied and positioned another arrow on his well-waxed string.

"Fire," came the order, shouted over the heads of the townspeople.

Jesse released, trying to will the arrow into the centre of the target. Unfortunately, the flying shaft flew over the target and buried itself into the ground.

The third arrow was more successful and it almost hit the centre of the target. Jesse emerged from the packed lines feeling confident. He saw Aman waiting for him and headed over.

"Hey, Sloth, get over here!" shouted Aman.

Jesse saw the baker's assistant emerging from the crowds of people.

Sloth lumbered over to them thankful to find his friends. The bakery assistant often stayed with them during the practice. He was very good with a bow despite his smaller frame and had even given Aman and Jesse some good tips. Jesse shook Sloth's hand as he approached. Sloth had been abandoned by his family on the street on account of his frail body. Jesse and Aman had always tried to keep an eye out for their friend.

"Thanks for giving me the tip about the reject cakes, mate," he said to his friend.

"No worries," said Sloth. "It's not like the baker needs to have anymore, right?"

He said this with a wolfish grin on his face, surprised at himself for being brave enough to say it. He looked around to make sure the baker was not in earshot.

"Over there," said Jesse laughing and gesturing towards the stave training. The baker was laughing with some recruits from the Dao dojo at some young women training with staves.

The morning wore on. Jesse and his friends took a drink while resting on a small hill. Jesse kept casting an eye on the situation on the training area. It was getting slowly worse; the 'training' was now being taken over by the recruits. The town guards were now just focusing on the archery training. Jesse kept catching one or two of the troublemakers looking at him every couple of minutes. The townspeople took the day as an opportunity to relax and enjoy the time off. A few of them took the training seriously because they were looking for a job as a town guard. For the average merchant, the day was just an excuse to speak to their neighbours. Although the actual training was not very fruitful, it did help to create a good community atmosphere within the townspeople.

As Jesse and his friends went for one final practice, they wandered into the crowd and shoved their way to the waiting queues of archery recruits.

Suddenly, Aman grabbed Jesse by the shoulder.

"Where's Sloth?" he asked concerned.

He was scanning the crowd for their friend.

Jesse whirled around looking into the crowd of people. He heard loud sounds of cheering coming from the practice arena. Looking over, his worst fears were realised.

"He's over there."

Jesse pointed out, gesturing towards the staff training.

Aman grimaced at the concept as the two of them made their way through the crowd to find him, hoping they were incorrect about their friend's situation.

"They must have grabbed him when he went to relieve himself," suggested Aman.

"It hardly matters anymore," said Jesse. "We need to go and get him, if he's there."

Sure enough, they found Sloth standing in the middle of the training area.

Sloth had been given a staff to defend himself with. Several dojo recruits surrounded him and were approaching with their own staffs.

"Stay here," Jesse ordered swiftly to his friend.

"I can help," argued Aman.

Jesse took a moment and analysed his options.

"I will cause a distraction; you go in and grab him," the young recruit replied.

Aman nodded and thrust his way through the crowd to get to the other side of the melee of people. As the crowd was moving in to witness the potential fight, the town guards were nowhere to be seen. A few recruits were dotted throughout the crowd. Two Khopesh fighters stood tall over the crowd watching and saying nothing. A group of Dao recruits moved in closer to catch a glimpse.

Jesse stalked forward. He could feel anger swelling up inside, he was fighting hard to control the rage and maintain his rational mind. Why was no one helping prevent this one-sided battle? He caught sight of one of the sneering faces surrounding his long-time friend and his proposed plan was starting to slip from his mind.

The leaders of the bullies were now looking at Jesse approaching through the crowd.

"Give me that!" Jesse barked at a shopkeeper holding a stave.

The shopkeeper was in no hurry to argue with him and almost threw it at Jessie. The young fighter launched himself into the open arena eager for some justice.

"Hey!" he shouted.

"If you want to fight one-v-eight; I can supply that."

Everyone in the training arena moved away, leaving a large space, not wanting to become involved, but eager to watch, nonetheless. At this point all the training had stopped. There were some people still firing arrows far off who were not aware of the commotion but everyone watching fell silent. One of the trainees hit Sloth in the stomach bringing the unfortunate man to his knees.

He will be first to fall, thought Jesse. He could feel his anger coursing through the muscles in his arms and legs; he tried to shrug it off and kept his focus. The eight recruits surrounded him each waiting for someone else to strike first.

"What? Do you cowards want me to strike first?" announced Jesse, to the watching crowd.

He was trying to attract as much attention as possible giving Aman as a big a window as he could.

That did it. Jesse knew it. Questioning their bravery was so easy to exploit.

The person directly behind him swung first. Jesse blocked it simply and deftly sent the attack back at the coward. The unfortunate opponent flew backwards from the force of the retaliation. The other bullies did nothing, afraid to strike next.

Jesse stood there and laughed loud and long; the sound echoing round the silent arena. His would-be attackers seemed unsure of what to do next.

Jesse turned and looked at the leaders who were not even part of the fighters surrounding him. They stood a distance away smirking at the result of their actions.

"Can't you guys get your kicks doing something else?" Jesse announced.

"You're interrupting our fun," answered one of the leaders.

He grabbed his staff and marched forward, then accelerated swiftly and swung at Jesse's midriff. Jesse ducked underneath the blow, spun and jabbed at the coward who had hit Sloth. The blow was so fast the unfortunate precipitant did not see it coming. He fell over backwards out cold. This triggered the others to join in.

Jesse retracted his stave back to use it to block three attackers at the same time. The leader attacked again, clumsily but quickly. This blow was aimed at his head. Jesse ducked underneath and caught another attacker in the leg flooring him. A swift kick to the face finished him off.

The red mist of anger fell over Jesse's eyes. Fuelled by the injustice of the situation the young fighter moved instinctively allowing his training to flow through him. Aman and the plan were extinguished from Jesse's mind.

Jesse half turned and stepped over another attack from someone else. The bully in front of him swung hard, Jesse met it with his own. The force of the attack broke both their weakly-built staves. Jesse saw another attack coming and took the force of the blow on his hands and then ripped the stave from the owner. Using the momentum, he hit another attacker in the face with the butt of his newly claimed weapon.

Jesse spun the stave around and stepped back assessing what was left. The leader was still on his feet and four others. Four more guys lay on the floor, three out cold and one nursing a broken nose. Someone else must have been taken out by accident in the mayhem. Jesse stopped and breathed heavily clearing the adrenaline out of his system. This was going to have consequences. He noticed Aman had got in and smuggled Sloth out, no doubt taking him back to town. The rest of the bullies joined his opponents leaving ten of them altogether.

"I think it's time to go home," announced Sensei Thatcher interrupting the squalid combat.

Jesse turned to see his Sensei standing in the muddy quagmire of the training arena. The old man's eyes were lit up with anger.

Chapter 6

"Sensei," announced Jesse and he fell kneeling to the floor; his hand directing the stave to point to the sky.

Jesse's opponents fell back as Sensei Thatcher walked towards his errant pupil.

"Drop it. Your actions deny you the honour of wielding it," ordered the teacher. Jesse's weapon fell to the floor.

"Get up. We are going now."

Jesse came to his feet and started walking out of the training area, his head bowed.

Jesse's mind that had been swimming in righteous anger emptied suddenly and instantly. 'What had he been doing? Was this what his skills were meant to be used for?' Jesse had never seen his master so angry. The old warrior was barely leaning on his wooden quarterstaff; he strode ahead forcefully leading the way. Jesse had not dared to meet his eyes with his own preferring to look at his feet instead.

One of the attackers took a step forward, perhaps to interject. Thatcher fixed a look of pure wrath on him and with a flick of his wrist revealed the tattoo on his arm. The young trainee cowed immediately and fell back into his group of fighters retreating from the superior officer in his presence. The rest of the bullies turned away and merged into the crowd around them.

Jesse carried on walking. The townspeople dispersed sensing the training session to be over for the week. Jesse had a million thoughts flowing through his mind. Sensei did not like excuses and from past experiences he knew it was better to take the consequences of his actions. Thatcher pushed Jesse forward with the end of the quarter-stave.

The two of them paced onwards continuing towards the outer town gate. The passing crowd gave them a wide berth not wanting to involve themselves with the two fighters.

"This way," instructed Sensei.

He gestured past the gate and to a group of buildings outside the city with the end of his staff. Jesse followed the order, wondering where they were going, but not daring to question.

Thatcher went ahead and Jesse followed behind. The two of them wove their way through cheap residential houses until Thatcher stopped and knocked on a very ornate wooden door. The door swung open and a very old man stepped into the doorway. His beard was plaited and Jesse could see a tattoo on his head. It looked like the blacksmith guild but seemed to be two wooden chisels crossed instead. The old man beckoned them in.

Thatcher turned around and said, "Make sure that you always know a good carpenter."

After saying this, he winked at Jesse. The young fighter caught sight of a small smile sliding onto his face. Jesse relaxed slightly; perhaps some of that wrath had been an act.

Stepping into the doorway the first thing that caught Jesse's attention was the fine wooden detail on everything. Every piece of wood the shack was built out of had been finely carved with minute drawings. Not just the planks in the walls but also the wooden rafters above their heads. Jesse was surrounded by thousands of small etchings each expertly done by a skilled hand. It all reminded Jesse very acutely of Thatcher's chosen weapon.

"May I?" asked the short old man, holding out his right hand.

Thatcher tossed his sacred weapon across the small shack. The old man caught the weapon with relative ease before running his fingers all over the fine woodsmanship lying on the surface. Jesse noticed the strange man had his eyes closed as he examined his own handiwork. The carpenter broke into a broad smile. Before passing the weapon back over. The man spoke.

"Thank you, I love the memories."

There was a brief pause before the bearded man spoke again.

"Your order," and as he spoke, he waved his hand to the back of the room.

"Excellent, I hope it's top quality." Thatcher stated.

Jesse noticed his master was starting to get excited. The old man's eyes were shining in glee as if he was about to spar with his student.

"Of course," the carpenter said, with a little frown on his winkled face, as if the very idea of him doing subpar work was sheer folly.

Sat on a work bench half cast in shadow was a wooden staff. Jesse could tell this one was different; it was larger than the ones he had trained with. The staves he was used to sparring with were just over two metres but this was at least three metres in length. Thatcher strode forward and picked up the weapon. He ran his fingers all over it, examining all the natural bumps, feeling the weight and testing the balance. The wooden stave was too big for him, however. It towered over the warrior but somehow, he managed to make it look smaller with his presence alone.

"It's excellent as always, Grimshaw." He complimented.

The tiny old man nodded at the statement as if it was a concrete fact. Thatcher paid him well before complementing him further and then left with the large weapon.

As they exited the building, Thatcher said to himself loud enough for Jesse to hear, "Often a good carpenter is more important than a good blacksmith."

The two of them travelled back to the dojo, Jesse following quietly. Thatcher again led the way, carrying both staffs (the larger resting on his shoulder). The other people on the street gave them a wide berth, many of them aware of what had happened earlier. By the time they got back to the dojo, the day was morphing into night. The sun was disappearing over the horizon painting the sky in red and orange colours.

Thatcher went into the dojo and sat down in the middle of the training floor. Jesse, recognising the lesson, sat opposite him. The two of them sat in silence each contemplating their next moves. This was the sensei's way of handling disagreements. Jesse had come to appreciate the time in quiet thought. It showed that Sensei was interested in coming to an understanding but it also signalled his disagreement. As per usual Jesse waited until his teacher was ready to speak. If he instigated the conversation then the teacher would ignore him and then normally wait longer. Jesse played over his decisions in the day, was there a way to get Sloth out of there without using his skills?

"The greatest warrior is the one who has no need to be one."

This had always been the cornerstone of the Sensei's lessons. While they spent countless hours honing their combat skills, Thatcher also encouraged Jesse to solve his problems without using them at all. Jesse considered these thoughts and many more as the two warriors sat together for a good hour and a half in complete silence.

Sensei Thatcher sat in quiet serenity with his new weapon balanced on his crossed legs. He seemed to be drinking in his pupil taking in every facet of him. Every flaw and failure of his childish student flashed in his mind's eye but at the same time they fought with all the strengths and qualities portrayed within his pupil. Finally, he spoke.

"I understand the situation you found yourself in and honestly I don't know what I would have done in that situation," the old teacher spoke truthfully.

Jesse was about to speak but then decided not commenting would be smarter. He kept his gaze to the floor so he missed the flicker of a smile in his master's eyes. The teacher marvelled at his star pupil for the restraint he was showing.

"I think it is time you told me everything." Thatcher stated.

Jesse paused for a moment and then, deciding honesty was the best policy, started with his visit to the blacksmith.

"I went to the blacksmith and asked them about constructing me a weapon," he started.

The old sensei gave no reaction.

"They told me that they needed to bring in an expert to construct such a weapon. They warned me that it was going to be expensive as there would be a lot of metal used in the process. After that, Aman and I went to the village training. I like to stay away from the stave fighting as it seems to be a consistent place for conflict so I was improving my archery skills. They grabbed Sloth at some point and I went in to cause a distraction."

"Well, you succeeded," interrupted Thatcher.

Jesse paused, expecting the Sensei to continue but he sat there waiting.

"Aman went in and grabbed him while I had them all distracted," finished Jesse.

There was a pause as it seemed the old sensei was pondering the information.

"A few questions. Is he worth it, Sloth, I mean?" asked the old teacher.

Jesse felt a stirring of passion well up.

"Undoubtedly," he argued.

This time he did catch the flicker of a smile on his master's face, giving him confidence.

"But what would have happened if you had been seriously injured? It could have put an end to all the work you have put in for yourself." Thatcher debated.

"What is the point of this training if not for this type of situation?" argued back Jesse.

The Sensei, impressed with his pupil, did not speak immediately.

"Are you ready for me to be honest?" asked the old man.

Jesse nodded, confused as to what his sensei had done.

"I have failed you as a master and I apologise," Thatcher said humbly.

Jesse was unsure of what to say. How had he been failed?

"I inadvertently involved you with the politics of the situation when I signed you up for the tournament next month. This put a lot of pressure on you, so much so that you went to the blacksmith yourself. That is something that I should have been there for. The truth is I involved you as a quick quip to score an easy point against an opponent. It was not my intention to bring you to Lord Faircastle's attention just yet."

Jesse said nothing; his Sensei was being uncharacteristically loquacious.

Thatcher followed up quickly with, "I do think you are able to win though or I would not let things play out the way they did. I have been selfish with you. The truth is you were good enough to win the tournament long ago. But I wanted you around for myself. The minute Lord Faircastle sees your potential he will steal you away."

Jesse was unsure how to feel about this. Was he good enough to be one of the Lord's warriors? Why had Sensei Thatcher been holding him back? Was it envy or jealousy? Jesse took one glimpse of his Sensei and saw the old master apologising to him. He knew it was for neither of those reasons. Perhaps, the ultimate reason would emerge in the future.

"Master, I will always be loyal to you," spoke out Jesse, honestly defending the man who had taught him everything he knew.

"No, your liege Lord is Faircastle," replied Thatcher, correcting his pupil. "He has the right to see all the warriors in his dojos."

His eyes burned straight into Jesse's.

"Loyalty is the most important currency you have in this world. Promise me, Jesse. That long after I'm dead that you will continue to serve the lord. While he has his faults, they are nothing compared to other rulers."

The conversation now had an immediate serious tone. Jesse nodded, sensing the importance of this topic. Thatcher calmed himself before continuing.

"The truth is I also have been hampering you as well. You have been using the incorrect tools."

At this, Thatcher jumped to his feet. Jesse matched him; the younger fighter taller than his teacher.

"Look," said Thatcher and he gestured to their difference in height.

"You are nearly a foot and a half taller than me. It makes no sense that you use the same weapon as me. I gave you the smaller weapon to curb your growth so I could keep up with you. I wanted to see the content of your character first before instructing you in the finer techniques."

Jesse considered this new information. The quarter stave had seemed very limiting to him recently. Also, he was often worried about breaking them, so he had curbed his strength of force when training with them.

"This is a long stave and a weapon worthy of both your character and physical stature," Thatcher continued.

He passed the long staff over and Jesse took it feeling the weight and the potential tensile strength.

"From now on we train for the trials, but more importantly we train so you can protect the lord from all threats, interior or exterior." Thatcher stated.

Jesse nodded at this.

With that final statement, Thatcher strode over to the side of the dojo, retrieved his favourite stave and started back towards Jesse.

"Now. Defend yourself, my student!" barked Sensei Thatcher.

Jesse gripped the wooden staff tightly ready for the oncoming sparring session.

Chapter 7

Jesse awoke as his usual routine dictated. He rose at the breaking of the dawn and headed to the mill. This time while he was delivering the grain, he did not see Sloth. The baker gave little indication that he even noticed Jesse. He took the delivery quickly and passed Jesse a small pouch along with his usual misshapen fee. Jesse found he had been paid with a few coins as well as the dodgy unsellable bread cakes; perhaps the baker had remembered what had transpired yesterday. He shuffled off quickly with barely a word. The baker's daughter gave Jesse a smile as he disappeared. Jesse left quickly and headed straight to the blacksmiths in order to receive his usual fee. However, instead of heading back to the dojo with his money, he walked to the logging camp.

It took him a while to get there, as it was located very near the forest, some distance outside of the city. Even though it was still fairly early in the morning some workers were already there, digging new cutting trenches or sharpening their large, vicious tools. The trees they had felled yesterday still needed splitting and they used their large two-man saws to cut the trunks into more reasonable pieces for travel.

One of the men, who had a very scraggily beard, signalled Jesse so he headed over.

"We need you for conveying messages," the foreman instructed Jesse.

He indicated where Jesse should head. Some distance away from the action was a raised platform away from the forest. Five foremen were milling around setting up for the day's hard work. It was from here that the hundreds strong workforce was controlled and organised.

Jesse would be running around sending messages to the different groups of the lumberjacks. He had done this a few times before whenever the usual messenger was unavailable. The chief foreman was setting up his command post. Jesse would be working for one of the men under him. The logging workforce had two branches; one side dealt with felling trees and the other in preparing the lumber into the timber that was ordered.

The chief foreman was in charge of meeting quotas from all over the east of Pangaea. This forest was the main supply of commerce for the town. While there were many other lumber yards, this was the largest and most efficient. The rainforests to the south of the continent were also capable sources of wood except they had more dangerous animals living there. The lumber that came from there had the reputation of being cheap but unreliable.

As Jesse approached the raised platform one of the foremen leapt off it. She headed towards Jesse.

"I hear you are fast," the head foreman said.

She offered Jesse a hand to shake and he obliged.

"We have a lot of work ahead of us today so I need you to be fast on your feet."

Jesse nodded. The head foreman seemed satisfied and turned away to go and speak to some workers milling around in the distance. The head foreman stuck out from her compatriots on account of her gender but she seemed more than capable in her role. The workers respected her greatly and were quick to follow her orders.

After about half an hour, the menial workers from the town started marching into view, many of them looking as if they had just woken up. There were more foremen which herded them to their different positions organising the woodsmen into the different teams they would be working in.

One group got to work cutting the trees to manageable pieces using the cutting trenches. The workers laboured in pairs cutting the tree with a two-man saw. One of them climbed on top of the tree and cut from above and the other man sawed from below. The men took turns pulling the saw through the tree. Despite the briskness of the morning air, pretty quickly they were red in the face from the effort and sweating profusely.

"Go tell team three I want a thicker trunk!" the head foreman yelled.

She had a list of orders in her hand and was reading them while examining the trees from a distance. She seemed to be receiving instructions from the chief foreman standing next to her. He was overseeing both sides of the operation whilst the two head foremen managed their respected halves.

Jesse took off at pace and raced to get to team three. The foreman for the group had a number three on his top for reference. Jesse saw a gap in one of the worker groups and rushed through. A couple of workers were startled by him as he whipped past clearly still waking up. Jesse got to the team quickly and relayed the message. Team three had been eyeing up a thick looking tree but apparently that was not up to speck. They shrugged and headed for another bigger one further into the forest. Jesse raced back where the chief foreman had another message for him to deliver.

The morning wore away quickly for Jesse as apparently this was the day that two foremen had mixed up the jobs they were carrying out. One worker almost got crushed by a falling tree and one of the hand-saw workers got trapped under a log for a few minutes. By midday the usual messenger had arrived. He was a taller lad than Jesse and he looked lightning fast with his muscular build. Jesse got paid several silver crowns slightly more than he was owed.

"That's for putting those savages in their place," the head foreman muttered to him, before disappearing off to go yell at a delivery wagon that was late.

Jesse guessed she was referencing the incident that took place yesterday; apparently, the word had been spread around the town quickly. As he headed back into town, he noticed a lot of the residents were looking him in the eye and nodding politely to him which was a welcome change from the usual cold indifference. Jesse had always found the townspeople distant, many of them choosing to ignore him unless they needed him for something. When he was younger, scrabbling out an existence in the gutter, they had shunned him but now they were starting to acknowledge him.

The journey back to the dojo was harder as his legs were screaming with the early morning effort, he had put in. The town guards let him through, and one of them even patted him on the back, clearly impressed with him from yesterday.

"I told everyone in the tavern last night," the guard whispered to Jesse as he passed.

He made sure to check that no one else was listening before saying.

"Those brutes deserved whatever you did to them."

Thatcher's recruit trudged up the hill a little weary from the morning's work.

Jesse nodded at Aman as he walked past the blacksmith yard. The young smith saw him but made no such gesture as he was focusing on one of the blacksmiths who seemed to be lecturing about the exact order the smith tools had to be laid out in.

As Jesse entered the dojo, any happiness he had felt from this morning fled immediately. Sensei was lying on the floor face down, covered in blankets.

"Sensei!" shouted Jesse as he raced to his side.

The old man was still breathing but his heartbeat was very thin and weak.

"Where were you?" an angry voice burst out.

Jesse jumped to his feet at the intruder. A familiar face appeared from the kitchen at the back. Sensei's daughter Locke was carrying a bowl of warm water. He had known her ever since she had been old enough to travel to her father on her own. She wore her long brown hair tied back tightly in a long ponytail.

"It's your job to look after him. I can only visit every now and again," she scolded Jesse.

Kneeling down next to her father, she started mopping his forehead with a warm wet towel. Jesse did not say anything; he sat there worrying about his teacher. Thatcher had been getting more and more ill as the months passed by. This was not an illness that was getting better, if anything it was getting worse. He would periodically collapse every couple of weeks as if his body had shut down.

Locke could only visit her father every now and again as she was a warrior in another city a few days journey away. Jesse spotted her chosen weapon leaning in a rack near the door. Locke was a student of the Qiang spear and she served at the pleasure of the Baron Jackson. The leaf shaped spear head stood out among the rows of wooden staffs and around it hung a red horsehair tassel. Being a few years older than Jesse, she had a much longer time to train than him and Locke was a branded warrior in her dojo. Locke's mother had divorced Thatcher years ago and had remarried a wealthy merchant in the state's capital. Locke had been given the finest training money could buy and enrolment in the best dojo. Some of the biggest dojos required regular payments for the opportunity to learn.

Locke ignored Jesse and continued to nurse her father. Jesse knelt next to his master until early evening. Locke stopped after she felt satisfied that he was past the worst of it and then disappeared into the back to go and cook 'proper food', as she called it. Apparently what Jesse and Thatcher ate on a regular basis was not up to standard.

Eventually, Thatcher stirred and Jesse helped him sit against the closest pillar. Locke ran forward and gave him a large hug as only a daughter can give to her father. Jesse got up and started doing exercises with the long stave as Thatcher tutored him from the floor. He was starting to enjoy the longer reach it was affording him. Thatcher made him face a wooden training figure and jab at it. Jesse was to aim his strikes as close as possible without touching it. While

Jesse trained, Locke appeared with some vegetable soup. She handed a bowl to her father who accepted it gratefully. The two of them ate while Jesse trained hard, swinging away, barely scraping the training dummy.

After a while Thatcher asked, "How's your mother?"

"She's happy," said Locke.

"Good," replied Thatcher.

That was apparently all they were going to discuss between each other in regard to that topic. Thatcher switched to an easier thing to talk about.

"How's your training?" he asked her.

"Great, I'm one of the top students," Locke answered. "Mistress Lin says that I have a natural talent."

"I wonder where that came from," said Thatcher, smirking over his spoon.

Locke gave him a disapproving look.

"It comes from me working hard." She stated.

"How about trying out my pupil?" suggested Thatcher.

"He's got the trials in a few weeks' time."

"I wouldn't want to embarrass him too much," replied Locke.

She was the one with a smirk on her face now.

"Well, I bet I have higher standards than Baron Jackson," said Thatcher, with a smile on his face.

"Alright then," said Locke. "But I will make sure I go easy on your 'only' pupil."

"That is all I ask," replied Thatcher.

Both father and daughter wore a smirk now.

She got up and walked to the weapon rack; ignoring her chosen weapon and picking up a duelling wooden staff. She swung it through the air to test the weight of it out of force of habit.

"Don't be too disappointed when I mop the floor with you," she said, before taking a defensive form.

She paused with her arm in front of her and the practice staff pointing away from Jesse behind her.

Jesse turned and swung wide grasping the end of his long stave. The attack had a very long reach due to the length of the stave. Locke leaned backwards, avoiding it. The staff missed her nose by inches and then using the momentum, started forward rapidly. Jesse had to quickly move backwards to avoid her initial attack but the blow never came. Locke paused and Jesse saw another smile on her face. He retrieved his weapon and readied himself. Locke spun to the left but then jabbed forward. Jesse deflected the attack and then countered with his own. The blow went towards Locke's head. But again, as gracefully as water, she slid around the attack. This same formula played out several times. Locke would attack quickly and Jesse would block it but fail to use the moment to his advantage. The female warrior seemed to be impossible to strike. Her body would move unnaturally away from every one of Jesse's attacks.

For Jesse it felt like she was playing with him. Toying with him like a ball on the end of a string. Locke continued the random attacks but began to speed up the frequency. Before long, Jesse was standing still, continuously blocking attacks as Locke spun around him. Her movements were extremely hard to track as she moved in a unique pattern unknown to Jesse. The blows kept raining in and gave him no time to plan ahead. It was all he could do to stop them hitting him. Slowly he was starting to give way under the pressure, his feet steadily being forced backwards. Locke continued to lay down the pressure from all sides. Jesse found himself not thinking or acknowledging the attacks coming in; he blocked them on pure instinct. The world around him became a blur as the two fighters were the only thing left in existence, a mass of spinning staffs wielded by two expert fighters. The eerie moment was shattered by Thatcher.

He banged his staff on the floor indicating the end of the fight. The sensei was now on his feet. Locke broke off the engagement and spun away. Jesse fell to his knees exhausted from the combined effort of the day. Every muscle and bone were screaming out for relief. Thatcher helped him to his quarters and the young protégé fell asleep immediately on the nearest bunk.

"What did you think of him?" asked Thatcher, once he had closed the sliding door for the sleeping quarters.

"You trained him well. Towards the end I was throwing in real attacks and he blocked them decisively," replied Locke.

The young warrior replaced her practice weapon in one of the racks on the wall. She grabbed her weapon and started running through a basic training regime to help her cool down. Thatcher sat back down to watch his daughter practice. He noticed beads of sweat forming at the brow of her hair line.

"I worry about him. I haven't got much time left. The medic said the problem is my heart and the medicine can only delay it for so long," spoke Thatcher.

There was a pause between the father and daughter, neither one sure what to say. Locke turned through the air, jabbing her elegant spear at an army of invisible enemies. The horsehair tassel rotated around the tip of the spear as she moved.

"He is every bit your student. He even does that annoying thing you do and sits in silence all the time!" moaned Locke.

Thatcher smiled.

"Thanks for that. He doesn't get much competition here," he said to his daughter.

"I have to go early. I'm only here to deliver a message from the Baron. They expect me back in three days."

"I appreciate the visit. Thank you."

Silence fell as Locke continued her exercise and Thatcher fell asleep watching the drill. Lying against the pillar in the centre of the dojo, it pained him to have to mislead his devoted student and his only daughter.

Chapter 8

The following weeks for Jesse were very busy. Whenever he could, he earned more money with odd jobs. Every morning he was up early delivering the grain and then selling on the subsequent pay cheque – honey bread. He found himself doing a multitude of menial jobs. Jesse even covered for Sloth in the bakery one day when he had been too ill to work. But to Jesse all of the hard work was worth it, the opportunity to have his own forged weapon was closer than ever.

During the village training Jesse had taken charge of the stave teaching. After discussing it with the town guard, it was concluded that would be the best decision. Jesse made sure that everyone was at least training and he had put an end to the petty bullying. The other trainees from the rival dojos avoided him, choosing to practise their archery skills instead.

For Jesse, he saw it as a good opportunity to trial his teaching techniques. He would after all have to teach his own students at a certain point when he had his own dojo. He was used to learning one-on-one from Thatcher and Jesse started off teaching in a similar style. He had to abandon this quickly however, as the volume of people wishing to learn was too much to allow these one-on-one sessions. Jesse was forced to have everyone practice altogether echoing his own movements. Ironically, now he was training exactly like the Falchion dojo. For Jesse he viewed this as a failure, he did not believe that he was teaching his students very effectively at all, but this was the only option left open to him.

Thatcher was also pushing him harder and harder in training. The old warrior would take any opportunity when Jesse was not working to further educate his pupil. Thatcher focussed on Jesse's offence nearly all the time.

"If you can defend yourself against a branded warrior like Locke, you don't need much more practice in that at the moment."

Thatcher referring to the tattoo on Locke's arm only motivated Jesse to earn his own. He would throw himself wholesale into any training given to him.

Jesse would always start off jabbing at the training dummy. He had improved tremendously with his constant use of it. Now he could miss the figure by millimetres while still attacking at full power. Against Thatcher however Jesse was still struggling, the veteran warrior was painting circles around him. Jesse was yet to land a hit and Thatcher kept on finding counter blows, quickly penetrating Jesse's guard. Jesse was starting to worry about the upcoming trials; the other dojos were going to throw their best warriors at him, each young fighter hoping to achieve the rank of warrior. When Jesse confessed his thoughts to Thatcher, his Sensei seemed a lot less concerned.

"You'll be fine, you needn't worry," said the Sensei. "Your defence is definitely good enough and we are improving your offence."

Jesse still spent the time before he fell asleep worrying about losing in front of the whole town. His dreams were filled with the faces of the bullies laughing at him being beaten to a pulp by an unknown brilliant fighter.

The following morning, he almost failed to wake up and had to rush to the granary mill at top speed. He got to the bakery ten minutes late even after running flat out up the hill with the flour sacks. As each day passed Jesse felt more and more worn out, forcing his weary body to train and work endlessly.

With a week to go before the trials, Jesse and Thatcher were training in the dojo when there was a knock on the front door. Thatcher went over and answered the knocking. Jesse continued his training while keeping an eye on who the visitor was; it was rare for the dojo to receive any guests. Aman was stood there in the slowly falling rain.

"The expert blacksmith has arrived and wishes to discuss the details with you and your student," reported Aman.

He was speaking in a very formal tone to Thatcher; not knowing the old warrior as well as Jesse. The young trainee bowed his head slightly to Thatcher as he spoke to him, signalling the older man's authority.

"We will be along in a few minutes," answered Thatcher.

Aman nodded and turned away heading to deliver the message back to his masters.

"Get your things. We are going to the blacksmith," ordered Sensei Thatcher.

Jesse rushed to get the money he had saved; he had just over thirteen gold sovereigns. He kept it all in the box and carried it under his arm. Quickly grabbing a travelling cloak that was hanging on one of the beds, Jesse pulled it on. When he entered the dojo training area, Thatcher was dressed in his best clothes and carried his favourite wooden stave. He also carried a battered scroll in his hand.

"Before we go," said Sensei Thatcher, pausing for a moment.

He turned to look Jesse in the eyes.

"There will be a discussion debating price and specifications. Remember they want us to give us their business; we need to make sure we use that in our favour."

Jesse nodded; he felt a little anxious. Hopefully they would accept the money he had saved. The two of them left the dojo and headed down the street. The rain increased slightly as both fighters pulled their travelling cloaks around themselves tightly. Thatcher led them to the blacksmith guild.

There was no one outside the guild; Thatcher and Jesse strode between the anvils and forge fires. There were canvas structures built over the forges in case of poor weather. All of the workers were absent; the smith tools lay vacant waiting for a master to pick them up.

When they entered the workshop, Jesse was surprised. All of the blacksmith students were lining up along one of the walls apparently preparing to watch the following negotiations. The smiths were all sat on one side of the hall. One of the tables had been moved so they were facing the two fighters as they came in. The other wooden tables and benches had been cleared leaving the floor space empty. Thatcher took a seat on the bench opposite the blacksmiths. Jesse was about to line up behind him.

"Sit next to me," instructed Sensei Thatcher.

Jesse was surprised; he was not used to sitting at the table while the discussions were going on. He sat down facing the experienced blacksmiths. Most of them he recognised from the last time he was here. Although one was significantly different than the others, they towered over him with muscles protruding from every possible point on their bodies. The older smith was long and lean with a thin strip of beard flowing down below his chin. His muscles were still visible except they were a lot more subtle and he seemed to command a certain amount of respect from his fellow compatriots.

"Welcome," said one of the local blacksmiths.

He extended a hand forward and shook Thatcher and Jesse's hands.

"We are excited to forge this weapon for you," the smith continued.

"I'm afraid that we have to change the specifications we are looking for," said Thatcher, interrupting quickly.

He unrolled the parchment that he had been clutching in his hand. Jesse saw a blueprint for a metal long staff. On the weathered parchment was a drawing of the weapon with several labels highlighting different parts. He wondered where Sensei had got this from.

The blacksmiths all leaned forward to read the plans. Some of them were finding it hard to mask their excitement of the new potential knowledge. Thatcher passed it forward and gave it to the old thin blacksmith. He took it rapidly and muttered something in forge-talk to his fellow smiths. The old blacksmith's aged eyes broke into life as they examined this previously unknown document. The other smiths either side of him leaned in to examine the scroll.

"Intriguing," the old blacksmith said in the common tongue. "These are old specifications, but just to check you are now looking for a long stave not a quarter stave."

"We are," replied Thatcher, firmly.

"Well, just to warn you the price is going to rise."

Thatcher didn't react. Jesse panicked momentarily but he looked over to his Sensei and the calm being displayed on his master's face relaxed him.

"Can I ask, where did you get the plans from?" inquired one of the other blacksmiths.

"They were passed down to me from my Sensei," replied Thatcher.

"Hmmm," commented the blacksmith.

"I am very excited to start forging this weapon for you," carried on the old blacksmith.

He was still eyeing up the old document, he seemed to have burst into life once he had seen the plans. The old blacksmith's face was split in half by a broad smile which seemed to be stuck there permanently.

"Unfortunately, the price is going to be twenty sovereigns."

"For me that seems too high," replied Thatcher. "I've given you those plans to look at. That is a document that includes a lot of information and I am willing to bet there is knowledge on there that you did not even know."

Thatcher's tone was becoming more and more firm and this was accentuated by his voice echoing back off the high ceiling. The old warrior got to his feet.

"This new weapon is not particularly complicated to forge as you do not have to make a sharp edge. Now, I understand that you need to get the combination of elements correct for the compound metal. However, with all these factors the price does not need to be that high."

Thatcher stopped and then sat back on the bench using his quarter stave to steady himself. Jesse continued to sit in silence also, the two of them putting on a brave front.

The blacksmiths opposite started discussing with each other in their own dialect. As they debated in forge-talk, the old blacksmith said nothing sitting in the middle. Eventually the conversation ended and one of the other blacksmiths spoke.

"The price will be eighteen gold sovereigns."

Thatcher paused for a moment before saying, "Fourteen."

One of the blacksmiths on the end snorted at this and started arguing with his fellow smiths again.

The old blacksmith stood up causing the others to fall silent watching the old smith.

"I'm going to be honest with you. I do not get to create a weapon like this very often at all."

The old blacksmith paused for a moment before continuing. "The blueprints are very useful indeed. If you would let us keep them then I can authorise fourteen sovereigns."

"Master," Jesse whispered to Thatcher, "May I?"

A thought had just come to him.

Thatcher sat back and gestured for Jesse to continue.

"I am happy with fourteen. However, I want Aman to help forge it."

The old man looked a little taken aback; clearly unsure of whom Jesse was talking about. Jesse caught sight of Aman lined up on the right-hand wall, he looked shocked.

"He would have to be made a smith for that to happen," said the blacksmith on the end.

The large man seemed to find this idea outrageous.

Then the blacksmiths fell into an even louder conversation. Thatcher sat there not reacting allowing his pupil to finish the negotiations.

"Done," announced the old smith, interjecting the argument and shaking Jesse's hand immediately.

He seemed almost eager to finish negotiations. The other smiths burst into uproar again arguing with each other and with the old smith.

The old man walked round the table approaching Jesse.

"I prefer to make the deal with the recipient of the weapon," he said. "You drive a hard bargain, young warrior."

"Oh, I'm not a warrior yet," corrected Jesse.

"You will be with the weapon I am making for you," announced the old blacksmith and one of his long bushy white eyebrows lifted up to fix an eye on the young fighter.

He seemed to be eying up Jesse almost as if he was taking in his measurements for a new tunic.

Jesse handed him his box of money that he had worked so hard for.

"This is just over thirteen," he said, getting ready to apologise for the missing money.

"Here," said Thatcher and he handed Jesse a purse filled with silver sovereigns.

Jesse was startled. *Where did Sensei get the money?* The old smith took the box and shook hands with Jesse again.

"I'm looking forward to this," he said. "I've not forged a staff like this for twenty years."

Aman ran over during the chaos. He hugged Jesse like a cave bear.

"I'm going to become a smith," he said; tears streaming down his face.

Chapter 9

Over the next few days, Jesse and Thatcher trained even harder. Jesse only left the dojo early in the morning to complete his usual grain delivery. Thatcher focused further on Jesse's offence, drilling into him the perfect technique and reminding him that his footwork needed to improve. They would only have a few days with the forged weapon until the trials.

Jesse was feeling more and more confident as the days fell away. Every now and again he would slip an attack under Thatcher's guard and the old master would have to physically dodge the attack. The other day he almost hit his master, the attack brushing his shoulder. Thatcher bounced to his feet and Jesse thought he was about to be scolded. But the sensei congratulated him; apparently Jesse used the length advantage of his weapon correctly. That evening Jesse attempted on his own to re-create the scenario but he could not quite work out what he had managed to do.

On the evening of the third day, the two of them were training hard when there was a knock on the door. Jesse opened it while Sensei Thatcher rested for a moment. There was a blacksmith trainee who bowed when he saw Jesse.

"Your weapon is ready," he reported. "Please, feel free to pick it up whenever you wish."

The trainee disappeared down the alley and Jesse turned around to report the news.

"Can we pick it up now, please?" begged Jesse; he was desperate to get his hands on it.

Thatcher would have to go with him to get the long stave as he was unable to walk the street with the weapon. The old man took a deep breath and nodded.

Jesse ran to his quarters to get changed, his adrenaline surging. He rushed to the door ready to go. Thatcher walked over slowly apparently taking in the moment. Clutching Jesse's shoulder the two of them left the dojo.

It took them a few minutes to get to the blacksmith quarters. Jesse was trying to rush them but Thatcher refused to walk any faster than normal. One of the trainees saw them coming and hurried inside.

There was one blacksmith hammering away on a blade lying on an anvil. Several trainees were gathered around assisting him in various ways; one feeding the forge fire, one handing the smith tools and another two watching intently. The blacksmith ignored the two visitors as they passed him. He carried on hammering away, all of his attention on his masterful creation.

Jesse and Thatcher entered the main building. There was a committee waiting for them inside. The old blacksmith was resting inside and sitting next to him was Aman. Aman was sporting a brand-new tattoo on his skull. His normal hair had been shaved off, but replacing it was the crest of the blacksmith guild. It had been branded on his face as well signifying his importance to the guild. He looked very tired as if he had not slept for many nights. Resting on the table was a weapon and Jesse's eyes were drawn towards it. The long staff glinted in the firelight from across the room. At the sight of it, Jesse's heart skipped several beats; it was a work of art. Each facet of the pole had been meticulously worked on. Several symbols formed together to forge a pattern that flowed from one of the ends that fell down the shaft. The streams of detail intertwined with each other before meeting together at the other end. For Jesse the weapon was breathtaking and it belonged to him. Him!

Thatcher sat down opposite and Jesse, after a moment, joined him sitting on his right.

The old blacksmith spoke; he too looked very tired and exhausted.

"Your order is completed; may the weapon serve you well."

Aman picked up the metallic stave and passed it forward. Thatcher took it politely.

"We take receipt of the weapon. Thank you for the hard work and the experience you have poured into it," Thatcher replied.

With that the handover ceremony was over and the tension broke over all the people sitting there. Thatcher immediately passed the weapon to Jesse.

"You cannot leave this building with this weapon," he warned.

Jesse nodded, barely listening. He was far too interested in the weapon in front of him. It was the same length as his wooden long staff. Somehow though it was only slightly heavier which was strange. Surely it would be much heavier as it was made from metal. He weighed it in his hands, imagining the patterns of attack he used. How would this affect them?

Aman rushed around the table and hugged his friend.

"Thank you so much mate," he said. "You have given me my dream. He's taking me back to Blacksmith HQ."

Jesse broke into a smile for his oldest friend; he was glad that Aman was achieving his long-held dream.

For as long as Jesse had known him, they had both watched the warriors march through the streets. Jesse had wanted to wield their forged weapons but Aman had wanted to forge them himself. They had countless arguments about what was better, wielding or forging the weapon. Jesse had always maintained owning the weapon was more important.

Aman always retaliated with, "Yes, but you will only have one, I will have thousands."

"How does it weigh so little?" asked Jesse, his attention focusing once again on the magnificent creation in his hands.

"I'm not allowed to say much, it involves mixing metals," Aman replied.

He refused to say any more than that. Thatcher was shaking hands with the old blacksmith. They stood back and watched the young warrior start drills in front of them. The old blacksmith stood there with a broad smile on his face, enjoying this moment for the young man.

Jesse stopped drilling and bowed low before the expert blacksmith.

"Thank you very much," he said.

"It was a pleasure; I do not get the opportunity to forge these types of weapons often," replied the old man. "I saw it as an education for myself as well as for my new blacksmith brother."

He laid his hand on Aman's shoulder. The youngest blacksmith in the town had joined him.

"I only know of about five such weapons in existence and I forged three of them. Yours, however, is unique because I have never forged a staff this long before. Enjoy the weapon, young warrior, and remember. The path to being a tyrant is often the easiest," the old man warned the young fighter.

Jesse saw the intensity in his eyes and it brought his euphoria back under control.

Jesse passed the weapon back to Thatcher. The two of them gave their final thanks and they left to continue their training. Jesse felt a burst of pride at seeing the weapon in Thatcher's hands as they headed back to the dojo. The thick metal made a dull sound as it hit the mud caking the street.

Chapter 10

The day of the trials had arrived and Jesse had been up for several hours already. He had rushed his morning delivery, completing it in record time, sprinting back to the bakery with the sacks of grain on his shoulder. Jesse mentioned to the disgruntled baker that he may have to give up the job after today. The baker turned away, muttering dark comments under his breath; clearly disappointed with losing such a reliable delivery boy.

By the time Jesse had sold the buns to the usual blacksmith, the dawn was still breaking. He rushed back to the dojo to fit in some more training. Over the last three days Jesse had fallen more and more in love with his new weapon. It was starting to feel like an extension of his arm: a good sign according to Sensei Thatcher.

Jesse had been excited to find out that engraved on the metal staff there were images of bygone ancient victories, masses of warriors fighting each other for one square inch of ground. While the images lacked the identifying facial features of the fighters, Jesse could make out a myriad of different weapons being brandished. The images of warfare lay underneath the ribbons of detail Jesse had spotted at first. Although he had no idea who the warriors were, they did give him a sense of confidence when he held it.

Later, Sensei Thatcher had told him that the battles were depicting the heroic victories of King Jeroboam. They had been fought four hundred years earlier. Jesse had also identified two small marks at the base of one of the ends. They were two smith sigils identifying the makers of the weapon, should other warriors admire the handiwork. Jesse could tell which one was Aman's. It was a symbol comprising of a capital A and M creating a zigzag pattern with the two symbols attached to each other. The other rune was a combination of an F and an R. It stood for Friedrick according to Thatcher.

Jesse continued his warm-up training trying to make as little noise as possible. Sensei could be quite grouchy if woken up too early.

"Jesse," interrupted the old Sensei.

Jesse stopped moving and slowly turned around. The older fighter was standing in the doorway of his personal quarters. He was dressed for his visit to the palace. The veteran warrior was wearing plain black silk robes. They were the ones he wore whenever he went for the high table meetings.

"We need to get there early," informed Thatcher. "We eat on the road."

Jesse nodded and handed Thatcher his staff so his master could transport it to the arena. Thatcher had his favourite wooden one in his hand and clutched Jesse's with the other.

Once outside on the street, Jesse had to match his sensei's pace once again. The old warrior was, of course, not in a rush to get anywhere. Each of them tucked into a half a honey cake as they climbed, the gates of the palace court looming over them.

The crowd had not yet begun to pack in, as they had arrived earlier than normal, so it was relatively simple to access the front gate. The waiting warrior on the palace gate let them in without checking identification. They were apparently expected.

The open court was bereft of people and Jesse thought it looked a lot bigger than last time. Once again, they crossed the sands of the arena. This time though when they got to the seats, Thatcher beckoned Jesse to follow him inside the palace. He also passed the weapon back to Jesse who carried it in his right hand. They made their way up to the large palace doors that stood tall over four metres high. Another guard stood to attention as they passed.

Jesse took a deep breath as he crossed the palace threshold for the first time. Inside there were four branded warriors each armed with a Khopesh blade. As Thatcher and Jesse passed them, one of the guards peeled off and followed. Thatcher knew where they were going and led the small party through a heavy looking door, unveiling an impressive room. There was a grand throne sat at one end of the room. It was covered in animal skins but was currently vacant. Thatcher stood fast and waited in silence and Jesse joined him standing still. The guard stood by another door at the side of the large chamber and proceeded to watch carefully. The rest of the hall had been mainly laid bare exposing the large wooden beams that made up the exoskeleton of the massive building. Jesse marvelled at the engineering that had gone into the structure.

Over the next ten minutes, the other lieutenants entered with their recruits who were doing the trials. Lieutenant Raúl had brought seven recruits. Raúl gave

Jesse a look of displeasure as he stood by the throne next to Thatcher. Lady Emma brought three recruits with her. She instructed her fighters where to stand and then joined her fellow lieutenants. Master Manish brought four pupils with him.

As the final lieutenant took his place, the door at the side of the room burst open and Lord Faircastle appeared. He was dressed in more animal furs. The large leader beamed happily at the sight of these potential recruits. Then he stood with his lieutenants in front of his throne. Hanging at the leader's side was his mighty blade. The cutlass was massive in size and must have been significantly heavy, although Faircastle acted as if it was nothing, as it hung within reach of one of his large, callused hands.

The appearance of Lord Faircastle had distracted Jesse for a moment but he spotted two other warriors emerging from the doorway behind Faircastle. One of the fighters was armed with a cutlass but unlike the others in the room he had a large mane of thick grey hair. The fighter wore a wolfish smirk similar to Lord Faircastle's. Behind him was a warrior similar in size to Lord Faircastle, he was armed with a Khopesh blade, he too wore an excited grin.

Lord Faircastle's presence filled the large chamber. He clapped his hands together evidently pleased with the fighters he was witnessing. While he stood head and shoulders above everyone in the room, his many layers of clothes helped him to appear bulkier and taller still. This included the large fighter Jesse had seen last month. Tareq had arrived with Mistress Emma ready for his next opportunity to join Lord Faircastle's warriors. Lord Faircastle ran his eyes over all the recruits lingering momentarily on Jesse and Tareq.

"Welcome all," announced Lord Faircastle.

Jesse instinctively fell to his knee holding his treasured weapon straight up next to him. Jesse's eyes found the floor in reverence. A few of the young recruits followed suit showing their respect for the lord of Rugged.

Lord Faircastle continued but his eyes caught on Jesse.

"You are all here to receive the treasured mark of The Warrior. Unfortunately, there will be only one of you skilled enough to receive the mark today."

Lord Faircastle went to on to explain the order of the draw. Apparently, Tareq was the favoured winner because of his prowess last time. So, he was at one end of the bracket but Lord Faircastle had put Jesse at the other end, apparently believing Jesse to be the next favourite.

Lord Faircastle then strode through the recruits and his lieutenants followed. His two bodyguards followed on either side of the hall. Jesse caught the bodyguard with grey hair looking at him suspiciously.

The recruits then followed behind, Jesse sticking to the back. He used the time to prepare himself mentally. All the years of training were building up to this. Thousands of important pieces of information from Sensei Thatcher flowed through his mind. Jesse thought about his footwork, the various different defensive styles and where his hands should be positioned for optimum effectiveness.

He was still stuck in his thoughts as they went outside. By this time the entire Falchion dojo had joined them. As the recruits flowed forward to create a show for the waiting crowd Jesse was taken aside by Thatcher.

"Jesse, focus," said the Sensei, shaking his only pupil to snap him out of his mental state.

"Listen," he continued. "You are capable of beating all of the fighters in this tournament. If I didn't think so then I wouldn't have brought you here."

Jesse looked up into his Sensei's eyes and saw the fortitude in them. He nodded.

"Okay, Sensei," he said, breathing easier.

Thatcher took his seat. Jesse stood next to him, a silent sentinel watching the show being completed for the crowds' amusement. To Jesse it looked like the public crowd was larger than last time. The hungry populous had spilled onto both sides of the fighting square. Jesse couldn't make out any individuals but it looked like there were several blacksmiths watching and quite a few of the town guards.

The drumbeat was reaching its crescendo again and the trainees made their final pose. The young recruits left the fighting sands and took their seats on the floor.

"Welcome one and all," announced Lord Faircastle to the entire plaza.

The familiar smile shone out. Jesse saw the other competitors moving forward so he joined them. The sixteen of them then bowed in front of their liege-lord.

"Congratulations to all of the applicants for being selected. Make sure you give it your all. The last thing you want to do is leave today disappointed because failed to do so. First two fighters step forward," Lord Faircastle said the first part loud enough for the fighters to hear, but the final question was fired loudly across the seething plaza.

The crowd let loose a cheer at the announcement. The tension was already beginning to rise.

Jesse strode onto the field and stood in the middle. His first opponent stood opposite several metres away. Both fighters bowed towards Lord Faircastle. Faircastle signalled he had seen them and with a flick of his wrist started the fight.

Jesse dug his feet into the sand of the arena. His opponent was from the Falchion dojo and was carrying a thick one-handed cutlass. The fighter lunged forward quickly but to Jesse it seemed distinctly slow compared to Thatcher and Locke. Jesse blocked the attack and sent the fighter spinning away. Jesse's much thicker weapon was giving his block greater force than the sword. The cutlass wielding warrior seemed very confused but continued the attack. Jesse could hear the public crowd muttering to one another as he defended the simple attacks away from himself. The muttering got louder and louder as the skirmish continued. Eventually after another three minutes, as the warrior started to tire, a loud voice boomed out across the pitch.

"Finish him," yelled Lord Faircastle.

Jesse realised in that moment what he was doing wrong and immediately went on the attack, cursing his own stupidity. He launched a low attack. The defender had to block the blow with two hands. Too slow though, he did not see the next attack coming. Jesse brought the other end of his staff through catching the fighter in the face. The fighter fell to the floor, clutching his broken nose, blood streaming from it. The blood signalled the end of the fight. Rapturous applause burst out from the watching crowd.

"Apologies Sensei," said Jesse as he approached his seat.

Jesse realised that he had let the fight go on too long. He had reverted back to his defensive ways instead of finishing the fight quickly.

"It sounded like you were toying with him," replied Thatcher.

He had got another recruit to describe the fight to him.

"That was not what I meant to do. I just fought it like one of my training sessions with the townspeople," explained Jesse.

"Yes, but you are a Warrior. On a battlefield you do not have time to educate your opponent."

Thatcher said this last comment with a smile on his face. Jesse caught Master Raúl admonishing his pupil for looking so foolish.

He resolved to make the next fight much quicker. The subsequent competitors were already fighting and as the first round continued Jesse analysed his potential opponents. To Jesse it did not look like there was much competition, the only one who seemed like they were a challenge was Tareq. He seemed to have gotten stronger and quicker in the last month but he still fought recklessly, leaving himself open to attacks. Jesse had to catch himself for thinking too confidently, as Sensei liked to say, confidence is a stumbling block that few see and fewer still conquer. It was better to be cautious in this situation.

By the end of the first round, Jesse had found weaknesses in all of his opposing fighters but also found things for him to watch out for.

The next round began and Jesse found himself face to face with a Khopesh fighter. The opposing fighter followed the offensive style of his dojo and launched himself into an attack. While he was in his forward movement, Jesse swung his metal stave forward, forcing the fighter to block the attack. The Khopesh blade dealt much better with the force of the staff. Swiftly, Jesse used his next attack to strike the inside of the fighter's leg. His feet loosened off the ground and as the fighter fell, Jesse struck the back of his head, knocking him out.

The whole fight had taken a matter of seconds, the large crowd erupted into cheers and whooping. Jesse caught sight of Aman with Friedrick watching the fight. Aman was cheering as loud as he could while the expert blacksmith gave Jesse a curt nod of acknowledgement.

Jesse looked back towards the lieutenants. Lord Faircastle seemed to miss the entire engagement as he was draining his large flagon for the fourth time that day. He seemed to see the funny side of the situation, as he burst out laughing and shouted something directed towards Thatcher, who answered in return.

Jesse could hear nothing except the crowd. He caught sight of Mistress Emma who just sat on her chair with a blank face watching him. Eventually, she looked away to accept a cup of mead from one of the servants on the side. Jesse found his seat, cleaning his weapon of the dirt and dust it had accrued. Two assistants ran on the pitch and retrieved the downed fighter. Thatcher said nothing for a while, allowing his pupil to take in the moment.

"Just be careful you don't finish the tournament too fast or my lord might miss all of your fights," he said after a few minutes.

Lord Faircastle burst out laughing again at this quip.

"Yes, I would be grateful," he replied, his eyes gleaming with the hint of intoxication.

Tareq easily beat his next opponent. The crowd cheered but Jesse noticed slightly less than for him winning, giving him a little boost of confidence.

The other fights took longer as the fighters seemed to lack the stamina Jesse possessed. His next opponent was a Dao sword fighter. The young fighter seemed to have fast reactions and would dodge any attack that would come at him.

After a small break the next rounds started. Jesse again strode onto the field. There was even a smattering of applause from the public section. The Dao swordsman looked a little worried as he took his place. Lord Faircastle signalled the start of the fight, his flagon nowhere to be seen, presumably being refilled.

Jesse instigated the attack, launching a jab at the fighter's head. The Dao swordsman dodged, but barely, Jesse's training had paid off. He now had another potential attack to add to his repertoire. Jesse saw the Dao blade fly towards his head. So, he blocked the blow deftly and attacked from the side. The Dao warrior spun swiftly but similarly to the other fighters not quite fast enough. Jesse launched another attack from on high swinging downwards. The swordsman was forced to block the blow with his blade, his second hand coming up to assist the first. The weapons clashed and the swordsman collapsed to his knees with the force of the attack. Jesse swung again, this time from the left side. The swordsman had to spin away on his knees again barely dodging. Jesse caught sight of his face; there was genuine fear from his predicament. Jesse thought through several options and decided on one less violent. Feinting to the left of the swordsman's head, he moved at full acceleration. Jesse had not yet used his top speed. The fighter had even less time to react than normal. He went with the feint and prepared to deflect the oncoming attack but it never came.

Jesse swung and struck home catching his opponent in the hand. The warrior was forced to drop his blade and Jesse kicked it away. The Dao warrior was left kneeling in the dust, Jesse waited for the surrender.

The warrior had other ideas and attempted to kick out at Jesse's legs. Jesse blocked it with his long staff and then he heard a bone breaking crunch. The warrior was left clutching his foot yelping in pain. Lord Faircastle called an end to the fight as Jesse's opponent was unable to compete. While the Dao swordsman was helped off the pitch, Jesse retook his place next to Thatcher.

He was now ignoring the cheers of the crowd, choosing instead to focus on this final fight. If he completed this, he would pull himself out of his poor social standing and join the lord's warriors. He had spent his entire life in the pursuit of this aim. The endless hours of practice and pain fell away as it had all been worth it to put him here in this moment. Ignoring Tareq's fight he chose to quietly contemplate. He ignored Lord Faircastle's coarse jokes. He ignored the crowd cheering. He ignored the spill of blood on the floor signalling the end of the match.

Jesse stood there silently until the fight was signalled. Thatcher had also left him alone allowing his pupil the time to prepare himself mentally. Jesse strode forward, ready to seize hold of his destiny. He looked up to see Tareq glaring at him. He seemed to always be angry. There was not time for Jesse to consider why, before the incoming attack was launched.

Jesse easily sidestepped the attack and let Tareq pass him. Tareq thought he saw a hole in Jesse's guard and attacked again. Jesse caught him in the stomach, punishing the foolishness. Tareq launched several attacks at once. Jesse blocked them all and countered with his own. The muscled warrior was forced to block for once, put on the back foot. Jesse was starting to mentally tire, he was fighting automatically, allowing his subconscious access. Tareq let out a bellow of rage and grabbed a handful of sand launching it in Jesse's face. Jesse closed his eyes before the cowardly attack hit. Completely blind, Jesse then blocked the next attack and swung back. The blow caught Tareq in the jaw forcing the large fighter to spit out blood.

"Enough!" shouted Lord Faircastle, through the melee of the combat.

The duel was over, blood was the sign. Tareq ignored him and charged again. It was at this point that Jesse felt anger rising within himself again. He had just ignored a direct order from his liege-lord. Several older warriors were now making their way forward to stop the fight. Jesse realised they were not going to get to him in time. He blocked the incoming attack with the far end of his long staff and launched himself forward. He skimmed across the sand with such agility that Tareq could not react at all. Jesse drove the staff into Tareq's foot, bringing his opponents head down. Then with the swiftness of Locke he brought his staff up and caught Tareq in the jaw as it was coming down. With a final flourish he disarmed the warrior by shattering the bones in his wrist hand. Tareq fell backwards completely finished; his weapon flying far away across the sands of the arena.

Jesse was about to take a step forward before a large body moved between the two fighters. It was Lord Faircastle. The semi-drunk man had moved faster than anyone else. All mirth and jokes were wiped away. The large man was seething with rage at the ignored command.

He had drawn his blade about to dispatch the wounded fighter for the crime of insubordination. Thatcher appeared next to him.

"I don't recommend doing that in front of the entire town, my lord," he muttered.

Lord Faircastle took a moment. The entire plaza held its breath.

"Lady Emma, take this disgusting piece of human waste out of my sight. I never want to see him again," he ordered.

Lady Emma nodded, clearly embarrassed. She clicked her fingers and two recruits from her dojo appeared and bundled off the unfortunate fighter. Lord Faircastle breathed heavily before turning to congratulate his newest warrior. Jesse was kneeling behind him; collapsed from mental and physical exhaustion. The lord smiled as Jesse knelt before him paying homage quite by accident.

Chapter 11

After a few minutes, Jesse got to his feet, using his weapon to steady himself. His heartbeat had slowed dramatically. The crowds were pouring out of the plaza, the event now over. Jesse paused for a moment, feeling a little unsteady, his body felt spent of energy. He spotted his Sensei in a conversation; he was talking away leaning on his wooden quarterstaff. Thatcher stopped speaking to Lieutenant Manish and turned to greet Jesse, seeing his student approaching.

"Congratulations, young pupil," he said.

His face broke into excitement for his protégée.

"Come on, get up. We have to get your mark," he said to Jesse.

The old warrior seemed to be in a hurry for once.

"Where are we going?" asked Jesse.

He was still feeling fairly out of it but he scrambled back up to his feet, grateful for his long staff which he steadied himself with.

"We need to see Mamma Zamora," Thatcher replied.

Refusing to explain himself any further, he led Jesse to a small house outside the castle walls. The crowd had more or less disappeared from the palace gates. A few enthusiastic merchants were finishing up deals before heading home. The sky was starting to darken over; it was vacant of any clouds. It looked like it was going to be a cold night.

The house they were heading towards was even more ruinous than their dojo. The roof had at least three decent sized holes which would easily allow rain to fall through. Outside the shack there was a wooden porch and on it was an old woman weaving baskets from bulrushes. The old lady had her long-knotted hair weaved into several long strings which enveloped her in a mass of billowy cloud. She saw them coming and left her work on the floor before beckoning them both inside with a thin, aged finger. Thatcher entered the house but first removed his shoes. He gestured for Jesse to follow suit. The young warrior copied his master before entering. The street behind them laid empty, leaving total silence.

Inside the house, baskets were stacked high against the walls. In the middle of the main room was a wooden couch with a single arm rest. The old woman sat on a wooden stool next to it. She faced away from her visitors and she seemed to be fiddling with several strange tools lying on a nearby table. Jesse made his way into the room cautiously. He eyed a few of the most heavily stacked piles unsure of whether they would collapse on him. Jesse spotted that the baskets had been woven several layers thick. Satisfied that the tottering piles were more solid than they looked, he followed Thatcher further into the room.

"It has been several years, Thatcher," Mamma Zamora said. "I never thought I would see you again in here."

"Likewise," replied Thatcher.

He went over and embraced the old woman, as if she was an age-old friend.

"Take a seat, Jesse," continued the Sensei, turning to smile at his victorious pupil.

Jesse sat down with his arm placed on the rest. His hands felt small grooves, evenly spaced for his fingers. He realised the wood had been worn smooth by countless other warriors sitting where he sat.

The old woman looked him dead in the eyes. Jesse could make out specks of grey within the cloud of blue.

"So, you are Thatcher's pupil. I have heard rumours for years about you. Interesting, Thatcher, decides to bring you out now."

The old woman produced a sweet smile on her face and Jesse could make out that she still possessed most of her teeth. Zamora whipped around to examine Thatcher behind her, expecting an explanation.

"Come on, Mamma. There is no secret agenda," said Thatcher, waving away her curt theories.

The old woman gave him a knowing look before rolling up Jesse's sleeve. Her yellow fingernails seemed to move independent of each other, like she had two five-legged spiders at the end of her arms.

"I am about to give you Faircastle's mark. Are you resigned to this fate?"

Now she was talking to Jesse directly. Jesse looked into the old woman's eyes and nodded. The following tattoo would mark him for life and signal his allegiance for years to come. The old woman nodded. She unveiled several metal needles from her dress and laid them out on a little table next to her.

"Get the ink!" she ordered Thatcher and she gestured towards a cupboard at the back.

74

It took Thatcher a few minutes to find the correct ink. There were several dusty vials sitting on the shelf. While they were waiting, the old woman was massaging Jesse's left arm. She moved suddenly and quickly with every movement. Jesse felt his weary muscles in his left arm relax and unwind. Mamma Zamora hummed an old ditty to herself as she moved.

Thatcher came back with the ink and put the bottle on the little table with a saucer. The old woman uncorked the bottle and sniffed the contents before pouring a small amount on the saucer.

"Brace yourself," she warned.

The old woman shot a serious look at Jesse. Jesse nodded and swallowed nervously.

Mamma Zamora started penetrating the warrior's arm with one of the needles. Dripping in ink she inserted it under his skin. Jesse had to grit his teeth from the pain.

As the ink was forced under Jesse's skin, Thatcher grabbed his pupil's free arm. Jesse's fingers dug deeply into the veteran warrior's hand trying to expel the pain.

Jesse forced his eyes away from the old woman and her toil to look at his Sensei. Thatcher met his eye line and Jesse saw raw willpower burning away within them.

"Your fealty?" spoke Thatcher.

"Is yours," replied Jesse.

"Your will?" spoke Thatcher.

"Is yours," replied Jesse.

"Your life?" spoke Thatcher.

"Is yours," finished Jesse.

The warrior's oath was complete. Thatcher nodded to Jesse, the two warriors sharing the moment. Mamma Zamora toiled away ignoring the two of them. Jesse felt the pain ebbing slightly away, his body was flushed with adrenaline. With the sealing of the oath, he was now a warrior in his own right.

Fresh warriors swore to their lieutenant who then swore on their behalf to the reigning lord. Thatcher repeated the oath three times in total. He grasped Jesse's hand halfway through the painful procedure to repeat the process.

After Jesse replied in the exact same way, Thatcher repeated the entire oath once again. However, at the end of this swearing of the oath Thatcher added something.

"Your life?" spoke Thatcher.

"Is yours," finished Jesse.

"So, it will be," replied Thatcher, in confirmation of the promise that the two warriors had forged.

He turned and left the hut.

Thatcher sat outside on the porch finishing off the woman's basket. He was apparently very familiar with the weaving technique the old lady was using.

Jesse clung on through the pain trying to keep his cries to himself. The room spun in a haze of fire and wicker baskets.

After an excruciating hour, Mamma had created a black circle high up on Jesse's arm. She then called Thatcher in.

"I need to see yours, so I can get it accurate," she stated.

Thatcher sat down next to her and pulled up his sleeve. There were three different tattoos on there. The top two were crossed out with a black line. The bottom one was the image of a circle with two weapons crossed in the middle. One was Lord Faircastle's chosen weapon; a cutlass; the other was Thatcher's quarter stave. Jesse tried to make out the other marks on his Sensei's arm but it was hard. Not only was his arm in extreme pain, causing his eyes to water, but the two older tattoos had faded slightly. The only weapon Jesse could make out was a war tomahawk. These tattoos displayed Thatcher's past allegiances to previous lords.

After another hour the old woman was finished. On Jesse's arm was now the symbol of Lord Faircastle; a cutlass lying across a circle. The weapon lay to the right. Jesse spotted that Thatcher's mark also had his chosen weapon crossed with Faircastle's cutlass.

"I will finish the tattoo when you become a lieutenant in your own right," said Mamma Zamora, as if guessing Jesse's thoughts.

Thatcher stood Jesse to his feet.

"I now add my part to the oath," he said.

Zamora turned, clearly intrigued.

"Protect the lord," Thatcher spoke. "If the lord is dead, protect the people."

Jesse nodded, drinking in the order. There was a moment of silence but it was fleeting. Thatcher turned and thanked his old friend for her time and the two warriors left.

"Farewell," shouted the old woman as they left, looking at Thatcher as she spoke.

"You will see her again. I'm sure of that," said Thatcher to Jesse.

Jesse nodded. He hoped he would get the opportunity to become a lieutenant. Immediately he felt shame flush through his mind. For that to happen then Thatcher would have had to be dead. Or Jesse would have to defeat him in single combat. Jesse flashed a look at Thatcher to see if he had read his mind as the old man would often appear to at the most inopportune times.

"You never know, you might take your students there one day."

The old warrior had a smile on his face when he said this. Jesse realised that his Sensei was dreaming out loud.

This gave Jesse a moment to pause. Would he ever have students who would learn from him? And if so then what would he teach them? Thatcher had taught him so much, how could he remember it all?

"Definitely not for a while," Jesse replied quickly.

He missed a sad smile slide onto Thatcher's face. His old Sensei said nothing as the two of them headed home, the sky now dark above them.

Jesse woke early as usual but the rest of his morning routine was going to be different. As one of Lord Faircastle's warriors, he had responsibilities to the lord and he was expected to present himself to the lord for his new duties. Taking his metal long stave, Jesse exited. It felt strange to carry a weapon around the town. He had spent many years wondering what it would feel like. Jesse realised that yesterday evening he had travelled back to the dojo carrying his own weapon. He was so shattered that he had not even realised this.

Jesse winced suddenly as his new tattoo caught against his shirt. The mark was still very red and sore. Jesse decided to go down to the river to wash it in case of infection (He needn't have worried; Mamma Zamora was a genius in her craft). He started making his way down the hill and out of the town.

As he approached the outer gate, the guards saw him coming. They opened the gate quickly. There was urgency in their step Jesse had never seen before.

Jesse walked towards them instead of his usual blistering pace.

"Good morning, gentlemen," Jesse said with a smirk, feeling very pleased with himself and clutching his beloved weapon in his right hand.

"Good morning, sir," one of the guards said and the man even bowed his head slightly.

The other guard was more anxious to say something.

"I saw you yesterday," he blurted out.

"Oh," replied Jesse, saying nothing but his eyes betraying his excitement.

"You looked amazing. We were just saying that we had no idea you could fight like that. When you floored that guy in like a second, I was amazed," the young guard carried on.

"Well thank you for showing your support," replied Jesse.

He wondered if this was going to be how people were going to react to him. How would other people in the town react to him? With his new role there would be some seniority shown to him now. How would his friends react to this?

The first guard spoke.

"We decided that a few of us guards would come to see you and support you, since you have been a lot of help with the town training."

The older guard shook Jesse's hand.

"Congratulations, sir," he said.

The guard seemed genuinely pleased for Jesse.

Jesse made his apologies and left heading into the market district. The conversation made Jesse feel exuberant and his body flushed with adrenaline. The different stalls were yet to set up for the morning and Jesse saw no more people on his journey through Rugged. He headed through the fields once again aiming for the fast-flowing river.

A figure passed him on the road. It took Jesse a moment to realise that it was Sloth. The small man was carrying two heavy bags of grain up the hill.

"Well done, mate. Sorry, I could not make it up the hill to see you yesterday," said Sloth.

He was sweating profusely from the effort of carrying Jesse's usual load.

"Don't worry about it, mate. Are you alright with those?" asked Jesse.

"I have to get used to it," said Sloth, stalwartly. "So, don't help me. Anyway, catch you later."

Sloth continued up the road towards the bakery. Jesse thought he was doing really rather well considering his small size. He seemed to be in a hurry so Jesse carried on towards his destination choosing not to distract him further.

The river was several metres wide and was quite strong so Jesse stayed to the bank. After washing, paying special attention to his new mark, Jesse got out and headed back up the hill. It would look good to arrive early at the palace on his first day. The town was starting to wake up all around him. The woodcutters were leaving to go to work. A few of them were awake enough to recognise Jesse and congratulated him on his new tattoo. He received several slaps on his shoulders, and while each one sent shooting pains through Jesse's left arm, he felt the intended praise.

As Jesse passed the bakery, he saw Aman and his new teacher on the road. They were wearing long cloaks and carrying heavy travel bags. Jesse wondered where they were going.

Aman saw him as well although it was easier to spot Jesse carrying his long-staff in the middle of the high street.

"Where are you going?" asked Jesse, concerned for his friend.

"Master Friedrick is taking me to Blacksmith HQ in Haven City," said Aman.

The young blacksmith clearly looked excited. He was sporting a huge smile all over his face.

"Right now?" asked Jesse.

Friedrick jumped in suddenly.

"Yes, I'm due back in a few days so we're going to be late anyway. Congratulations, young warrior. I'm glad that my weapon has an appropriate master."

Jesse thanked the blacksmith for his talent once again.

"Don't worry about it," said the blacksmith. "Now Aman, I'm going ahead. Make sure you catch up."

The old blacksmith hobbled off along the road. Aman lingered with Jesse a few minutes more.

"I'm sorry I couldn't give you any warning," apologised Aman. "But this is a really great opportunity for me."

"No, I understand," said Jesse. "Go and be a talented blacksmith, just remember there are some of us back home wishing you luck."

Jesse gave his friend a hug before Aman turned to go.

"Just remember to keep an eye out for our friend," said Aman.

Jesse nodded in response. The blacksmith turned to go and set off at a run to catch up with his master.

Jesse turned away back up the hill; trying not to feel disappointed at his oldest friend disappearing from his life, potentially forever.

Chapter 12

The sun was rising in the sky by the time Jesse had made it to the palace gate. The warrior guarding the gate made a big deal of looking at Jesse's mark. It was still red and swollen making it difficult to read. Eventually, Jesse was let inside when the guard was satisfied that the mark was valid.

"Any idea where I'm supposed to go?" asked Jesse.

"Round the back," one of the other guards said and Jesse wandered around the palace.

The lord's castle was situated in the middle of the entire complex but as well as the plaza there were several sizeable buildings dotted around. A few of them seemed to be storage buildings. Jesse looked in at one of the windows and saw racks of leather armour piled high.

Jesse had never been on this side of the palace before so he made his way around the complex cautiously. Behind the palace was another large building that seemed to be an old dojo. That too appeared to be a storage unit except it held numerous training weapons. There were stacks of wooden swords and various other practice weapons. A few warriors were starting to gather around outside. The elder warriors were limbering up giving their muscles a chance to warm up. The younger warriors were standing around conversing.

Jesse noticed that many of them seemed to not wear a sleeve on the left arm so their warrior's mark was revealed at all times. Jesse made a mental note of that for the future.

Since the warriors who were there early seemed to be waiting for something, Jesse started his own warm up. Practicing his footwork, he spun swiftly, swinging his long-staff around. Jesse decided to try to emulate the type of foot technique he had seen from Locke when she had beaten him. Her whole body had moved like it was a single piece of cloth, gracefully moving with the wind but still remaining a single piece of material. Jesse imagined an enemy attack slicing through the air towards him and he moved to avoid it. As he allowed his body to move with the attack, he threw out his own to counter his faux opponent.

"What is he doing?" asked one of the Dao warriors who had just arrived.

The confused warrior was speaking to the others who arrived early. Jesse ignored him and carried on.

A few of the waiting warriors had stopped warming up and they were now watching the newest recruit turning in the air.

"I think he is trying to copy the water movement technique," said one of the older warriors.

He was from the cutlass clan and his weapon had definitely seen combat. A large battle scar was present on the blade and it was followed by a similar mark on the fighter's right arm. The wound must have been serious as the gash looked deep. The older fighter also sported a roughly cut grey haircut.

Jesse slowed his movement and with a flick of his wrist, he caught the end of his staff and flung it into the air. The long-staff flew over his head and the end hit the floor. The weapon stood there momentarily, about to fall, but before it could, Jesse retrieved it. Pausing for a brief moment, his eyes flickered to the watching audience. The spectators turned away quickly pretending to not have noticed Jesse. The scarred warrior met Jesse's gaze and flashed his younger compatriot a smile before he moved away as well.

Jesse turned away before sitting on the floor moderating his heartbeat to calm it down; a favoured meditation technique taught often by Thatcher. The other warriors that were arriving ignored him and Jesse got a bit of peace.

Eventually, after another ten minutes the training area was filled up with warriors and Jesse stood to join them. He noticed that generally the different dojos avoided one another; however, the older warriors seemed to stick to each other regardless of their dojo allegiance. Jesse caught sight of Rodrigo standing with other warriors from his dojo. The young warrior looked very at ease within his group. The fighter had long blond hair that landed at his shoulders and his blue eyes were set back in his face. Once or twice, Rodrigo caught Jesse looking at him. The next most inexperienced warrior did not react to Jesse's looks.

Mistress Emma appeared from the large training hut and the general talking ceased. The gifted lieutenant stood at the entrance of the building for a moment saying nothing leaving an awkward moment of apprehension for all the warriors. Then she spoke.

"Double time around the complex, let's go!" she barked.

Her command echoed off the sparsely built building around her magnifying the noise.

At once, all the warriors turned towards the right and started jogging around the perimeter of the palace grounds. Jesse shoved his way through the crowd, attempting to get to the front, but he soon gave up as the crowding warriors left no gaps to slip into. Many of the large fighters were jogging shoulder-to-shoulder experienced at travelling in a unit. Carrying his staff against his shoulder, Jesse kept pace with the warriors around him.

As they made their way around the first corner of the palace wall, Jesse saw a potential opening. The crowd was starting to spread itself out making it possible for each warrior to have space for themselves. Jesse stayed back until halfway through the first lap, so he had some idea of the distance and he could pace himself. The column of warriors snaked its way around the palace. Jesse picked up his pace as the first lap got towards the end.

Mistress Emma had not moved since giving the order. She was waiting for the warriors to appear. She watched the fighters run past her.

"Faster!" she ordered harshly.

Jesse passed the warrior on his right and dug his heels in as he started the next lap. He noticed that a few of the other runners were keeping pace with him. In all there were a good two hundred warriors running altogether. Jesse again increased his pace aiming to be towards the front of the group. He caught a glance from the scarred older warrior who had watched him earlier. He carried his blade over his shoulder, similar to Jesse. The warrior was a good ten to fifteen years older than Jesse. His competitor gritted his teeth and drove forward, reacting to Jesse's new pace. As the second lap came to an end, Jesse and the other warrior had moved up to the first half of the runners who reached their destination.

"Brace yourself," the older warrior said under his breath to no one in general.

"Again!" ordered Mistress Emma.

Standing tall, she gazed across the group of warriors and she did not look impressed. Her lip curled up in disgust at the state of some of the warriors who were starting to wheeze and cough.

The group started off again. This time Jesse began quickly, he was tired of the pace that was being set for him. By the end of the third lap, Jesse was in the lead group. The older warrior was just behind him keeping pace. There were about twelve warriors in the lead group and they looked amongst each other, wondering who would set the pace for the final lap. The older warrior passed

Jesse and strode ahead setting a brutal pace. Jesse now had to work hard to keep up. He moved his staff onto his other shoulder to make it easier to run. Freeing up his favoured arm to help him build momentum, Jesse caught up with the warrior and matched his speed.

The halfway point of the lap approached and Jesse attempted to increase his pace once again. At this point though three or four warriors passed him with ease, they too had sped up. Jesse strained to keep up with them but he was left behind. Apparently, these warriors had saved themselves for this final lap.

The lead group reached Mistress Emma and Jesse arrived shortly afterward. The young warrior had to remind himself that these warriors were the greatest fighters in Rugged. Of course, he could not beat them yet, they had years of experience on him. The older warrior stood near Jesse, looking very unfazed by the exercise. While others were trying to catch their breath, he was just stood there as if the whole thing had just been a light jog. He stretched his leg muscles breathing quite easily.

The rest of the warriors arrived in small groups lagging behind. Mistress Emma started chastising the warriors who were coming in towards the end. Once everyone had arrived, Mistress Emma ordered the fighters to line up in pairs. A few warriors headed into the building behind her and retrieved a huge haul of wooden weapons. Jesse laid his forged staff against the building and managed to spot a wooden quarterstaff leaning against one of the walls of the dojo. It was not the correct size for him but he decided it was better than nothing.

The pairs of fighters were lined up facing their partner; they formed two parallel lines.

Lady Emma gestured to one side of the warriors and announced 'offence' then pointed at the other side and said 'defence'.

The warriors on Jesse's side audibly groaned at the idea that they were defence. They all lined up facing an opponent. Jesse was paired with a young warrior from the Dao clan who looked confident; he was going to get first taste of the newest pledge. The warriors on Jesse's side took defensive positions, although to Jesse they looked very shoddy. Many of the fighters had their feet in all the wrong places. *If Sensei Thatcher was here, he would be very unimpressed,* thought Jesse.

A lot of the fighters on Jesse's side looked anxious. All the warriors were using wooden training weapons but it was still going to hurt if they got hit.

"Proceed," announced Emma.

She seemed to be analysing the offensive side carefully. The warriors charged. Jesse easily blocked the oncoming attack. The rest of the defending fighters stopped once they were hit. Jesse focussed on his skirmish. The Dao warrior continued the pressure but just could not break through. He started to get desperate as the other training fights stopped allowing everyone to watch him. Jesse saw an opportunity to counterattack and took it; deflecting the next attack so the training blade spun off at a strange angle. Then Jesse struck, catching the opposing warrior in the stomach with the butt of his staff. Jesse was careful not to hit too hard; this was a training session after all.

The warrior went down to his knees trying to catch his breath.

"What are you doing?" roared Lieutenant Emma.

She stormed over towards Jesse. Her face lit up red from anger.

"You are on defence!" she shouted.

She stood a foot taller than Jesse and her face towered over him.

Jesse said nothing, all though a thousand retorts floated through his mind.

"Again," shouted Mistress Emma.

The warriors lined up again ready for another attack. The teacher stalked back to the end, focusing on offence. She gave several pieces of advice to different warriors about their attack criticising their posture or their ferocity. Jesse's opponent rose to his feet, clearly embarrassed.

"Proceed," was the command and the attack began again.

This time Jesse's opponent was a lot more careful. He attacked cautiously, making sure not to allow any openings. Jesse stood there blocking the flurry of attacks. Again, all the other fights had finished and the other warriors were watching this unfortunate attacker trying to break through Jesse's impossible guard. Once again, all eyes were watching. Jesse refused to finish the fight because apparently Lady Emma did not want him to go on the offensive. He was not about to deliberately lose. The skirmish continued for another two minutes. The warrior attacking him started to get desperate once more and Jesse could see several opportunities to finish but he did not take any of them.

Mistress Emma stopped the skirmish with a short-barked order. Jesse's opponent looked grateful but he received an earful from Lady Emma. She fixed a glare at Jesse and then changed his opponent. This time it was a large warrior from her dojo. He was called Vulcan and his face bore a look of determination. The fighter had a wonky nose and a few teeth missing. He brandished his Khopesh with a snarl.

The attack began again and Vulcan charged full tilt at Jesse. Jesse slipped under his attack and turned on his heel, ready for the next manoeuvre. Vulcan attacked from on high and Jesse deflected it to the right; once again slipping through to stand in his original position. This carried on several times and each time the taller warrior got more and more worked up. He started to snort with effort and rage, with each attempt failing.

"Enough!" shouted Mistress Emma.

The two fighters stopped, one catching his breath.

"Switch," announced Mistress Emma and the two sides swapped over so Jesse's side was on the offence. The training continued on a few hours. Each time Jesse was on the defensive the opposing fighter could not break through his guard and since Jesse was not allowed to counterattack the skirmish would never end. Jesse found the offence more challenging as he had focused on this less with Sensei Thatcher. After a few hours the fighters took a break.

The older warrior with the long arm scar came over and sat down next to Jesse.

"You need to teach me some techniques," he said to Jesse.

He reached out a hand and shook Jesse's. A few of the older warriors joined them. Mistress Emma had disappeared for a few minutes.

"You have really upset her training this morning," said the warrior.

The old fighter seemed to be amused by the idea.

Jesse smirked at the concept.

"I'll give you some tips if you help me with my long-distance running skills," he replied.

The old warrior nodded at this and laughed.

Over the next few days Jesse kept his head down during the training, preferring to hang around on the peripheries of the conversations going on. He used the time to analyse the training that was going on. Lady Emma liked to train brute force tactics and she focused on stamina training. However, when Raúl took over training on the second day, he focused on strength training and open skirmishes. Here all the warriors fought together in two sides against each another, Raúl apparently preferring to mimic an actual battle format. Jesse would often find himself against a few warriors at the same time. He managed to avoid finding himself face down in the dirt just beating his opponents to make his team victorious. Master Manish preferred to focus on technique in his training sessions. He would have the warriors drilling repeatedly until they could all complete a series of movements perfectly together.

During all this training Jesse found himself very confused indeed. All of these different techniques being taught by different teachers left his head swimming.

He did learn the identity of the scarred veteran. His name was Weaver and he had been fighting for Lord Faircastle for twenty-two years making him one of the most experienced in the army. The two of them had talked at the end of the final training session of the week. For the fourth day the warriors would train at their own home dojos.

"The good thing about the different training styles is that everything is covered," argued Weaver.

Jesse had brought up his thoughts on the training practice.

"I suppose you are right," replied Jesse. "But I can't help think that, that could be a lucky coincidence."

Weaver smirked at this.

"I think Faircastle sees over all the training," he said.

The scarred warrior gestured towards the balcony above their heads. The palace looked out over the warrior's training area. Jesse caught a glimpse of the ruling lord disappearing out of sight.

Their conversation was interrupted by a palace guard coming over.

"You are needed in the palace tomorrow," he said to Jesse.

Jesse nodded, unsure of the nature of the request. By the time he had turned around, Weaver had gone leaving the young warrior to walk home on his own.

Chapter 13

Jesse had hurried home to deliver the news to Thatcher. The old warrior had retired early to his quarters and Jesse could hear his trademark snoring once he had entered the dojo.

The young warrior grabbed a quick dinner before getting an early night himself. While lying in his bunk he considered who may have requested him. Perhaps he was to receive a dressing down from Lady Emma; she had been less than pleased with him disrupting her training this week. Jesse worried about it for a good while before falling asleep on his bunk.

It was a fettered sleep, his usual dreams interrupted with different lieutenants yelling at him for various supposed crimes. By the rise of the dawn Jesse had already been up for a few hours choosing to train instead of winding out the last few hours of possible sleep. As a consequence, he was ready to leave on time. Casting one eye on his master's quarters to establish if Thatcher had risen, Jesse left and headed to the palace.

The journey up was also filled with creeping dread as Jesse's mind played out various scenarios that could be about to take place. He had never heard about a warrior being dismissed so early but maybe it could happen. The guards let him through the palace gate, this time they were warriors from the Falchion dojo.

One of the guards took him into the palace and up a flight of stairs. The walls of the magnificent building had been decorated with tapestries depicting images of famous warriors and glorious victories. The palace guard approached a door and then gestured for Jesse to enter. Jesse knocked and then opened the door.

The reigning lord was sitting on a chair watching the clouds pass by.

"My lord," said Jesse kneeling down.

"I see you have made your presence known in the training sessions," said Lord Faircastle.

Jesse looked up, Faircastle's tone was stern but Jesse could see a flicker of mirth in the lord's eyes.

"I'm sorry, my lord. I apologise if I have been a hindrance," replied Jesse.

Several warriors from Lord Faircastle's dojo were talking amongst themselves outside in the courtyard unaware of the conversation taking place above them.

"What am I going to do with you?" queried Lord Faircastle out loud.

He stroked his beard while he said it, as if to appear to be thinking of an idea. Jesse knew better, the lord would not have called him up if he did not have an alternative plan.

"It appears that you are not well fitted for our training sessions," said the lord.

Jesse got up from the floor and examined the room. There was a guard in the room, however he seemed quite relaxed. The stationed warrior was roughly shaven but he had allowed his white hair to grow thickly though on the top of his head. That too had been cut brutally as if in a hurry. The warrior was armed with a cutlass and he fixed Jesse with an imposing look as if daring Jesse to try anything.

Jesse switched his gaze to Lord Faircastle who had paused for a moment to wolf down a small loaf of bread. His breakfast lay on a small table between the lord and his newest warrior.

"Unfortunately, Master Thatcher rarely produces students and when he does, they don't really fit the mould of our other warriors."

"Sir," said Jesse, interrupting. "I would like to continue training as I think I can learn from them."

"Really?" queried Faircastle.

"As far as I can see no one down there is capable of breaking through your defensive technique. That makes you impossible to train. You need an opponent who is better than you to train."

"I agree, my lord, but I can learn things down there other than fighting techniques," replied Jesse.

"Like?"

"Like stamina and teamwork."

Lord Faircastle raised an eyebrow to this and thought for a moment.

"I may have a solution."

Jesse listened carefully wondering what it was.

"I will recruit you as one of my bodyguards. Frankly, it would be nice to have someone with such a good defensive technique watching my back."

Jesse was surprised to hear this and apparently so was the guard standing in the room. He seemed to stir at this idea but said nothing.

Lord Faircastle seemed to like this plan as he nodded to himself thinking it over.

Jesse knelt and said formally, "If that is your decision, my lord."

"Stop kneeling all the time," said Faircastle. "I'm too tall for that and it just looks ridiculous sometimes."

He said it with a smile. Jesse got up, smiling back.

"Jude, take him to get acquainted with the others," ordered Faircastle.

He said it quietly though, as if he was worried about other people listening in.

The warrior behind Jesse came forward and offered his hand.

"I am Jude. I head up Lord Faircastle's personal security."

The old fighter's eyes were darting all over Jesse. He gripped Jesse's hand tightly signalling his apprehension at the situation.

Close up, the warrior seemed even older than Faircastle. His weathered skin was stretched tightly over his muscular body. He broke into a wolfish grin, partly emulating Faircastle's.

"At least you know how to fight," he said to Jesse. "Congratulations, young warrior. This is an honour that few receive quickly."

Jesse returned the smile, glad of it as it allowed him to relax.

Jude took Jesse into a side room within was a table and six chairs around it. There were three other warriors sitting there. Each of them seemed to be experienced veterans. The youngest warrior was the Khopesh warrior but even he was ten years older than Jesse. He saw another cutlass blade and a Dao blade. Jesse noticed one of the warriors was Weaver.

"Well, we wondered why we had all been gathered together and this is the reason," announced Jude, as they entered the room.

"We are all members of Lord Faircastle's personal security," explained Jude to Jesse, turning to speak to him.

Jesse exchanged looks with all the members of his team. They seemed friendly enough except for the Dao clan member who gave Jesse a cold look. He sat at the end of the table, next to the closest door, which he kept shooting glances at all the time, as if he wanted to leave immediately or was expecting a sudden ambush. He wore a wide brimmed hat, hiding most of his face to everyone at the table.

"I am surprised you were selected so quickly," said Jude. "You have only just received your mark. Of course, we watched your victory last week."

"I didn't," commented the Dao swordsman.

Jude ignored him and carried on. The other members of the protection team followed suit and gave Jude all their attention.

"We know you are a warrior of the long stave. That will be very useful in protecting the lord. From my experience, long staffs are a very defensive weapon."

Weaver spoke.

"I saw him fighting earlier up close; he definitely has skills in defence."

Weaver winked at Jesse while fussing over his cutlass which was lying on the table.

"It is our job to protect Lord Faircastle wherever he is," continued Jude. "Now, our group mainly works in secret from the rest of the army. We find this helps us to keep the element of surprise."

Jesse noticed that the warrior with the Khopesh blade was nodding at this and was the only warrior in the room listening more intently than Jesse. He was a very large warrior; his enormous size was at least equal to that of Lord Faircastle.

"The only problem is most of our job involves blending in with the other warriors. And with your weapon you can't blend in."

Jude said nothing for a moment.

"He could switch weapons," suggested the Khopesh warrior.

"Then he loses the advantage of his training and he has to learn another weapon altogether," replied Weaver, disagreeing.

He explained this slowly to the other warrior. The warrior turned away and thought carefully about this.

There was a pause. Jesse decided to not share any thoughts but let the others decide.

"I think he should be visible next to the lord," said the Dao warrior at the end of the table.

He had his shoes up on the table and was spinning a knife through his fingers.

"Think about it, we use his visibility to our advantage. It makes it harder to spot us if he is the distraction," the warrior said it with a smirk on his face. "That's what we do with Hesutu, anyway."

The Dao swordsman gestured towards the large warrior down the table from him.

"That makes a lot of sense to me," replied Jude, thinking it through. "Normally Hesutu and I stick close to Faircastle, but with Jesse here, I can disappear into the rest of the fighting force like Weaver."

The elder warrior realised that Jesse was a little confused.

"Oh, we only have a few obvious bodyguards when we are out of the palace," explained Jude.

He said it with a kind smile on his face.

"We find it is easy to deal with any threats if some bodyguards are hidden," spoke up Weaver.

Hesutu nodded eagerly at this.

"We'll go through this in more detail later," said Jude. "But I need to introduce everyone to you. We are going to be working closely together for the foreseeable future. I believe you've met Weaver already. He helps to keep an eye on the Falchion dojo."

Jude gestured towards the scarred veteran. Weaver nodded at Jesse in response.

"He's been fighting with Lord Faircastle for many years side-by-side with me," said Jude.

Jude and Weaver shared a look of acknowledgement before moving on.

"The opinionated warrior at the end of the table is Diachi. I find it's best to ignore most of his snide comments."

Diachi huffed a little at the statement before going back to fiddling with the knife. He seemed to be inscribing something into the smooth wood of the long table.

"He has been stationed with us for the last five years and he helps keep tabs on the Dao dojo."

"Why do we need to?" asked Jesse, interrupting Jude. He was very confused by this; surely the threats would not be from the branded warriors.

"A lord is just as likely to be overthrown by their dojos as they are to be beaten on the battlefield," muttered Diachi. "I'd have thought you'd have known that."

The Dao swordsman gave Jesse an incredulous look as if he was shocked at such a basic question.

"Luckily, we only have to worry about three dojos, and not four, since your lieutenant neglects to train anyone," Diachi continued.

Jesse leapt to his feet to defend his Sensei before Jude interjected.

"Sit down, Jesse," he ordered.

The young fighter obliged taking his seat once again.

The older warrior then rounded on Diachi.

"Keep your comments to yourself," he ordered the smirking fighter at the end.

"Fine," answered Diachi, and with that he stood up and left the room, leaving Jude shaking his head, and sharing a look with Weaver.

"Is the meeting finished?" asked Hesutu, innocently.

"Almost," replied Jude.

Moving on from the interruption he introduced Jesse to the large fighter calmly sitting at the table.

"This is Hesutu, he is Faircastle's most loyal fighter," he said with a smile.

Jesse stood up to offer his hand, but Hesutu ignored it to come round and give Jesse a bear hug. Jesse was taken aback by the greeting.

"I have been fighting for Faircastle for my whole life," Hesutu said.

Jesse nodded as the large fighter enveloped him. His Khopesh blade lay out on the table.

"Me and Hesutu have somewhere we need to be anyway," said Weaver.

Jude nodded at this and Hesutu pulled back from the embrace. Jesse felt a little flustered by Hesutu and he sat back down. Jude sat next to him, waiting a moment for Weaver and Hesutu to leave.

"He's a bit simple, but I promise you he fiercely defends his friends," said Jude.

He smiled a little at this and he ran his fingers through his thick grey mane of hair.

"I do need to ask you something, Jesse," the older fighter now looked at Jesse closely.

"Keep an eye out for anything suspicious. Weaver came to me the other day and said he had heard murmurings from disgruntled warriors who are not happy about Faircastle."

Jesse flashed a look of concern at Jude.

"Nothing concrete yet," Jude hastened to add, "but we think the majority of them may be from the other dojos."

Jesse nodded slowly, taking it all in.

"I'll keep my eyes open," he replied.

Jude nodded in response, his smile returning.

"Well, I know that was a lot of information to take in all at once, but I am grateful I have someone else to watch Faircastle."

The older warrior rose from his chair before clapping Jesse on the back. The elder fighter left to get back to Lord Faircastle.

Jesse sat for a few moments to consider everything, his new role, his new team and his new responsibilities. How was he going to explain it all to Thatcher?

Chapter 14

Jesse arrived back at the dojo as the day was morphing into the late afternoon. The meeting had been illuminating but very confusing for Jesse. Now he needed to be wary of descent towards Faircastle in his fellow warriors, while protecting the lord of Rugged. He was happy to see the doors of the dojo; he was excited to give Thatcher the good news of his promotion.

Overall, Jesse was excited for the new role he had been given. Clearly, he was considered trustworthy by Lord Faircastle. This gave Jesse a small burst of pride and he entered the disrepaired building with a small skip in his step.

Sensei Thatcher was waiting for him. He had prepared a bowl of meat stew which he liked to make on special occasions. Jesse collapsed next to him and ate greedily. The meat was goat and Thatcher had paired it with the rustic potatoes that grew down in the fields outside the town.

The old master waited for him to finish politely. Eventually Jesse slowed his eating so he could speak.

"So, how was your week?" asked Thatcher after waiting patiently for several minutes.

Jesse went over the details of the week, starting with the training session. Thatcher had been away for a few days and was therefore unaware of the situation. The young warrior described the initial running warm up concocted by Lady Emma. Thatcher nodded at this, explaining that warriors may be asked to travel over large distances in not much time. Therefore, teaching the stamina for long distance running was important.

Jesse then went on and explained the sparring session he had experienced with Lady Emma.

"I don't understand why the fighters on the defensive lost so fast," stated Jesse.

"Well, I train defensive techniques first," explained Thatcher. "The way I see it, it means that the fighter has a higher chance of surviving on a battlefield."

Jesse nodded, understanding the logic.

"The other lieutenants however believe that offence is more important. It does look more impressive having offensive skills; however, it's not how I was taught or how I teach," Thatcher continued to explain.

Jesse thought about this for a moment, this may explain why the other warriors seemed surprised at what he had done. Since Jesse had a totally different education than them, he had been exposed to a totally different fighting style and strategy.

"I met Lord Faircastle again," said Jesse.

At this news Thatcher reacted.

"Why?" the old warrior seemed suspicious.

"He requested me at the palace, today," replied Jesse, lingering a moment for dramatic effect.

"He asked me onto his personal guard unit," announced Jesse with a flourish of the wooden spoon he was clutching.

At this, Thatcher's expression changed from intrigued to concern. He looked away worried.

"What's wrong?" Jesse asked.

This was supposed to be a good thing. Faircastle had spotted his talent early and was promoting him quickly. The old lieutenant did not reply. He seemed to be thinking something through.

"I was afraid of this," said Thatcher.

Jesse said nothing, waiting for an explanation. He was starting to feel disappointed with his master's reaction.

"The reason I didn't put you forward for the trials earlier is for this exact problem."

The Sensei paused again before continuing.

"I've known for some time that you were capable of passing the trials. That is why you passed fairly easily. You came under Faircastle's leadership, as soon as you became a Warrior."

Thatcher at this point started lowering his voice; almost as if he believed someone might be listening.

"Now, listen, Lord Faircastle is a fair leader. He allows his subjects to get on with their lives. He understands the importance of law and order. And trust me, Jesse, there are leaders in this land who couldn't care less."

Thatcher's eyes were very intense. Jesse leaned in, listening keenly.

"I've fought for many different rulers and not all of them care for treating their surfs fairly. Lord Faircastle does make an effort to install justice however..." At this Thatcher looked over his shoulder before continuing.

"He can be quite lazy and this focus on the lowliest people in his town means that other people can be unhappy at his rule. Currently, he rules through a show of force; however, that may not be true for ever. He doesn't trust the lieutenants around him."

Jesse nodded at this. It was the cycle of the world that inevitably a lieutenant would take over from the reigning lord. There were only a few realms that passed the lordship down through blood. Jesse remembered what Jude had mentioned to him, unrest within the other dojos.

"The other lieutenants have been slowly building up their forces. Faircastle probably sees you as someone to trust since you are not connected to the other warriors in his charge. That's why he probably selected you for his personal guard and of course your skills helped as well."

Jesse tried to take all of this in, could he perhaps have to defend the lord from his own warriors in the future? What were the plans of the other lieutenants?

"I'm sorry that you have been put in this position, Jesse," Thatcher said.

"You should not have had to worry about this for a long time. I hoped that was to be the case."

The veteran warrior broke off. Jesse noticed that he looked very tired.

"We'll talk about this later," he suggested.

Thatcher nodded, agreeing and Jesse helped him to his quarters. The old man fell asleep quickly and soundly. Jesse tidied up their mess and contemplated what had just been disclosed to him. It had not occurred to him that there may be potential threats from within the palace. Lord Faircastle of course would want the most trustworthy warriors close to him.

Jesse went to bed later that night, thinking through all the interactions he had with his liege-lord and the implications of his decision to become a warrior. He had made an oath of fealty to Lord Faircastle. What would he have to do in order to fulfil it? Eventually, Jesse fell asleep, worried for the future.

Jesse woke later than normal and he headed to the palace. He went straight inside as soon as he arrived. The palace guards took little notice of him; they were getting used to the newest warrior. Eventually, after wandering around for a while Jesse found a room which was double guarded, suggesting the lord's presence.

"Is he in?" Jesse asked.

The guards nodded.

"What's he doing?" asked Jesse.

"His usual morning training routine," replied one of the guards.

They seemed a little suspicious of Jesse and his early presence. One of them made a move to block the door.

"I have been requested," said Jesse.

He moved towards the door confidently. The guard paused for a moment before moving out of the way for Jesse.

Jesse nodded politely at the guard before entering. The guy was doing his job after all. It was probably a good thing he was suspicious of unknown warriors. He strode into the room. Jude was leaning against the wall by the door. He flashed a smile at Jesse as he entered.

Scattered around the chamber were several training dummies. Racks and racks of weapons lay along the walls, some forged and others made of training wood. There was even an archery range stretching out of the back of the room. The bay doors had been flung open allowing someone to fire an arrow out of the room and down the firing range. Lord Faircastle was lifting weights at one end. Jesse was impressed with the weight he was lifting easily. The expert warrior's back was toned and muscled thickly.

"Just stick to Faircastle today," ordered Jude.

Jesse nodded at this.

"The rest of us will watch your back," said Jude. "You might not see us but trust that we will be there."

"No problem," replied Jesse with a curt nod and he headed over towards Faircastle.

Jesse stood to attention in the middle of the room waiting for instruction.

Lord Faircastle decided to finish his set before acknowledging he had seen his warrior. The huge warrior pulled on a silk shirt before wandering over to Jesse.

"Good morning, young one," said Faircastle.

"Good morning, my lord," Jesse replied.

Lord Faircastle wandered over to one of the walls and grabbed two training weapons from the side. He tossed one of them to Jesse who caught it.

"It occurred to me last night that you have not lost yet in a duel in my presence. I worry that you might be feeling overconfident with your skills."

Lord Faircastle was wearing his trademark smile while he said this. Jesse placed his metal long stave in one of the training racks before returning to his position in the middle of the room.

"Defend yourself," warned the lord.

Jesse brought up his weapon just in time to catch the opening salvo. Faircastle laid out several attacks. Jesse blocked them barely; the veteran was putting a lot of force into the attacks. Jesse was not going to have long to get used to the practice blade. It was a roughly cut wooden blade carved into the familiar shape of Lord Faircastle's cutlass.

Faircastle paused for a moment before launching another assault. Jesse was better prepared for them and dealt his response accordingly. He even got a chance to slip in one of his own attacks. Faircastle avoided it. The large warrior seemed capable of extremely swift footwork. As soon as Jesse caught sight of his opponent moving that quickly, his heart sank. The warrior was toying with him; he was capable of beating him swiftly. He was just choosing not to.

Faircastle seemed to sense his opponent's apprehension.

"You see how frustrating it is to realise your opponent is capable of besting you but not finishing the fight," the warrior lectured.

Jesse's mind flashed to his first fight in the trials.

"Now I am going to pay you the respect of finishing you quickly," announced Lord Faircastle.

He took a step backward, preparing for the coming attack.

Jesse also took a step back, readying for the attacks. Faircastle moved quickly to the left side of Jesse. Jesse felt the first attack come in. The blow was sudden and impactful. Jesse felt his weapon loosen from his grasp. Faircastle brought the next attack from underneath. Jesse could not react fast enough and the attack blew through his guard. The training weapon caught him under the chin knocking him over as he hit the floor.

Jesse looked up to see Lord Faircastle standing over him.

"First lesson. If a fight can be won, win and move onto the next one. Because remember there is always another battle."

Jesse nodded, accepting the lesson. He heard a stirring from the other side of the room. Jude was standing by the door with the palace guards, apparently enjoying the fact that Jesse was flat on his back. Lord Faircastle ignored them so Jesse decided it would be a good idea to emulate him. He retrieved his weapon and got back to his feet for another lesson. Lord Faircastle spotted his warrior's choice and smiled.

Chapter 15

After another half an hour of Jesse being pummelled, Lord Faircastle went to his quarters and got dressed. He appeared from a separate room off his bed chamber wearing the fur of wild animals that were not indigenous to any land Jesse had ever been to. As Faircastle stalked the corridor, Jesse noticed that he was wearing a cape that followed behind him. It created the effect that Faircastle was even larger than he already was. He looked every inch a leader of men.

Lord Faircastle entered his throne room and sat down. Jesse stood to the side of Faircastle with Jude at the other side. While Hesutu was usually meant to be the visible bodyguard for Lord Faircastle, Jude had taken his place to keep an extra eye on Jesse on his first day.

There was a scruffy-looking serf waiting in the middle of the large chamber. He appeared very nervous as he looked at the large man sitting on the ornate chair. There were several other people standing at the side. Jesse recognised a few of them from the marketplace; these were the most influential merchants in the city. One man, who was to the left of Lord Faircastle, was carrying a large ledger. Jesse was sure he had seen the man around before, working in the marketplace, but he could not recall which stall he worked at.

"Speak!" announced Lord Faircastle to the unfortunate man standing in the middle of the room.

The man started talking but it was barely audible.

"Louder!" shouted Faircastle, starting to get annoyed.

"I have brought a message from the lord of the Bat's Anchorage," said the messenger half-tripping over his words.

"The reigning Lord Julius has decided to reject your offer of fealty. He believes that he does not need your aid; although he is grateful for the offer."

The messenger finished and seemed very nervous. Jesse guessed he was worried about potential violent reprisals on himself.

Jesse glanced towards his lord, watching his reaction. The large warrior sat in his chair; for a moment Jesse thought he saw a look of disappointment on the lord's face.

"So be it," Lord Faircastle announced to the room.

He gestured for the messenger to leave and the desperate man took the opportunity to flee quickly. He tried to make it look like he was not in a hurry but it was self-evident to everyone else in the room. He even tripped slightly as he rushed out of the large chamber desperate to escape the presence of Lord Faircastle.

The man with the ledger approached Lord Faircastle and the two of them conversed with each other. Jesse was surprised. He stole a glance at Jude but he made no reaction to this potential threat approaching the reigning lord. It seemed that Faircastle knew this man very well and trusted him. The two of them spoke in a very familiar tone.

"It seems like we will have to forcibly take the fishing grounds," said Faircastle.

"We don't have much choice; we have two thousand mouths to feed come the winter. The good thing about fishing is that it produces food the year round."

Faircastle nodded, agreeing with his advisor.

"We need to call a high table meeting. Send out the messengers, I want it this afternoon. The element of surprise will only be a factor for so long."

"Yes, my lord," the advisor replied and disappeared out a side door.

Lord Faircastle turned to Jude and said, "We need to go and make an appearance at the logging camp."

"Yes, m'lord," replied Jude. "Allow me to go and get a contingent of warriors to go with us."

"I don't want too many soldiers, Jude," warned Faircastle. "It sends the wrong message."

The experienced warrior nodded and disappeared out of the chamber. Jesse was left in the throne room with Lord Faircastle and two other palace guards. Each of the lord's dojos took it in turns to provide warriors to act as guards in the palace. The dojo providing security currently was Manish's. Lord Faircastle took a few moments to think.

He stood to his feet and retrieved his weapon which was leaning against his throne. His cutlass was an example of beautiful craftsmanship from the blacksmiths. The Sigil of Lord Faircastle was finely decorated around the edge of the blade and in the centre was an image of a large warrior wearing full plate metal. Jesse recognised it as Lord Faircastle ready for war. Only rulers could afford to hire an armour smith to fit them with armour, the metal being bought at a premium. Jesse wondered where Faircastle kept his.

Faircastle headed out of the main front doors. Jesse followed on behind. The two of them exited the palace and stood outside the large doors. The stationed palace guards seemed surprised to see them.

"Young one. How is your Sensei?" asked Faircastle.

"He's fine, my lord. I spoke with him last night," replied Jesse.

Faircastle looked worried for a moment.

"Is he feeling better?" he asked.

"He has missed several meetings this last couple of weeks."

Jesse thought about it. Thatcher had been ill more often recently. Normally he had an ill day every two weeks; however, this had happened more frequently recently.

"I'm sure he will be here this afternoon," said Jesse, hoping this was true.

Lord Faircastle said nothing else because his escort was ready. Jude had appeared with a selection of warriors. They seemed to be a mixture of all the dojos. Jesse scanned the faces and saw Weaver and Hesutu walking with them. The two of them made no reaction to seeing Jesse, although Hesutu caught Jesse's eyes for a brief moment. He could not see Diachi amongst the crowd. The group approached numbering twelve or so individuals. They made their way out of the main gate all together, Faircastle and Jesse in the centre of the mass of warriors. Jude had disappeared within the crowd of warriors and Hesutu had tagged on behind the lord.

As they walked down the hill on the main road; the group spread out a bit, taking up most of the high street. People walking past had to move to the side to allow them through. Lord Faircastle took the opportunity to talk to some people on the way down. Whenever he stopped, all the warriors froze waiting for the conversation to end. Faircastle seemed to know a lot of the richer merchants who lived in the upper town. He even talked to one of them for ten minutes about the cost of blue dye rising. Jesse was impressed; the lord seemed to know his subjects quite well. As they approached the outer gate, the town guards bustled to attention. The leader of the guard appeared, to speak to Faircastle.

"Good afternoon, my lord," he said.

"How is my fair city?" asked Lord Faircastle.

"It is doing well, Lord. We caught that pickpocket the other day," came the reply.

Faircastle seemed to be interested in the thief's identity.

"Turns out it was a filthy street child. He was robbing people when they lined up for the trials," said the town guard.

"Make sure he faces justice," ordered Faircastle in a gruff voice.

"Yes, my lord," replied the captain, saluting his lord.

The group moved on through the gate and they entered the market district.

Hesutu moved closer to Lord Faircastle and Jesse spotted it. He mirrored the movement and moved in. While the people in the inner city were vetted by the town guard, the citizens in the market were not. Anyone could be in the market district. Jesse noticed that Jude and Weaver were blending in with the warriors.

In fact, it took Jesse a few moments to identify them as they were difficult to pick out from the crowd. Clearly, they were very experienced at moving covertly. Weaver was loitering at the back of the group, having a conversation with a few warriors from his dojo and Jude was near the front integrated in a conversation with an older warrior from the Khopesh clan.

Lord Faircastle went straight to the butcher stall and started chatting with the owner. Jesse scanned the individuals who were standing near there. There were two ladies gossiping between themselves, oblivious to the people around them. There was a short balding man buying meat but Jesse recognised him from his frequent trips to the market. That was Carl the candle maker; he had a stall two over.

Down the side of the butcher shop was an alley. There was a crowd of children excitedly chatting away, staring at Lord Faircastle. They were also eagerly pointing at the weapons the warriors were carrying. Jesse gave a smile; this was him not so long ago. Something caught his sight though behind them. He ushered the children away quickly. They took the hint, glancing at his forged weapon.

Jesse looked closely. There was a figure crouching in the shadows. Jesse slowly moved closer; the stranger seemed to be watching Faircastle. As Jesse approached, the figure stayed put not reacting at all. His eyes, hidden under a large hat, met with Jesse's momentarily.

"Try not to give the game away, rookie," the mysterious man spoke.

Jesse recognised the hostile words and relaxed. Daichi was slumped on the muddy floor; he was dressed in filthy rags and to all intents and purposes looked like a village tramp. On his head sat a large cloth hat, Daichi's facial features were hidden by the soft brim. Jesse wrinkled up his nose; the experienced warrior had gone all out, he even smelled foul.

Jesse turned around and joined the group. The children had run to two of the warriors who were showing off their blades to them. Lord Faircastle finished ordering a large quantity of meat for the castle, which seemed to make the butcher very happy, and the group carried on down the road. The children followed behind, chattering away. They made sure not to get too close or the warriors would have shushed them away.

Lord Faircastle carried on chatting to random people that he met walking down the street. Jesse was very impressed with his ability to know a lot of the ordinary people's names. He even laughed with a few of them, his deep booming laugh echoing down the street. This invariably led to more people coming to say hello. They finally made their way out of the market district and through the residential area. Luckily, there were less people there so progress was a lot quicker. Although Lord Faircastle somehow started a chat with an old woman who was washing clothes. The giant of a man seemed to enjoy conversing with his people and he would ask them personal questions about their life. The people were all too happy to answer and Lord Faircastle would seem very interested and engaged with their responses. Jesse could see why Thatcher had mentioned his popularity with the townspeople. That was clearly evident.

The housing district gave way to the farm district. There were several people working away in the fields. They seemed to be watering certain sections of the crop. It was not due to be harvested for another month, normally Lord Faircastle sent extra workers there to make sure the harvest was collected.

"Take a look, young one," said Lord Faircastle.

He gestured towards the fields.

"The lifeblood of your city is right there. People don't stick around for long if there is no food."

Jesse nodded at this.

The forest loomed ahead. A few of the warriors in the group wandered in front as they approached. Jesse stayed put with Hesutu orbiting their lord. A group from the Loggers Camp broke off to meet them. Jesse spotted the head foreman. He brought two large lumberjacks with him.

"Wonderful of you to join us, my lord," announced the head foreman.

He gave a cursory glance at Jesse before meeting the lord's gaze.

"I thought I'd make a visit," said Lord Faircastle.

He fitted in quite well with the large loggers, being the same build as most of them. Some of the other warriors though were acting very cautiously around them. Jesse saw several with their hands lying on their weapons. Hesutu seemed quite relaxed so Jesse endeavoured to do the same. After all, he had known many of these workers for years. His opinion of them did not need to change just because of his new rank.

Lord Faircastle and the head foreman wandered towards to the foreman's station.

"We have a potential large order coming in from Pretoria soon," informed Lord Faircastle. "That will need special attention; the other orders can be delayed if necessary."

"When are you going to confirm the order?" asked the head foreman.

"In the next coming weeks," replied Lord Faircastle.

The two leaders sat on a hill watching the woodcutters toil away. Jesse could see that the female foreman had taken over so production did not cease. The warriors sat down as well around the both of them. Jesse preferred to stand and did so a few metres away from Faircastle. The head foreman may have been strong from his years of work but Lord Faircastle was trained in the art of combat so there was no perceived threat. After an hour of talking, where it was decided that they need another ten bow saws and a handful of other wood cutting tools, Lord Faircastle stood up. The procession of warriors wandered back to the city.

On the way back Jesse asked Faircastle, "Could you not have sent a messenger, my lord?"

Faircastle did not reply immediately. He paused a moment before answering.

"I've found a message is more fruitful if you are there in person."

Chapter 16

Jesse ran down the side street to get back to his dojo. Lord Faircastle, on the way back to the castle, had ordered him to go and get Thatcher for the upcoming meeting. After Faircastle's comments earlier, Jesse had been more and more worried about his Sensei all morning. As he entered the ramshackle dojo all was quiet inside. Jesse took off his muddy footwear; a habit formed at an early age when entering the dojo; and rushed to the living quarters. He slid open the door and peeked round.

Sensei Thatcher was in the kitchen making porridge. Jesse felt an overwhelming sense of relief wash over him.

"Are you alright, lad?" asked Thatcher, his face looking confused at Jesse's rapid entrance.

"Lord Faircastle wanted me to check and make sure you were coming to the meeting this afternoon," replied Jesse, catching his breath a little.

"I was planning on leaving in a few minutes," said Thatcher and he sat down with a bowl of hot porridge on the floor. Jesse sat with him.

"You can have some if you like." offered the old lieutenant and he gestured towards the piping hot pan.

"No thanks, I ate this morning," replied Jesse.

The two warriors sat together in silence for a few minutes while Thatcher ate. The old man concluded his meal and then tidied up his things. Jesse gave him a minute to go and get changed to go out.

"Any idea what this is about?" asked Thatcher as he appeared from his room.

The old warrior wandered across the training room to select his favourite weapon from the racks.

"I'm not sure, but it might have something to do with a fishing village," replied Jesse.

He was unclear about why exactly they needed a fishing village.

Thatcher nodded at this, half listening as he pulled on his travelling boots. Jesse did the same.

"How are you finding being part of the personal guard?" Thatcher looked at Jesse and Jesse could see a slight mocking tone bleeding through.

"It's very different to what I'm used to," replied Jesse, attempting to defend his position.

"Hmmm, hardly a good use of your fighting talents," said Thatcher, with a smirk.

"Well, I've only been at it for one day," answered Jesse, defensively.

"Well, I imagine you will see combat soon enough," replied Thatcher, looking away.

The two of them left the dojo and wandered up the road towards the palace.

"Congratulations by the way," said Thatcher. "It really is a good opportunity for you. You can learn a lot there if you are willing to watch and pay attention."

Jesse nodded.

"It says a lot about you that Lord Faircastle trusts you so quickly," finished Thatcher.

As they climbed the hill, Lieutenant Manish emerged from a side street and ended up walking with them.

"How are you, Manish?" asked Thatcher, with a friendly smile on his face.

"I'm very well, thank you," replied Manish, and he nodded his head at Thatcher. In a sign of mutual respect Thatcher repeated the gesture back to him.

"How are your students?" asked Thatcher.

Manish seemed to not want to engage in a conversation but he replied politely back.

"As whiney and preening as ever."

Thatcher smiled at this but did not reply immediately.

"We are summoned to appear at a meeting by Faircastle. Yet a part of me sees another hand pulling the strings," Thatcher theorised out loud.

Jesse could see that Thatcher had said this to bait a reaction from the normally serene lieutenant. A flicker of a smile appeared in Manish's eyes.

"Indeed," he replied, accepting he had now been drawn into a conversation.

"It wouldn't surprise me to find out that Victor had something to do with this," Manish commented.

Now it was Thatcher's turn to smirk, however he flashed this one in the direction of Manish.

"Congratulations to you for your student. You have a done a wonderful job training him, he is every inch a student of yours," said Manish.

"Thank you," replied Thatcher, taking the comment as a compliment.

Jesse was not sure that it was but he said nothing.

The three warriors trekked through the dry mud and they slowed as they approached the palace gates. Jesse said nothing through the rest of the conversation preferring to listen to the two experienced warriors. He wondered who Victor was; he was not one of the lieutenants in this city. How could he have the power to sway Lord Faircastle's mind? The two lieutenants continued to chat. They conversed about previous conflicts they had fought in. Manish was ten years younger than Thatcher and asked him about a battle he had fought in for Lord Pedro thirty-five years ago. Thatcher was only too happy to go over the details. Apparently, the battle had taken place over three days and by the end only five warriors had remained.

"I was promoted right after the battle to lieutenant," informed Thatcher a wild grin appearing.

He became very animated whenever he was talking about the past. It was like he was transported back to the glory days of his youth.

"You know, son?" said Manish, now speaking to Jesse. "Your master could have become a lord in his own right twenty years ago."

"It never interested me, I'm afraid," said Thatcher.

This revelation did not surprise Jesse. He had fought against his Sensei countless times and even though the old man was partially sighted, he had never bested him. The old warrior had spent a lifetime honing his skills on the battlefield.

The conversation ended when they entered the palace. The two lieutenants seemed to know where they were going so Jesse let them lead the way. Manish opened the door for Jesse and Thatcher to pass through.

The room had a long wooden table in it with several matching chairs dotted around it. Manish took a seat and Thatcher sat opposite. Jesse stood near the chair, at the head of the table, which he guessed was for Lord Faircastle. Two warriors from the Dao clan entered the room. They were both seasoned fighters and they sat either side of Manish. He muttered to them under his breath and they nodded to him. A minute later the door opened and Lady Emma appeared. Flanked by two of her warriors, she sat at the furthest end, away from the head chair. Again, her warriors sat either side of her.

Lord Faircastle was next to arrive; he seemed happy and he caught Jesse's eye when he saw Thatcher sitting there. Faircastle made his way around the table to sit at the head. Hesutu was flanking him as he entered the room and he stood against the wall behind Faircastle. Jesse made a move to copy him. However, Lord Faircastle leaned over and muttered to him.

"Custom dictates that each lieutenant brings two representatives from their dojos to the meetings. Go and sit next to your Sensei."

There was a pause when neither of them moved.

"That's an order."

He said it with a smile on his face and Jesse smirked back. He took one of the empty seats on either side of Thatcher. There was a small amount of muttering around the table from the warriors but none from the sitting lieutenants. Lord Faircastle leaned over and muttered something to Manish, who politely smiled in reply.

After another two minutes the door opened again and the final lieutenant entered. Master Raúl appeared, flanked by two warriors from his dojo. Jesse spotted that one of them was Jude. It looked strange to see an older warrior being led by a younger warrior but Jude seemed to take it in his stride. Jesse was once again impressed with the older warrior's professionalism. Many other warriors would have been unable to swallow their pride and accept a more inexperienced warrior to lead. Master Raúl took his seat and with all the lieutenants present the meeting was ready to begin.

Chapter 17

"The reason I called you here today is a time sensitive issue," announced Lord Faircastle.

He stood from his seat as he spoke. The other people sitting at the table all stopped speaking to each other and listened.

"Normally I would have waited till next week for the regular high table meeting. However, it became apparent to me this morning that we needed to convene immediately."

Jesse looked around the room. He was easily the most inexperienced warrior. So, this was a high table meeting. It was here that all the major decisions for the town were made. You only got a seat if you were a lieutenant or a chosen warrior from your respective dojo.

"I'm going to invite Victor in to explain the situation."

Lord Faircastle nodded at one of the guards by the main doors of the room. The guard opened the door and the official with a clipboard, that Jesse had seen earlier that morning, entered. Lord Faircastle took his seat as Victor made his way around the table. Jesse caught a few looks between the lieutenants. Master Manish caught Master Raúl's eye line.

"As our lord has stated we have a time sensitive issue," said Victor.

A few of the warriors around the table stiffened sharply when Victor used the word 'we'.

"We have projected that by the middle of winter we will run out of grain. This is caused by the fact that our logging services have expanded in the last two years. Last year, we had to stretch our stored food in order to meet demand. As a consequence, we will run out of food by mid-winter."

Jesse was surprised; he had heard nothing about a potential food shortage last year. The high table must have kept that information secret in order to make sure that people did not leave the town. The strength of the town was the people who worked there. But, with the current system of feudal lords the workers had a choice who they wanted to work for. The bigger towns were often seen as a place where a man could make his fortune. If Rugged did indeed have a food shortage, then people might be more inclined to move to another town or city.

"We have been making plans to secure more food sources and we were looking into the fishing stocks at Bat's Anchorage. Initially we offered to purchase large stocks, which they refused to let us do," said Victor.

"I thought that they didn't want to accept our price," interrupted Raúl.

"Yes, we have been in discussion with them for months, but they are refusing to budge on their prices," replied Victor.

He did not seem very impressed that he was interrupted, since he was not a warrior though he had no rank on the High Council.

"Therefore, the decision was made to try to incorporate them into Lord Faircastle's cabinet," continued Victor.

"Wait!" interrupted Lady Emma, standing up. "When was that decision made?"

She seemed annoyed and confused.

"Yes," said Manish. "I was not aware of this."

"It was part of our final offer," replied Lord Faircastle.

His tone made it clear that this did not need any more discussion. The opposition died down. Emma sat with a scowl on her face.

"This morning, the messenger delivered their final statement. Lord Julius refused the offer of fealty," finished Victor.

He stood back from the table in silence, every now again glancing at the metrics on the clipboard.

"Therefore, our only option is to go and conquer the fishing grounds," announced Faircastle.

"It's not our only option," replied Thatcher, disagreeing with his lord.

Jesse was surprised with his Sensei's opposition. Faircastle also did not look very happy.

"We can always go back and give them another offer," Thatcher suggested.

Faircastle did not look very impressed with that idea.

"Then we look weak," he stated.

Thatcher did not reply.

"We cannot ever afford to look weak," said Faircastle, his voice increasing in volume.

"We currently control the biggest lumber yard in the west. We can now demand our own pricing to our customers. We cannot allow a small colony like Bat's Anchorage to dictate terms."

His voice echoed against the walls of the room harshly.

At this point, Faircastle sat down and the discussion was ended.

Lord Faircastle took a moment to calm himself before continuing.

"We need to make an impact which will send a message to the other powers in this region. I make a move to send the army. It has been a while since we last sent the force out and it will send the right message," said the reigning lord.

"I second the idea," replied Raúl.

He stood to his feet, raising his hand.

To Jesse, the lieutenant had appeared opposed to the idea so he was surprised to see his support for the plan. At this point the other Falchion warriors next to their leader raised their hands. Lady Emma and her warriors joined them. Manish took a moment to think about it but then followed up with his arm. Again, his warriors joined him. Lord Faircastle gazed around the table acknowledging their votes with a curt nod. Thatcher declined to vote for the proposition and Jesse was put in an awkward position. Should he vote with his Sensei or should he vote with his liege lord?

On one side everyone else had voted with their lieutenant but maybe they voted in line with Faircastle. Jesse had to think fast, he decided to go with his gut feeling. He would go with Thatcher; it would show loyalty to his Sensei; as well as strength to disagree with Lord Faircastle. Jesse sat in his chair, refusing to vote in favour.

"All opposed?" said Lord Raúl.

At this point, Thatcher leaned in and spoke to Jesse under his breath.

"Keep your hand down," he muttered.

While he said this, he raised his own.

Jesse sat still looking around the table. Everyone else was watching him, waiting for him to vote. There was an awkward pause as it became clear Jesse was not voting.

"The vote passes," announced Raúl. "Which warriors are we sending?"

"I am happy to join the campaign," said Master Manish. "My warriors are ready to join the attack."

"How many warriors and lieutenants do they have?" asked Lady Emma.

"All reports suggest that Julius is the only warrior with a dojo," reported Victor, from the side.

Again, Jesse noticed the other lieutenants reacting negatively to this perceived intruder. Many of them grunted slightly and Lord Manish shot an aggressive look towards the accountant.

"How large is their militia then?" questioned Raúl. "I don't believe they have many. Not many other towns train their general populous which makes them weak defensively."

"We only need to send two dojos," stated Faircastle.

He took control of the conversation suddenly.

"Also, we need to leave some warriors back as well. Manish and Emma, I want to take your dojos and I request you are there as well."

"Happy to be so," replied Manish.

"Likewise," said Emma.

Raúl said nothing at the other end of the table from Lord Faircastle. Jesse could see he looked a little disappointed but the veteran warrior made an effort not to show it on his face.

"I myself will lead the attack," stated Faircastle.

He seemed to be thrilled at the concept; his eyes gleaming with excitement. Standing to his feet, he raised his fist in the air.

"And we will be victorious!" he declared.

Chapter 18

Thatcher pulled Jesse aside as soon as he could. The meeting had broken up with it being decided that the army would be leaving tonight; the raid would commence at dawn. The early attack was suggested by Master Raúl and Lord Faircastle had agreed. Manish and Emma disappeared quickly to go and muster their warriors. Lord Faircastle had stood up and was talking to Victor about something in the corner. They seemed to be in agreement. Right before everyone started disappearing; Jude had interrupted and asked if he could select some troops from the Falchion dojo in order to create the Lord's Vanguard. Raúl agreed and Jude disappeared as well to go and select the warriors.

Thatcher pulled his pupil to the edge of the room away from everyone else.

"Jesse, be careful, your position is very precarious," Thatcher warned.

He looked very worried.

"You can't vote against the reigning lord unless your lieutenant has. That's why I got you to abstain from voting. Listen, Jesse, I appreciate that you backed me up but it is not a smart move for you."

"I agreed with your argument, Sensei, that's why I voted with you," replied Jesse.

Thatcher allowed a smile to creep across his face.

"Just keep your head down, Jesse. That's all."

Thatcher let go of Jesse's shoulders and backed away.

"Just be careful out there," he said.

"Focus on your defence, it will keep you safe. Remember, they will not follow the code of single combat so be prepared for anything. Watch Faircastle's back; he'll be an obvious target for the opponent."

Jesse nodded, taking in the advice. Thatcher turned, left the room and Jesse joined Lord Faircastle. He stood back to allow his lord some privacy. Lord Faircastle was still discussing intensely with Victor. The man with the clipboard was debating with him. Jesse was surprised at the tone of the conversation. Victor was speaking to Faircastle with a surprising lack of formality considering Faircastle's position.

The conversation ended between the two of them and Lord Faircastle sat back down at the head of the high table. He seemed to be thinking something through. As Victor turned to leave the room, Lord Faircastle blurted out after him.

"Aye, Manish, is the best option."

Victor turned and nodded at his lord before bowing and leaving.

Jesse took the opportunity to speak to Faircastle. He would struggle to speak to him later with everyone else around.

"I feel like I need to explain myself, my lord," Jesse started.

Lord Faircastle listened without saying anything. Jesse could read nothing from his face.

"I didn't feel like I was qualified enough to vote. Since this was my first time sitting at the high table," Jesse lied.

Lord Faircastle said nothing. Jesse stood there not knowing what else to say. This was the best reason he could come up with.

"Normally warriors vote with their lieutenants, so it took a lot of bravery to not vote with Thatcher," replied Faircastle.

Jesse nodded and moved away from his lord. Luckily for him, Faircastle had seen his dissension as an indictment on Thatcher.

"And, Jesse," Faircastle continued.

Jesse looked at him.

"If you are at the High Table then you are qualified to vote."

Faircastle flashed a smile across his face. Jesse smiled back, relieved that Faircastle had bought the ruse.

Some servants brought some food in for Faircastle. They placed it in front of him on the table. Faircastle ate slowly, still contemplating what they had just decided. He only ate about half before offering some of it to Jesse.

"No thank you, my lord," replied Jesse.

"Nonsense," argued Faircastle. "You won't be eating for a while so take the opportunity now."

He gestured towards the chair next to him. Jesse sat and decided to finish off the bread on the plate. The two of them sat together, Jesse eating slowly and Faircastle thinking, the two warriors contemplating the future in silence.

The warriors congregated outside the palace in the plaza. Master Manish had his troops set up on the right side of the plaza. Lined up in rows of two, the warriors snaked out along the side of the sandy arena. Mistress Emma had her troops lined up on the left side. She had fewer troops than Manish. Emma commanded forty warriors and Manish eighty in total. All the warriors were kitted out in leather armour and were all armed with their chosen weapons. Emma's warriors stood taller than the Dao clan. They each clutched the unusual Khopesh blade, many of them choosing to lean it on their shoulders. The warriors jostled and shoved each other, eager to begin.

The Dao clan warriors were lined up quietly, each wearing their swords to the side of them. They stood at attention and waited for instructions from their lieutenant.

Lord Faircastle exited the palace with Jesse and Jude behind him. Jude also wore leather armour. It hung on the warriors tight, giving some protection, but allowed for a lot of movement. Lord Faircastle wore thick plated armour on his chest giving him more protection from arrows and other attacks. The armour itself was reflecting the reddening sky.

There was a smaller group of warriors in the centre of the plaza. They were warriors made up from the Falchion clan. There were only about fifteen to twenty. These warriors would be Lord Faircastle's vanguard. Faircastle strode past them and stood in front. Jesse moved to the front of the group, staying close to Faircastle. Hesutu appeared from the crowd and stood with Jesse; Jude blended back into the crowd. Jesse spotted Weaver was within the group, presumably Jude had hand selected him as well. He also caught sight of Rodrigo. The young warrior was forcing a determined look; perhaps he was feeling as apprehensive as Jesse was.

The sun was falling below the horizon but there were still streams of light peeking out. The town was shutting down and the march to Bat's Anchorage was going to be mostly nocturnal, so they could attack the settlement in the early morning. They would only have received the messenger the evening before and would not be expecting an attack so soon.

Lord Faircastle said nothing to the gathered warriors; he signalled his lieutenants and then turned to leave. His vanguard followed him; they marched behind through the palace gate. The Dao clan followed with the Khopesh clan bringing up the rear. The regiment of warriors marched down the main high street. There was not much conversation between the men as they travelled.

There were not many townsfolk still wandering around and the few that were cleared the road to let the warriors through. Jesse noticed there were more town guards stationed on the outer walls as they went through the final gate. There was even a warrior from Lord Faircastle's dojo stationed above the gate keeping watch. With the lack of usual fighters to guard the town, the rest of the warriors were on high alert.

The army strode through the town district and residents came out of their homes to watch them. Lord Faircastle led the way until they got to the farming district. He and the other lieutenants peeled off into the stables. The vanguard stopped waiting for Faircastle. The Dao clan paused as well but the Khopesh warriors moved forward to the front. The leaders of the army appeared riding steeds. The large beasts stamped and snorted angrily. Lady Emma rode to the front. Lord Faircastle moved to the middle with his vanguard and Master Manish moved to the back of the army.

The company moved forward quietly into the night. They crossed the local ford on the River Wyoming and headed south. There was very little conversation between the travelling warriors and they stayed in silence for mile after mile. After a few hours, night had fully taken over. The way going was difficult as the army was travelling in pitch darkness. Jesse could only see the soldier ahead of him and the soldier next to him. He could not make out the Khopesh clan who were in front and Jesse had not seen them for a few hours. He found himself travelling with Weaver who exchanged a look with him. The older warrior leaned in and spoke to Jesse.

"During the battle stay very close to Lord Faircastle," he muttered. "Just to let you know, Daichi headed ahead several hours ago."

Jesse nodded in return.

Weaver at this point leaned in very closely so none of the surrounding soldiers could catch anything that was being said.

"So, you probably won't see him," warned Weaver. "He will try to keep away from the main skirmish and get around the opponent's lines."

Jesse was surprised. That sounded extremely dangerous. Jesse reassessed his personal opinion of Daichi. Who was this fighter to take such risks?

"He's the best at covert jobs, he plays the scoundrel well," commented Weaver.

Jesse smiled back, expecting the comment to be in jest but Weaver's facial expression seemed to suggest the opposite. The bald-headed warrior gave Jesse a look of warning before falling silent.

The march continued for another three hours. Normally Jesse would be feeling tired as it was now the middle of the night. However, as every mile marched by, Jesse could feel more adrenaline pump through him in anticipation of the oncoming battle. After another few miles the army was brought to a halt.

"Get some rest!" ordered Lord Faircastle.

The warriors all sat on the floor of the grassy field, taking a breath.

"We have a few hours, get some sleep," declared Master Manish.

He had moved up the formation to speak to Lord Faircastle. Both the leaders dismounted and sat together. Lady Emma appeared and sat with them.

"I've set a watch," she informed her compatriots.

"Not long," stated Lord Faircastle in response. "And then we attack."

Chapter 19

Jesse was shaken awake; he had fallen asleep surprisingly quickly. It took him a moment to remember where he was. The muddy pool of water in the grass brought him to his senses. He jumped to his feet, his adrenaline wiping any tiredness from him.

Hesutu had woken him up; he made sure Jesse was on his feet and then walked away. Jesse found the quietest member of Faircastle's personal guard a little strange. It was rare to hear him speak and when he did it was just to clarify what he should do. Normally he would flash a smile at Jesse but Hesutu neglected not to this time perhaps because of the seriousness of the situation.

The warriors around Jesse were clambering to their feet. They kept quiet awaiting their next order. A few of them communicated using crude hand signals but silence reigned throughout the strike force. Jesse tried to see if he could spot Lord Faircastle. He was, after all, meant to be sticking with him. He scanned the immediate vicinity. The sun had still not risen in the inky black sky so he could not make out the settlement they were attacking. Lord Faircastle appeared in front of the troops. Jude stood next to him. He wore a determined look on his face whereas Faircastle seemed to be in his element. The giant warrior was looking more and more confident. He was instructing his lieutenants as Jesse made his way forward. Manish and Emma saluted Faircastle before heading towards their warriors.

Lord Faircastle drew himself to his full height and waited for his vanguard to ready themselves. A couple of the younger warriors were looking slightly dozy before being roused by the veterans around them. A few of the warriors nudged the fighters next to them to get their attention. The vanguard then all stood to attention on hearing the first order.

"The rules of engagement are as follows," announced Faircastle.

"Anyone carrying a forged weapon is to be dispatched. Any militia need to be incapacitated but try to keep them alive. Serfs are not to be harmed, there will be no pillaging."

After saying this Lord Faircastle's tone changed slightly. His voice fell to a deeper pitch and Faircastle's face sharpened. Every warrior knew that there was to be severe ramifications if orders were not followed.

"And of course, no one is to harm any Untouchables."

Lord Faircastle turned and faced forward ready to start marching. He paused a moment before announcing loudly.

"Forward, march."

The entire force moved forward together. Jesse and Hesutu followed Lord Faircastle and moved to his right and his left. The vanguard swarmed around him, surrounding him. Jesse saw Weaver move to the front with Rodrigo. Jesse could not see Jude but he assumed he must have been covering them from behind. As the light of a new day started to emerge from the horizon, Jesse could make out the other squadrons of warriors' way off to the left and the right. They marched off to attack from the flanks. All Jesse could hear was the tramping of feet across the dewy grass and the scent of salt rising from the distant ocean. Emerging from the disappearing darkness, Jesse could make out the settlement they were here to conquer.

Bat's Anchorage was a fishing village and as such was situated on the coast. Jesse could see about a hundred residential houses and a larger hall sitting in the middle. Behind the village was a sizeable port with numerous fishing vessels docked there. They were still too far away to see but to Jesse it looked like they had not been alerted to the invading presence. The streets between the small houses were deserted. Lord Faircastle increased the pace and his vanguard followed suit. There was a thin wooden palisade surrounding the settlement. The invading force made its way towards the gate. Lady Emma's forces arrived at the entrance first. The warriors at the front shoved the gates open swinging them forward. The gates appeared to be unguarded and unlocked. They freely swung open to allow the force entry. Four of Lady Emma's warriors easily manoeuvred the gates to the side. They did so slowly to minimise the squeaking of the rusting hinges.

As Lord Faircastle's vanguard made their way through, Jesse spotted a pool of blood lying to the side of the guard's station. Someone had been ahead of them clearing the way.

Lady Emma took her soldiers to the left of the village. Faircastle's force marched forward and was on course to advance down the main high street. Behind them, Manish and his warriors headed around to the right.

Then, suddenly piercing the cool night air a large drum was struck, echoing through the town signalling the resident warriors and the militia. They had been spotted. Jesse wondered who was up but he could not see anyone on the streets. The warriors from the Cutlass dojo fanned out to check the alleys between the houses for any incoming defenders. Lights were being struck within the dwellings. A face appeared at the window of one of the houses. The small child saw the terrifying faces of the invading forces making their way through their settlement. An older man appeared at the door of his house but was warned to stay inside or face reprisals. The white-bearded man fled back indoors.

As they approached the end of the high street, a militia force was massing by the large hall in the centre and dotted within the crowd were warriors armed with large axes. This was the defending force.

"Forward," muttered Faircastle and Jesse could see the lord was getting more and more excited.

The bearded man was beaming his broad smile except it seemed to be permanently stuck on his face. Under the circumstances it was starting to feel chilling, the mirthful smile undoubtedly terrifying the helpless serfs peeking out of the windows of their houses. The vanguard had to spread out in order to fill the high street. Jesse could see more anxious faces peering out of the houses. Serfs who had no experience of combat; they would be fine as long as they stayed in their houses. A few of the vanguard slowed to warn the residents of this and ordered them to stay in their houses again.

The militia standing in front of the great hall turned to meet the attackers. Jesse could see that some of them were armed with hammers and staves. Most of them were armed with wooden spears complete with a sharpened spike at the top. The warriors at the front were all armed with heavy battle axes. They appeared to be the branded warriors. Jesse pushed his way forward so he was side by side with Hesutu behind Faircastle. Lord Faircastle's force approached slowly before halting and waiting for the incoming order.

Jesse could feel his heartbeat in his ears. The tension of the moment lingered in the air as both forces looked at each other eyeing up their potential foes. The only sound that could be heard was a scuffle at the other side of the settlement towards the north. Master Manish had found some opposition.

Faircastle strode forward out of his troops and drew his weapon.

"Anyone who wishes to leave may do so now," he announced to both forces. Some of the opposing force seemed to be contemplating this. One or two militia men dropped their makeshift weapons and ran off. Lord Faircastle smirked.

Suddenly, an arrow appeared from behind the militia. It flew through the air, aiming right for Lord Faircastle. Jesse took a step forward but Lord Faircastle gave very little reaction. The arrow flew right at his chest and the mighty warrior struck it out of the air with the edge of his cutlass. The arrow hit the muddy floor in two pieces. Lord Faircastle looked back at his warriors. He gazed upon a crowd of determined and loyal faces.

"Kill them all," he said.

The vanguard charged, Rodrigo and Weaver leading the attack. After the first line passed him Faircastle followed as well. He was not afraid to lead from the front. Jesse and Hesutu followed, covering his back. The two forces hit each other with a sickening crunch. Jesse found himself facing an enemy warrior also armed with a staff. The opponent looked very worried and stood in a defensive position. Jesse wanted to stay with Lord Faircastle so he needed to finish it quickly. The experienced warrior had already dispatched an axe-wielding opponent. Faircastle had deflected the attack and then dispatched his enemy in retaliation with a swift thrust. Then he surged ever deeper into the crowd of fighters.

Jesse focused on his fight and jabbed to the right. The militia man swung to intercept but was too slow and was caught in the face by the attack. Jesse disarmed the unfortunate man and then knocked him unconscious with a third move. At least he would be alive to see another day.

Jesse gripped his chosen weapon tighter and moved forward to engage a branded warrior. There was a screaming shout from the far-left flank and Lady Emma and her warriors hit from the side. Jesse was sure he had seen an enemy militia man fly through the air as the flanking attack hit.

The closest warrior turned to meet Jesse and swung at his head. The attack was fast and Jesse ducked underneath and brought his own attack up from below. The enemy warrior caught the attack with the handle of his axe. He shoved it forward pushing Jesse back. Jesse recovered and stepped forward.

He launched a barrage of attacks with the end of his long staff. The enemy fighter blocked the first few but eventually he could not keep up. The first attack to penetrate hit his chest and then the blows rained in. He collapsed to his knees and Jesse was about to finish the enemy off when a blade appeared from behind and dispatched the unfortunate fighter. The body fell to the floor and Jesse saw Rodrigo standing behind him. Jesse did not have time to speak to him and turned towards Lord Faircastle. The large fighter had somehow fought his way through most of the opposition on his own and Jesse could see he was aiming for the enemy commander who was directing his troops. Faircastle was isolated as the defending forces had closed up the gap he had forced through.

Jesse moved forward to try to catch up with him. Rodrigo followed behind; he had been left behind by their ferocious leader as well. Hesutu had been forced to cover Faircastle's right flank and had been left behind.

Jesse cast a glance at the battlefield. The defending forces were being demolished; the militia were massively struggling and were unable to hold their own. All over the battle, militiamen were falling to the floor.

Jesse had to break through an enemy line to get to Faircastle. The young stave fighter took out two militiamen to burst through and Rodrigo dispatched a warrior to the side. Jesse's fellow fighter seemed to have a taste for blood. His eyes flashed whenever he drew it from his opponents. The two young fighters made some ground towards Lord Faircastle. They dodged around a flying opponent who had just been launched by the large warrior in front. Jesse blocked a potential attacker who was aiming at Faircastle's back. The young fighter swung again and with a twist of the wrist Jesse caught him in the throat. The enemy combatant fell to the floor clutching his neck attempting to breathe. Lord Faircastle broke through to the opposition leader. Jesse and Rodrigo followed through behind him, grateful they had caught up.

Lord Julius stood tall regardless of his warriors falling all around him. Two axe wielding fighters charged at Lord Faircastle. Rodrigo jumped forward and starting fighting one and Jesse met the other. Lord Faircastle walked forward to face his opponent ignoring the fights around him. He had eyes for only one man. The lord's blade was streaked with blood and specks of it were also lying in his beard.

The enemy force was collapsing on all sides. Lady Emma pushed her way through from the left; she clutched her Khopesh blade overhead. The force of her next stroke broke through her opponents block and gutted the unfortunate fighter. She then paused to watch the oncoming duel between the leaders. She too was flanked by her warriors.

Jesse finished his fighter fairly quickly; the warrior seemed slow and lethargic compared to Jesse's usual opponents. He dodged the enemy attack, then leapt forward to catch him in the nose and then one more attack sent the double headed axe flying away. Rodrigo gutted his opponent also easily moving quicker than his opponent.

Lord Julius stood isolated surrounded by opponents. In his clutched hand was a double headed axe. He looked fairly nervous. The rest of his force was either slain or captured. Master Manish had appeared with several captured archers.

"We could have avoided this, Julius," said Faircastle.

He tightened his grip on his blade as he spoke.

Julius looked around for an alternative option. His forces were finished and his town was conquered. All he could see were the faces of unfamiliar warriors glaring at him.

"Your only chance is to defeat me in open combat," stated Faircastle.

Julius accepted the reality of the situation. He stood tall in the face of his enemies.

"There will be consequences for this, Faircastle," he warned.

Faircastle smirked at the notion.

"Ready when you are," he stated.

Faircastle brought his blade forward and stood in a defensive position.

Julius strode forward attacking with a low sweep. Faircastle caught the attack on his blade. Even though his weapon was smaller than the opposing one, Faircastle threw the attack off. Julius spun with the momentum and launched another uppercut attack from the left. This one Faircastle dodged, moving faster than you would expect for one so big, and he jabbed at Julius. The enemy leader fell back in order to avoid the attack. Faircastle moved forward to press his advantage. He brought his blade upwards to catch his opponent. Julius spun the axe around to block the attack.

Faircastle smiled before executing his trap. The attack was a feint. The experienced warrior brought another attack in; it caught Julius in the shoulder opening a gash. Julius fell backwards grabbing his injured body. Faircastle paused to allow his opponent to be ready. Julius gritted his teeth and swung again this time however the attack was much slower. He was not able to use both arms. Faircastle easily dodged and struck true in the stomach. Julius fell to his knees bleeding from his wound.

"Consequences," he repeated weakly.

"I think you should worry about yourself," said Faircastle and he struck for the final time.

Julius' head fell to the floor never to rise again. The battle was over.

Chapter 20

The people of Bat's Anchorage had been rudely awoken by the sounds of battle but that was not the end of their unusual day. After the fighting was over, Lord Faircastle gathered all of the villagers outside the large hall. He announced his victory and assured the villagers that neither they nor their property would be harmed. He informed them that their daily routine would not change much; he still expected them to continue sourcing fish. Manish's regiment had been sent to capture the fleet of boats straight away so they could not be destroyed or to aid in retreating. Faircastle announced to the village that they would receive lumber supplies to help reinforce their settlement and to construct a new, larger fishing fleet.

After that, Lord Faircastle ordered the fish stores to be opened and shared out with everyone. Over the next few hours, large bonfires were started and villagers and warriors alike ate their fill. The bodies of the fallen warriors were to be buried outside the city. They did not have any casualties, except one warrior from the vanguard who had a sizeable gash in his arm.

By late afternoon, Jesse found himself; having eaten heartily; sitting with some fellow warriors by one of the bonfires outside the town. Lord Faircastle had ordered him to go and enjoy himself. He had personally congratulated Jesse and Rodrigo for their achievements in battle.

"Thanks for following me in," he said to both of the young warriors.

Lord Faircastle shone his famous smile before turning away to go and scheme further with his lieutenants.

A few of the warriors were now duelling with each other while other fighters watched. Some people from the village came out and sat down to view the show.

Rodrigo was sat only a few metres away from Jesse. He had finished eating and was resting on the small uplift of a hill. Jesse caught his eye as they sat.

"You've got some skills," Rodrigo said, mockingly.

Jesse looked at his fellow warrior, mischief in his eyes.

"Yeah, I can see why you'd admire them," Jesse replied, flashing a broad smile.

"It's just nice that you can learn so much from watching me", answered Rodrigo.

The two young warriors smirked at each other and carried on their conversation. Several duels happened while they talked. Currently the Dao warriors fought each other. Their movements were lightning quick as they sparred with one another. Lord Faircastle emerged from the village and sat by one of the larger fires. Manish sat with him as they ate and observed the duels.

"I don't think your techniques are that effective though," observed Rodrigo.

"What do you mean?" asked Jesse.

"You need to be more ruthless," replied Rodrigo. "You should have finished them off quicker and you could have made sure that they weren't going to get back up." Rodrigo said this with a serious look on his face.

"I didn't feel that was necessary," said Jesse. "They clearly were not a threat to me."

Rodrigo seemed to disagree with this idea but he turned away to watch the skirmish choosing to end the debate. A small crowd of the local villagers came out and grabbed some of the food that was roasting on the bonfire. They greedily ate and watched the latest fighters spar with each other. Jesse noted that several of them looked quite thin as if they did not eat much often. Rodrigo reacted angrily at seeing the local villagers.

"I don't know why they think they can join us," he said.

Jesse saw him starting to glare at the serfs. A few of the other warriors sitting around were also looking very unimpressed that the villagers had joined them. They started murmuring between themselves. Jesse realised he was going to have to do something to distract them.

"Fancy testing your skills?" Jesse asked Rodrigo.

The swordsman looked across at Jesse.

"I'm not sure, you want a taste of me?" he said, switching to a smile.

"I think you might be a tad overconfident," Jesse replied.

He clambered to his feet grabbing his staff. Rodrigo stood as well clutching his chosen blade. The two of them strode over towards one of the duelling areas. The other warriors standing around noticed the two of them and started discussing loudly amongst each other arguing over the victor.

Jesse took off his leather armour and Rodrigo did the same leaving it lying on the grassy floor. Rodrigo warmed up by spinning his blade around his body and Jesse checked his metallic long staff for mud. Losing his grip during this duel may very well lead to defeat.

Rodrigo attacked first as fast as lightning. The attack came from above and Jesse blocked while spinning the staff above his head. He used the momentum to attack back. Rodrigo reacted fast and swung low, ignoring the staff flying past his head. Jesse blocked again and the two fighters stepped away to catch their breath.

By now all the warriors were watching, including the lieutenants and the victorious lord.

Jesse struck quick attempting to surprise his opponent. Rodrigo wore a smile when he saw the move. He blocked the staff with the edge of his blade and moved in. Jesse spotted the immediate danger; Rodrigo was now close enough that he could not react fast enough to block any attack. He could only block if he moved before the strike came. He spun away while blocking with the end of his staff. His staff met the oncoming attack, he had guessed correctly. At this point several watching warriors started cheering.

Jesse and Rodrigo carried on. The grass beneath their feet churned to mud as the two fighters tried every move, they knew to overcome their opponent. Jesse had fallen back on his superior defensive form and after a while he could see a window opening. Rodrigo was starting to slow, with his attacks giving him more and more time to counterattack.

The young warrior launched another two attacks and charged again. Jesse blocked both deftly before locking his feet on the floor and catching Rodrigo in the stomach. The young warrior spun away clutching his midriff. He stood strong on his feet but Jesse could see a pained expression on his face. Rodrigo swung again but Jesse easily blocked it and moved in. He now had his opponent right where he wanted him. Jesse swung horizontally giving Rodrigo nowhere to dodge. The blade met the edge of the long staff but this time the stave broke through. Rodrigo's blade spun away and the owner fell to his knees. Jesse stepped away and several warriors cheered his success. A few of Rodrigo's dojo members came forward to help him. Jesse beat them to it. Rodrigo took the help before switching to his fellow clan members and leaning on them. He said nothing but he did meet Jesse's eyes before nodding in acknowledgement.

Jesse staggered slightly to the closest hill to take a rest. His hands were aching with the force of the impacts from the two weapons clashing.

"Not bad," remarked one of the villagers; who was wearing a large hat.

Jesse looked towards the stranger; the older man sat calmly on his own.

"Where were you this morning?" Jesse asked him.

"Just because you didn't see me doesn't me that I wasn't there," Diachi muttered. "I can assure you that if I wasn't here then you would have had a fun time trying to get through a locked gate."

Diachi pulled his blade out from the hidden sheath on his back. He started polishing it in silence. Jesse lay back allowing his hands an opportunity to recover.

"Did you enter the village this morning before we attacked?" he questioned.

"No, I got here at sunset yesterday," replied the mysterious warrior.

He replaced his blade after checking it for new scratches.

"Really? When did you leave Rugged?" questioned Jesse.

Diachi gave his team member a tired look, frustrated by the endless questions.

"I left straight after the High Table meeting."

Jesse was impressed; the warrior must have travelled fast.

Jude appeared from the village. He nodded to both of his fellow teammates as he approached.

"We are moving out soon," he informed them.

The leader of the bodyguard unit extended an arm towards Diachi who took the offer and he clambered to his feet.

"Come, young warrior," Diachi directed the comment towards Jesse. "Our work is never finished."

He turned and headed towards Lord Faircastle. Jesse used his staff to aid in his ascension off the floor.

"Any scratches, son?" asked Jude.

The scarred warrior seemed slightly concerned.

"No. I'm fine," answered Jesse. "Thanks for letting me have a break."

"Faircastle reckoned you deserved a rest," Jude mentioned. "I agreed with him, right up to the point you went and had another duel."

Jude smirked at Jesse. Jesse returned the smile.

"Couldn't help myself," he replied.

Diachi had sped up ahead and was now integrated himself with the warriors from his dojo. Jesse noticed though that Diachi did not speak with any of the other warriors. Rather, it seemed like he was just using them as cover to hide his presence like a chameleon altering its skin to hide.

The older warrior looked a little worried for a moment before looking back towards Jesse.

"Keep an eye on him," he said to Jesse.

"OK," replied Jesse, confused slightly.

"If it wasn't for his talents for espionage, I wouldn't have him anywhere near Faircastle," confided Jude.

He spoke softly now to make sure Jesse was the only one who could hear him.

Warriors that were scattered around the hillside were getting the new orders and starting to retrieve their armour and any other personal belongings. A few of them broke up the practice duels going on and the army formed up ready for the march back to Rugged.

"You know he was a Ronin?" said Jude.

Jesse was shocked. A Ronin was a warrior who had no feudal lord to serve. They wandered the countryside looking for work to survive. It was rare for Ronin to be rebranded by another serving lord. They were generally seen as cut-throats and marauders. Not warriors to be trusted.

"Why is he here then?" asked Jesse.

"Lord Faircastle was impressed by him. The man managed to gain entrance to Lord Faircastle's quarters in broad daylight. I was there, we entered after a high table meeting and he was sitting in the lord's chair. He fell to his knees swearing loyalty immediately and all Faircastle did was laugh. Within the week he was a branded warrior. He does have a talent for accruing information and look how he left the gates open for us this morning. No leader could deny his usefulness."

Jesse nodded; he would try and keep his eye out for the warrior.

"Thanks, mate, I'm glad I've got someone to trust," said Jude.

The older fighter seemed more relaxed. The two of them sped to catch up to Faircastle who was organising his troops up ahead. Jesse mulled over this new information; an untrustworthy Ronin within in the ranks of Faircastle's protection squad. Perhaps he was the source of the discontent for Faircastle.

Chapter 21

The attacking force left Bat's Anchorage a few hours after midday to give enough time to get back to Rugged. Master Manish had been left with most of his warriors to restore the status quo. Lord Faircastle needed the village up and running, producing more food. He had promised to trade the food for the receipt of large quality timber. The remaining leaders of the village had agreed as this meant they could build bigger fishing vessels. Lord Faircastle named a new mayor from within the village to be in charge. This was a token role as Manish would have the real power but the populous would be happier being seemingly ruled by one of their own.

The journey back was set at a slower pace and as soon as the sun began to set, the sky was filled with shades of red. This seemed to make a few of the older warriors nervous. Jesse heard a few of them mutter something about it being a bad omen. Jesse dismissed it as foolish superstition.

Regardless, the pace of the army increased as the warriors became anxious to get back, preferring to spend the night in their own beds. Jesse walked with the other warriors in the protection vanguard. Diachi was travelling next to him. The older warrior was still wearing his tattered merchant cloak sticking out in the crowd of leather armour wearing fighters. The Dao swordsman made no attempt to talk to Jesse throughout the journey, even ignoring several questions directed towards him. Jesse gave up and just focussed on the marching.

Eventually Hesutu joined them; the larger warrior towering over Jesse. He said nothing but flashed Jesse a quick smile. Jesse returned it and the large warrior smiled again before looking forward to see what was approaching ahead of them.

The town of Rugged broke the horizon and the pace quickened again; the warriors eager to get to the warmth of their homes.

It took another hour for Jesse to find himself standing outside his familiar dojo. His body ached from the exhausting day and a half he had experienced. He was about to pull the end of his long staff out of the oozing mud and enter the building when he heard crying from inside. Jesse started forward bursting through the wooden doors.

Locke was kneeling over her father, weeping. She did not even react to Jesse entering loudly. Jesse ran forward, his precious weapon forgotten as it clattered to the ground. He fell to the floor to examine his Sensei. The old warrior was lying peacefully on the smooth wooden dojo floor. His eyes closed to the world for ever.

Jesse's mind drained of all thoughts. Locke was now weeping silently next to him clutching her father's head. Jesse had no words to console her. He was still trying to process the loss.

"Where were you?" Locke spat.

Her eyes flashed with anger.

Jesse was about to answer her before realising nothing he could say would suffice. All he could muster was,

"I don't know. I'm sorry."

She carried on venting through her sorrow.

"He's been getting worse you knew that," Locke stated. "He only had you."

Jesse thought back. He had been so busy, now he was a branded warrior, that he had neglected his Sensei. He couldn't even remember the last time he had asked Thatcher how he was feeling. The priority had been getting Jesse ready for the trials. Jesse felt guilt swell up inside him. How self-centred was he?

The problems like who to vote with on the high table and who to trust in the personal guard seemed trivial now. His master, his teacher, his father figure was gone. The signs had been there; the old man had been collapsing more and more recently.

"The physician said he had a few more months," Locke continued.

She was now interrogating Jesse with her accusing eyes.

"What happened to the money I left him? I looked for the medicine but I couldn't find it in his quarters."

She paused, allowing Jesse time to speak. Jesse could not answer her; his brain ran through the options. Then he remembered the extra money Thatcher had produced at the blacksmith yard. Had that been for his medicine? Weighing up the options in his head Jesse decided to go with honesty.

"He may have spent it on me," he replied.

Locke said nothing at the response, maybe expecting this to be the answer. She finally stood up and went to her father's quarters. Jesse waited for her to return but she did not. He covered the body with a sheet from the recruit's quarters.

He realised he had tracked mud into the dojo. A grave insult for Thatcher; shoes always had to be removed before entering. Jesse tore off his shoes before tidying up the drying dirt. His mind flowed with a hundred thoughts.

The undertaker would be shut this late; he would have to go tomorrow morning. As a lieutenant, Thatcher was due a state funeral. He would have to inform Faircastle as well. After tidying up, he trudged to his room. As he fell asleep in his bunk, his mind turned over all the questions he had for the future. What would happen to the dojo? Who was in charge now? Was he a lieutenant now? And more importantly, would Locke ever forgive him?

The next morning Jesse rose early to get to the undertaker but also to avoid Locke. He did not know how she would react to him. After visiting the doddery funeral director Jesse walked to the palace to inform Faircastle. With news of this magnitude, he saw fit to interrupt the lord in his sleeping quarters. However, the reigning lord was already up and doing his morning training regime.

"He must have died in the early hours of yesterday morning," Faircastle said, after hearing the tragic news.

The ruler seemed shook for a moment; he ran his hands through his long beard as he thought through several different things at once.

Jesse nodded.

"Does his daughter know?" asked Faircastle.

"She was the one who found him," replied Jesse.

Faircastle grimaced a little at this news.

"I will inform the other lieutenants," he replied. "You go and sort out the funeral details."

Jesse nodded. As he left the room, Weaver and Jude were standing by the door. They offered their condolences, which Jesse accepted politely, before trudging back to the dojo.

The undertaker was there ahead of him moving Thatcher's body along with one of his assistants. Jesse told him to send the bill to the palace. The undertaker nodded before placing the body carefully into a coffin. Locke appeared at the door of her father's quarters. She said nothing but she watched the whole scene play out with her arms crossed. Her previous weeping was portrayed on her face;

her eyes were red raw from the mourning. She wore a blank look on her face as if she did not know how to react or couldn't believe this was even happening. When the elderly undertaker had left, she went back into her room.

For the rest of the day, Jesse organised the details for the funeral. He got the village spokesman to say something about him. He also worked out with the undertaker where in the graveyard he would be buried. On the way back to the dojo Jesse picked up a few pieces of food for dinner. He decided to go with one of Thatcher's favourites, rabbit and potato stew. When he got back to the dojo, Jesse prepared and cooked the meal exactly the way Thatcher had taught him, making sure to sear the meat before including it in the stew. The starchy potatoes caused the watery stew to thicken and after an hour the meal was ready to eat.

Jesse thought he would be eating alone but Locke emerged from her room, her eyes a little less red. She sat down and grabbed a bowl full. She continued to ignore Jesse's presence and Jesse chose to keep up the silence. The two of them ate thoughtfully. Jesse must have made it right as Locke took a second bowl full after eating the first suspiciously. The young fighter felt his body itch; this was normally the time of the day when Thatcher would get him to train and give him pointers on how to improve his form. He glanced towards his staff still lying on the floor where he had left it the night before. Did he even feel up to training? Would it be disrespectful?

Locke spotted what Jesse was looking at and she caught Jesse's eye. She nodded at him. Jesse took this as her permission to train. He walked over and retrieved his weapon.

He started running through his practice regiment, first training his jabs and then moving onto his footwork. Locke finished the second bowl and laid it on the floor watching Jesse train. Every now and again she would nod, agreeing with something Jesse had done. Jesse eventually moved onto the training dummy and tried to strike as close as possible whilst still avoiding it. After firing off a flurry of attacks, which all flew past the dummy, avoiding it by inches, he turned around. Locke had disappeared again into her quarters. Jesse finished his usual training regime before tidying up his dinner and heading to his quarters himself.

Chapter 22

The funeral started at midday the following morning. Thatcher's body was laid on the back of a horse drawn cart. The wagon had been covered in flowers. Every now again, the odd blooming plant would fall off, as the cart's wheels dipped into the bumpy holes in the road. The unfortunate flora would land on the muddy high street only to be trampled by the people following.

The procession started on the outskirts of the town and worked its way up the hill, thus allowing everyone a chance to pay their respects. A large crowd of warriors strode ahead, making sure a path was clear. Jesse and Locke trailed right behind the wagon. They were dressed in long black cloaks which Locke had produced from her father's quarters. Locke now wore a look of defiant strength; her eyes showing no sign of weeping. Jesse himself was yet to cry and he was starting to wonder if there was something wrong with him? Behind them walked Lord Faircastle and behind him the two lieutenants that were stationed in the town.

Some distance after, Mistress Emma and Master Raúl followed with the members of their dojos. They marched up the hill, slowly following the funeral procession. The people of Rugged came out to watch the respectful march. Many of them donned black articles of clothing. The forest workers were even lined up with their families. The people stood still, watching the procession up the hill, showing their respect by stopping their busy schedules. As the wagon passed on through the market section, the forest workers set off to the forest, their work waiting for them.

Jesse kept his eyes to the floor, not looking at anyone. He was struggling to comprehend the sudden loss. The old man had given him purpose for many years. The two of them had met on the streets.

Jesse had managed to make a few measly coins completing a job for the shoemaker. He was feeling very pleased with himself and was already planning on what he would eat tonight. Up ahead there was a disturbance. Several of the older street lads were up ahead. Jesse was about to skirt away when he realised, they were leering at a smaller figure.

The group of bullies normally hunted down smaller children to steal from, but today they had picked a different target. One of the older bullies called Bulk lurched forward swinging a fist. The small figure moved suddenly and a wooden staff emerged from his long robes. Bulk was flung against the wooden wall of the closest house, knocked out cold. The fighter continued his peerless offensive, flooring two more of the older lads. A few others turned to run and one slipped in the filthy mud and turned to face his doom, fear painted on his face. The fighter paused in his attack; Jesse was standing in the way.

The older boy scrambled up and ran off, grateful to escape without a beating. Jesse stared down his opponent. Thatcher gazed at the defiant look on the young boy's face and knew immediately he had met his new student.

Over the years, Thatcher had taught him how to think, how to process the world around him and more importantly how to fight. Jesse was unsure of what he was going to do now without him. Thatcher had taught him to be distrustful of everyone around him for his own protection. No longer did Jesse have anyone to share his thoughts with. He would often analyse his actions and choices with Thatcher.

He still had so many things to learn from the veteran fighter. Jesse thought back to many of the manoeuvres he had seen Thatcher practising. The old man had promised to teach him these things, now that was never going to happen. Perhaps for Jesse the biggest loss was that he now felt no one was watching his back. With Thatcher dead, Aman leaving and Locke not talking to him, Jesse felt more alone than when he had been living on the streets. As the procession passed the alley where they had met, Jesse felt a sense of anguish pass through him. He was alone in this world.

The tears began to accumulate at the corners of his eyes. He wiped the residue away with the edge of his cloak. Locke's eyes flickered upwards to catch the movement before looking elsewhere.

The shopkeepers and stall owners had not started trading yet this morning in preparation of the procession. This did little to improve Jesse's mood. While the people were showing his Sensei respect this morning, by the afternoon these trades' people would be back at work; their lives continuing on, ignorant of what had been lost. Jesse tilted his head slightly as he caught sight of Locke walking alongside him. She too had her eyes to the floor silently mourning her father.

Her parents had separated when she was young but she still remembered her father. As soon as she was old enough, she made regular journeys to Rugged to visit him. Jesse understood that her new stepfather was a rich merchant who had funded her career in the martial arts. Locke had initially struggled to get on well with him thanks to the upheaval. Thatcher had helped her to improve her relationship with her adoptive father. Jesse wondered in that moment what was going through Locke's mind. She was his daughter. Was her grief greater than his?

The procession entered the inner gate and the townspeople were replaced by the wealthy class who resided in the upper town. They too stood in silence watching the dead lieutenant's carriage pass by. A few of the women and children dropped individual flowers on the road for the carriage to pass over. As they approached the blacksmith quarters, the smiths stood on the side of the road. Jesse recognised a few of them but did not react to their presence.

Jesse did notice that the forge fires were not burning. Evidently the blacksmiths would not be working today. Jesse accepted this gesture of respect more than all the others. As the carriage arrived at the palace gates it turned towards the right and followed the wall. After another five minutes the houses gave way to a small plot of green land. Littered across the green turf were several marked graves. The carriage came to a stop near a neatly dug hole.

It was at this point that the sky broke and rain fell upon the funeral. Jesse and Faircastle approached the carriage and with great reverence started sliding the coffin towards the edge. Emma and Raúl rushed forward to help and between the four of them they carried the coffin the short walk to the graveside. Jesse looked around; all of the other warriors had left. Only a small group stayed watching the miserable scene.

Jesse joined Locke at the other side of the dugout grave. The town crier appeared from behind the carriage and stood at the head of the hole. He started addressing the small crowd of people present. In amongst a few warriors Jesse could see Jude eyeing suspicious individuals. The older warrior was keeping his eyes trained on a small old man. Jesse recognised him as the carpenter he and Thatcher had visited. Jesse also spotted Mamma Zamora; she was seated on the floor watching the service. Perched in her mouth was a long reed pipe she was smoking slowly. Her eyes were focussed on the coffin, perhaps replaying events from her memory from so long ago. Jesse spotted Hesutu standing behind Faircastle; the warrior also wore a look of sorrow on his face. Weaver stood in the dwindling crowd watching the scene. Jesse felt a little better knowing his team were here; Diachi was nowhere to be seen.

"Lucian Thatcher had a victorious career," began the town spokesman.

The slightly tubby man was also wearing black and was clearly enamoured with his listening audience. It was not every day he got to speak in front of Lord Faircastle. The lord was peering inside the hole in the turf, ignoring the speaker.

"He was one of the five survivors of the battle of Bosworth Beacons. How he managed to survive in that hellish battle no one knows. But it must have given him strength of character because the noble warrior had it in spades. Many times he would have a sharp word for people around him."

Jesse smiled inwardly at this. At least the town crier had done his research. Lord Faircastle wore a smile at this as well.

"He had the skills of a deadly fighter and the wisdom to know when not to use them," remarked the portly gentlemen.

"No one present will be able to forget him till the end of their days," he finished.

The undertaker emerged from somewhere along with his subordinate and using a series of ropes started lowering the coffin. The coffin reached the bottom and the small audience started peeling away. Zamora stood to her feet and went over to Locke and spoke to her. Jesse started thanking people for coming. He thanked Faircastle first and then the individual lieutenants. Faircastle gave him a small smile of encouragement before turning and walking back to the palace, Jude following in his wake. Hesutu rushed over to Jesse and gave him a large hug; the fighter incapable of voicing his thoughts but still doing a better job at comforting Jesse than anyone else. Emma gave Jesse a curt nod. Raúl barely acknowledged the words of thanks before disappearing as well. The old carpenter turned and disappeared amongst the older warriors who had stayed to witness the burial before Jesse could thank him.

Zamora had finished talking to Locke and headed towards Jesse. The young fighter was about to open his mouth to thank her for coming but the old woman interrupted him.

"Don't worry about what you are going to do," she said. "I think he would have trained you to think beyond that. Yes?"

The old woman exchanged a firm look with Jesse before doddering off, her pipe still smoking in her mouth. Jesse turned to look at Locke. She seemed to have decided something as her body language changed. She strode over to Jesse forcefully and looked him straight in the eyes.

"Come," she said and Jesse followed, wondering what Zamora had said to her and also how Locke knew her.

She led them both back to the dojo. The building creaked as they entered.

Locke rushed into her father's quarters and after a few moments she emerged with her usual travelling bag. She had discarded the funeral cloak and looked dressed for a journey.

"This is all yours now, Jesse," she announced. "Make his dojo proud."

Locke even smiled at this and a wave of relief broke over Jesse. He had been worried about her for the last few days. This was the warrior he knew. Locke passed Jesse but stopped at the threshold.

"Oh, he'd want you to have this," she stated and threw a wooden stave at Jesse.

Jesse caught it instinctively and realised what he had. It was Thatcher's chosen weapon; the ornately carved wooden stave that the older warrior had poured thousands of hours into. Jesse caught sight of wooden lettering etched into the side. It read 'The Bosworth Beacon's Fifth.'

Jesse looked up to thank her but Locke had already disappeared into the hastening night. With that Jesse was alone, but he did not feel it with the staff in his right hand. Thatcher was still around, etched into the weapons and the walls. With Locke gone, he was finally alone.

The young man felt a vast void open up within himself. Emotion poured in to fill the gap. Jesse fell to the floor; hand over his eyes, tears falling.

Chapter 23

For the next three weeks Jesse was kept very busy so he had little time to reflect on anything else other than his work. When he was not guarding Faircastle, he was training to protect the lord in various scenarios. Hesutu and Daichi attacked him with various weapons and Jesse had to defend Weaver who was unarmed. The training was meant to be effective as it was designed to simulate a hectic battlefield or marketplace. Jesse had to use all his skills to keep the two more experienced warriors at bay. Jude leant against a wall and threw out a lot of information at Jesse. It was a mixture of instructions and random facts. After the various skirmishes, Diachi and Hesutu collapsed to the floor, breathing heavily, both of them failing to penetrate Jesse's guard. Jude would then interrogate Jesse on what he had told him during the fight. Jesse quickly began to listen to the barrage of random information. Most of it was information that was inconsequential but Jude would expect it repeated verbatim. Apparently, this would help him be able to take in a lot of information at the same time, a critical skill to have in an emergency according to Jude.

During all this extra training, Jesse had managed to persuade Lord Faircastle to let him leave the palace and go and train the townspeople every week. Jesse was keen to keep this task still going. He needed to improve his teaching methods; they would be very helpful when he had his own dojo.

Jesse had tried several of Thatcher's training methods but they seemed to be very extreme. Most of Jesse's early training had just been focused on defence. Thatcher had spent hours throwing out attacks as Jesse was expected to block or deflect them all. The first few months had been exhausting and very painful for Jesse. He guessed that most people would be unable to get the training regime he had.

Thatcher had been correct to focus on the defence first, as this was the most important skill for the potential recruits. It would keep them alive longer on the battlefield.

Jesse had the inexperienced townspeople line up and complete techniques to help train their muscles to have the stamina for a prolonged fight. The irony of the fact was that he was training them the same as Raúl had. The townspeople stood in ten rows of ten fighters each and as Jesse moved so did, they, in a very eerie dance. Jesse felt that he had no alternative as he was teaching so many students all at once.

The previously disruptive trainees from the other dojos focused their attention on the archery. Once or twice, Jesse had to wander over to speak to a few of them because they were being troublesome. The trainees nodded and listened to Jesse while staring at the quarter staff in his hand, a few of them eyeing the brand on his arm. Jesse had taken to carrying around Thatcher's chosen weapon. He found that the wooden weapon was less intrusive than his metal one when out and about. Carrying the wooden stave would also give him a sense of comfort. Jesse could feel the presence of Thatcher whenever he wielded it.

He used his metal long staff when training on his own in the empty dojo, whiling away the spare time he had, honing his technique. Jesse would lose himself to the practice, often training long into the night, preferring it to lying in bed alone with his thoughts.

Jesse had found the dojo lonely and vacuous without his Sensei. The empty rooms lay barren and creaking. He had moved into Thatcher's quarters. The room had presumably been left as Thatcher had had it. It seemed that Locke had taken a few things, probably personal, their absence obvious from the gaps in the layered dust. There was a slightly bigger bed than the ones in the communal bedrooms but other than that Thatcher had lived in the same shabby existence as his students. There was a large selection of parchment with a lot of writing on them. Unfortunately, they had no worth to Jesse as he was unable to read. Perhaps he would try to get someone to read them to him in the future?

Jesse left the crusted parchment to one side and searched through the various clothes that had been left by Thatcher. He found two uniforms for different army units but Jesse did not recognise the Sigil on the sleeve. Presumably, the fiefdoms did not exist anymore. He often fell asleep on the strange bed wondering whether he knew his Sensei very well at all, surrounded by all these strange belongings.

Three weeks after Thatcher's death, Lord Faircastle called a high table meeting. All of the lieutenants were present with their second and third in command. Master Manish arrived last; he looked weary from travel. He had come from Bat's Anchorage for the meeting. He was visibly unimpressed with the idea of having to go straight back afterwards. Lord Faircastle informed him of this but Manish threw a lot of angry looks at Victor who was standing in a corner, clutching his trademark clipboard stuffed with pieces of parchment. Jesse was stood next to Jude at the back of the room behind Faircastle.

Thatcher's old chair was left vacant and Jesse felt a twang of pain at the idea. The old man seemed to him to be the voice of reason on the council and the only one to disagree with Faircastle. What decisions would be made without the old sensei being involved?

The discussion at the meeting carried on and the warriors talked about the food situation which was a lot more positive. Manish had got the new settlement back on track quickly. There were even a few boat masters hard at work building a new fishing galleon from the fresh timber which had recently arrived. Apparently, morale was very high in the village. Lord Faircastle seemed very pleased at this news. He then announced that he would be travelling to Pretoria to speak to Baron Jackson. Jesse stopped his own idle thoughts to listen to the news.

"I will be making my bi-annual visit to the dear Baron myself," reported Faircastle.

He stroked his beard while informing his lieutenants. Jesse had come to realise this was a sign he was anxious. The mighty leader made no further outward sign of his true feelings to the people at the table.

"Raúl, I will need you and the rest of my Falchion dojo to travel with us," stated the bearded warrior.

Raúl nodded and then started discussing the details with his lord.

Pretoria, thought Jesse; he had only heard about the famed city. It was one of the remaining five walled cities left standing. The others had been destroyed or abandoned. It was also where Locke was stationed. Jesse had heard nothing from her in the last few weeks. Maybe he would get to see her. She was the only one he could talk to about Thatcher.

The meeting ended and Manish hurried out quickly, eager to get back before nightfall. It had been decided Lady Emma would look after the town when Faircastle had left. Jesse guessed he would also be going as one of Faircastle's bodyguards. This was why he had been training hard for the last few weeks. There had been no mention of what was happening to the spare empty dojo, where did that leave him? He was a branded warrior with no chain of command?

Jesse looked across to Lord Faircastle. The mighty warrior was in deep debate with his dojo leader about how many warriors were necessary to bring.

Regardless of all this, Jesse was looking forward to seeing the fabled city of the Baron Jackson. It was said to be one of the marvels of the world. Perhaps some of the emotion escaped onto his face.

Jude looked across at him.

"You won't be that excited when we get there, young warrior," he muttered to Jesse.

The older warrior flashed a look of warning.

"The city is as dangerous as any battlefield you will find."

Chapter 24

Jesse left his dojo as the morning broke. He carried his travelling supplies and both of his fighting staves. His metal long-staff was tied into his travelling backpack. He carried Thatcher's intricately detailed quarter staff in his right hand using it to aid his ascent up the hill. The butt of the staff was driven into the muddy floor firing mud on to Jesse's travelling boots. He had found the pair in a closet in Thatcher's quarters. They were perfect for long journeys and Jesse had been glad to see them. The young warrior made sure to lock the dojo before leaving. It took several minutes to get the key turned in the lock; it had not been used in many years.

Yesterday, Jude had pulled all of the security team together in a side room of the palace. It had been decided that Weaver and Jude would travel with the other warriors from the Falchion dojo. Faircastle clearly wanted to make a statement and bringing his dojo would do that. This would give the two falchion warriors a cover for going. It was decided Hesutu and Jesse would stick close to Faircastle, being the front facing bodyguards.

"I have organised transport for myself," stated Diachi.

He refused to say what; Jesse came to realise that it was just standard policy for the shady warrior. The other members of the team seemed used to this and did not comment further. As the mysterious fighter left, Weaver and Jude exchanged looks, the two experienced fighters sharing a nod between themselves.

In the palace courtyard many warriors were milling around. Groups of fighters were adjusting their backpacks of supplies. A few of the younger warriors were still quite dozy, the odd one rubbing their eyes to force their body to react.

Jesse caught Rodrigo's eye. The young warrior gave Jesse a familiar nod of acknowledgement. Jesse returned the greeting before making his way over to Jude who was standing by the palace gate. Jude was wearing his full leather battle armour; eager and ready to go as ever, his venerable blade hanging at his side perfectly polished. He also wore travelling boots except his were perfectly polished. Jesse realised that his own looked very battered and worn in comparison.

The waiting warriors stood around preparing themselves for the long march as the final fighters appeared. Master Raúl arrived with two warriors flanking him. He rubbed his rough-cut goatee as he approached. The lieutenant had cut his long hair down so it only fell to his shoulders. He spoke to some of his warriors getting them to tidy up a few uniforms. The warriors from his dojo gravitated towards him. Raúl made a comment and the fighters around him laughed in reply.

The lieutenant had his students lined up ready to march just as Lord Faircastle appeared from the palace. He emerged with two palace guards from the Khopesh clan behind him. Mistress Emma followed behind as well, to see her lord off. Faircastle shook her hand before turning and signalling his waiting troops. The mighty lord led the warriors out of the palace gates and through the town. The Falchion dojo followed behind Faircastle, Hesutu and Jesse. Raúl caught up with Faircastle and the two veteran warriors walked together.

The travelling warriors made their way out of the city. The troops marched their way down the main highway. The town had not yet risen so they only saw a few people on the street. They would not make it to Pretoria in one day; therefore, the pace was not hurried. Camp would be made as the sky darkened and then they would get to the city in the late morning the day after. Once they had left Rugged, Faircastle and Raúl fell back into the mass of warriors and the two leaders marched in amongst all of the fighters. Jesse and Hesutu stuck behind Faircastle. Jude and Weaver were blended into the other warriors from their dojo. Every now and again, Jesse caught a glimpse of one of them.

Jesse looked over at Hesutu; the Khopesh warrior stuck out as the only member of his dojo. Jesse realised that was something they had in common, both of them were often alone. The shy giant did not really fit in well with his fellow warriors, even those from his own dojo. He was often silent and with his head down, choosing not to interact.

For the first few hours of the march, the large fighter said little and he seemed to be daydreaming.

"Are you alright, mate," asked Jesse.

Hesutu looked across and calmly nodded.

"You look a little worried," inquired Jesse.

The large fighter nodded once more and tried to speak several times before forcing his words out.

"I'm worried about leaving my mum alone for too long," he replied.

Jesse was a little taken aback but showed nothing but concern on his face.

"Is she well?"

There was a large pause.

"She's been getting better."

"Glad to hear it," replied Jesse, smiling.

At this, Hesutu broke into a smile as well. The large man found his compatriot's smile incredibly reassuring. The two of them talked for a while, Hesutu spoke to Jesse of his home situation. Apparently, he was the main bread winner for the family; his parents were both incapable of working. His mum was inflicted with the coughing disease and his father had been crippled several years ago from a logging accident. The people from the logging camp came and brought them food every now and again but they mostly had to look out for themselves. His mum had worked as a laundry maid for several years but now she was too ill to work at all.

For Jesse it was a glimpse into a world he had never experienced. He had no recollection of his own family, and had grown up watching his own back, not having to be that concerned about anyone else. Hesutu had to be mindful of his family as well as himself. Many times, he had wished for a family to have of his own, maybe he would have had a different life if he had.

On the road ahead of them was a wagon transporting timber from the forest. The warriors took a while to catch up with the delivery. It was being pulled by two very large crag-horses. The horses both stood at three-and-a-half-metres tall; towering over the warriors as they swarmed around the delivery cart. The beasts of burden snorted at the intruders as they passed them. Their heavy breathing forced large quantities of steam out which jarred with the cool morning air.

There were two people sitting at the front and one sleeping in the back. As Faircastle walked around to the front one of the delivery men spoke to him.

"Good morning, my lord," he said politely.

Jesse looked up; the sun was soon to reach its zenith; morning was giving way to afternoon quickly.

"Where are you going this fine morning?" asked Faircastle.

"We are headed to Pretoria to deliver this lumber to the miners," replied the worker.

He seemed surprised to be speaking so freely with his lord.

"What a coincidence," replied Faircastle, "we are heading there as well."

"I assume you would be grateful for a guard to take you there. You never know what you might find on the road," Faircastle continued.

The delivery worker nodded surprised by the turn of events.

"Would you like a seat, my lord?" interrupted the other driver at the front.

He bounded to his feet and gestured towards the bench he was sat on.

"I'll be fine, my good man, but thank you for the offer," Faircastle said and then smiled beneath his broad beard.

The two delivery workers nodded and the assistant sat down. Faircastle marched ahead and his warriors followed surrounding their leader. The wagon moved to the back of the convoy. Faircastle checked the pace and slowed it slightly to include the lumber delivery. The man sleeping in the back stirred slightly as the wagon went over a pothole.

The rest of the day was whittled away with the warriors pacing towards their destination. The open landscape was broken intermittently by hills and small pickets of trees. There was the odd isolated farm but most people stayed near the established settlements for protection. The hills started increasing in number as the well-trodden road started winding through them. In the distance, Jesse could make out a mountain range appearing over the looming horizon.

As the afternoon wore on, the mountain range appeared to be rising to meet them. There was not much to report except towards the end of the march the convoy passed a small group of weary travellers. Some of the rugged and ragged men were clutching forged weapons. A whisper ran through the marching warriors, these men were ronin. Immediately the travelling fighters reacted against the perceived threat. The marching warriors all packed in tighter to protect their lord.

In days past they were warriors, but they had likely been expelled by their liege lord or made destitute when their lord had been killed in battle. The land was littered with men and women like this. As fiefdoms and settlements changed hands frequently, this often left warriors with nowhere to go. Ronin was notoriously untrustworthy. They were often hired for assassinations or by warlords to raid and pillage. Some reigning lords might also hire them to bolster their own forces in order to gain the upper hand over their opponents.

Jesse caught sight of one of them adjusting his travelling cloak. The weary man was clutching a strange looking flail. Jesse saw the fighter wore a tattoo on his left arm that had been etched out in black ink. Raúl hung back and spoke to the ronin perhaps to gain news from across the supercontinent. Jesse spotted that the Dojo master kept one hand on his weapon at all times.

Soon after that, the caravan stopped and made camp. Several fires were started to warm the warriors for the coming night. Jesse collapsed in front of the biggest one with Faircastle who was choosing to rest as well. He continued to give out several orders to set up a night watch. Raúl joined him and the three men ate their travelling rations while discussing amongst themselves. Jesse knew that Faircastle must have trusted Raúl a lot to place the fighter in charge of his dojo. The two warriors talked fairly pleasantly but Jesse noticed a hint of formality coming from Raúl. It was if the lieutenant was selecting his words carefully.

Jude sat alone on one side of the fire, choosing to sleep immediately instead of eating. Jesse finished his ration of salted meat and a semi-stale bread roll. He was about to join Jude in resting when a cloaked figure sat next to him.

"About to rest up?" asked Diachi.

He smirked at Jesse around his hood.

"Where have you been?" asked Jesse, he had not seen him at all during the march.

Diachi looked quite fresh and alert, as if he had just woken up.

"I have my ways," Diachi replied, flashing Jesse a wry smile.

"Any problems on the journey?" asked Diachi, flashing a look at Faircastle sitting across the fire.

"None we need to be worried about," reported Jesse and then at once remembered the travellers on the road.

"There were a few ronin on the road as we came up this hill."

Diachi took in the information, nodding.

"Something to consider," he replied, while peering back down the road.

"I think Jude was worried," Jesse said. "I caught him flashing a lot of nervous looks at them."

"He needn't worry," replied Diachi. "There are not many good ronin around here. The established settlements see to that. There isn't enough knife work for them."

Jesse raised an eyebrow at this statement, unconvinced.

"Trust me. I used to be one," informed Diachi.

"What?" replied Jesse, feigning confusion.

The other warrior was not convinced.

"You knew that already. Who told you?"

Jesse did not reply immediately, wondering whether to divulge that information.

Diachi did not wait for an answer.

"Not everyone is as they seem," he said.

His voice lowered, making sure no one else could hear.

Diachi nodded towards Jude sleeping some distance off.

"You trust him, but I find it suspicious that he is fine with what went down with Raúl."

Jesse felt uncomfortable for a moment; he hoped that Jude really was asleep at the other side of the fire.

"You know he was next in line for the dojo. Faircastle passed him over for the promotion, preferring him to stay as his personal bodyguard. He then proceeded to give the role to a younger fighter while Jude was lying on the medicinal bed after saving Faircastle's life."

Diachi pulled up his sleeve revealing his tattoos. Above Lord Faircastle's mark was another one that had been etched out, similar to the flail warrior on the road.

"I was not taught the ways of the Dao blade by Manish. His blade brother taught me in another settlement. When my master was killed, I took up the unmarked road. When I learned that my master had a blade brother here; I ended up enlisted again."

Diachi stood back up.

"I'm heading to Pretoria now. So, I can get into the city at daybreak. Tell Jude you've seen me when he wakes," Diachi said.

He seemed very perturbed by the conversation and then as mysteriously as he had appeared, he disappeared into the thick darkness. Jesse realised that he really did not know Diachi at all. The fighter's past history had made Jesse suspicious from the start but now he wondered about Jude as well. If indeed Faircastle cast him aside for role of lieutenant, then surely the fighter would be angry about it. The veteran had showed to Jesse no outward sign of malice towards Faircastle.

Jesse spent the next few hours thinking, Lord Faircastle had fallen asleep a while ago. The lord was surrounded by other warriors sleeping near him, making it almost impossible for any potential assassins to make their way through without disturbing anyone.

Jude stirred to his right and sat up. Jesse informed him of what Diachi had told him to say and Jude nodded. Jesse left out Diachi's suspicions of the leader of the protection squad.

"He's headed to Pretoria right now," finished Jesse.

"Get yourself some sleep, now," Jude ordered. "I'll stay on watch for the rest."

Jesse did not need to be told twice; he fell asleep with his back to the fire, clutching his two staffs. His mind blurred with accusations and potential deceptions.

Chapter 25

Jesse was shaken awake by Jude the following morning. Jesse rubbed his eyes; he could make out the other warriors moving around. The camp was being packed up. Fires were being quenched and belongings found. Jesse got to his feet and grabbed his travelling bag; he tied Thatcher's wooden quarter staff into it. The young warrior clutched his long staff and looked around for Lord Faircastle. The leader was organising his warriors into rows; ready to start the march. The lumber delivery workers were also adjusting the reins on their large steeds. They had slept with their stock throughout the night.

Jesse moved his way forward through the rows of fighters towards Faircastle. Hesutu was already stationed behind him. The friendly warrior smiled at Jesse as they waited for the order to be given to march. Maybe there was someone to trust in this army.

A few minutes later, the march began again. Faircastle and Raúl led the warriors initially before falling back into the mass of fighters. The armed warriors led the way down the road and the lumber wagon followed behind; the two delivery workers sat atop of it.

The road wound its way through some more hills before changing into stone. Jesse was astonished as his feet felt the new terrain. The city of Pretoria must indeed be an impressive city if they had the time and resources to construct a road. The highway immediately turned into a straight line cutting through small hills and thickets of trees. The pace increased thanks to the flat and smooth road.

The oncoming mountain range loomed larger and larger as they approached. This was the beginning of the King mountain range. The Kings snaked their way up most of the continent for thousands of miles. Pretoria was situated at the south most point of the mountains. Because of its location it was also the entrance to the passage north.

By midday, Jesse could make out a large settlement nestled at the foot of the closest peak. The first thing Jesse could see was the giant stone walls surrounding the city and protecting it from attack.

Pretoria was the foremost producer of stone from their quarry. They exported stone to cities across the continent. The city also leased masons to build the structures. Pretoria was one of the oldest cities on the continent; it used to be one of the provincial capitals of the Empire founded by the legendary King Jeroboam.

As they approached the city, the stone walls loomed over their heads, the towering mountain backing up behind them. Lord Faircastle and Raúl made their way forward through the crowd to stand at the front of the warriors. Hesutu and Jesse followed. The city was surrounded by farms and before the oncoming warriors made their way through them, Faircastle organised the troops.

He created an initial line of ten warriors to lead the march. Jesse was stationed behind them in front of Lord Faircastle and Master Raúl. Hesutu was stationed behind and was then followed by the majority of the other warriors. Jesse noticed that the initial line of warriors included Weaver, Jude and Rodrigo.

The visiting warriors started moving forward through the farms towards the main gate. The workers in the fields ignored the visitors. They stayed with their heads down working diligently. Jesse spotted a few overseers dotted around; they looked at the visiting warriors eagerly. The heavy wooden gates were already open to allow the visiting warriors access and Jesse noticed that several merchants were negotiating entrance fees with the guards. They were waved through and so was the delivery cart which disappeared quickly. The workers were eager to get to their destination.

As Jesse made his way through the city's threshold, he noticed the thickness of the stone walls. Each wall was a few feet thick, the stones that made it up had all been individually carved. Masterful hands had set the thousands of stones together with barely any space between them. Jesse marvelled that this was the work of men.

The gate opened onto a large space with market stalls littered around. Small crowds of people huddled around the market sellers buying various different items. Jesse saw the warriors on the front row clench their weapons which were tightly hanging from their side. Jesse walked forward clasping tightly his metal long staff with both hands, ready for anything that might happen. They were now firmly in enemy territory. A large group of strange warriors appeared from the crowd and surrounded Faircastle's force. Some of them were armed with long spears forged with steel while others were armed with a short sword and a rectangular shield big enough to block the whole fighter. They were branded warriors and they watched the visitors with suspicion.

"Move forward up the hill," commanded Lord Faircastle from just behind Jesse.

The front line of warriors hesitated for a moment before moving forward. The enemy warriors followed the route moving in tandem. The crowd ahead split apart moving to the side of the road. Jesse noticed that the main high street was also paved. The side streets spilling off the main road were not afforded that luxury. Jesse could see the typical muddy pools formed by many people travelling over the same ground repetitively.

The warriors made their way further into the bustling metropolis. The market stalls turned to open shop fronts and the further they got into the city, the nicer the clothing became on the ordinary citizens. The gradient increased slightly as the market district turned to residential homes. As the strange procession passed a large looking inn, several of the patrons fell out, clearly intoxicated. They were shouting to themselves, riling each other up. One of them walked into the outer group of the Baron's warriors. Angrily he turned to face the intruder to his frivolities. He attempted to shove his way through the warriors armed with forged spears. One of the soldiers spun his spear with a sudden movement and caught the unfortunate man in the stomach before spinning and kicking him in the head. The drunken individual collapsed to the floor bleeding from his forehead. The townspeople did not act surprised to this series of events, in fact several of them turned away. The drunk's friends came forward and dragged the man away down a side street.

Jesse forced his eyes to the front as the houses were starting to increase in size and some of them were partly constructed from stone. After another ten minutes' walk the houses were all made of stone. They were placed away from each other allowing for ornate gardens to be well maintained in front of them.

Jesse had never seen houses like this. How much expense went into these buildings? Any one of these was better than all the houses in Rugged. The road again opened up onto a large courtyard which had a sand duelling arena in the middle. Around the edges of the plaza were large buildings each with their own symbol emblazed on them. Jesse saw a long spear on one, the short sword and large shield and the duelling spear that Locke was proficient in. Warriors spilled out of the buildings to witness the foreign fighters. Jesse realised quickly that most of them were pointing at him and eyeing his rare weapon.

The procession led across the plaza and headed towards an old wooden dojo. The lead soldier pointed towards the building before bowing curtly towards Lord Faircastle as the leader passed him. Faircastle acknowledged the courtesy with a nod of his head. Once all the warriors were inside the building, the doors of the dojo were closed but not locked, presumably to create the illusion they were not under arrest, but in practicality they were. With so many soldiers stationed nearby, they were under house arrest.

It was only at this point Jesse realised that Diachi was standing next to him. Again, Jesse was impressed that the experienced fighter was able to join them even under heavy guard. Diachi gave Jesse a curt look before focusing attention on Lord Faircastle.

The lord seemed mildly diminished in this shabby accommodation. He drew himself to his full height; not far from brushing his wild hair on the ceiling and addressed his warriors.

"There is nothing to worry about, they always place their visiting warriors here," he stated.

Jesse noticed that Faircastle did not say this with quite the same confidence that he would back in his own palace. Apparently, his lord was human after all and was every bit as suspicious as he was. The mighty warrior was stroking his beard thoughtfully.

"Spread out and make yourself at home, we are going to be here a few days," Faircastle informed them.

Jesse caught Jude beckoning him and he went over, Diachi joined them.

"There will be guards stationed all around the clock, so we do not need to set up a watch ourselves," Jude said.

Diachi frowned for a moment before shrugging his shoulders as if to say 'fine'. Jesse was not very convinced, they were in enemy territory, surely now would be the time to definitely set up a watch. But he said nothing.

"I have been here many times before. It's not as bad it seems," stated Jude, presumably to make them feel better.

For Jesse, he felt very anxious. He was under house arrest in a large strange city surrounded by potentially hostile fighters.

Chapter 26

Within an hour the visiting warriors were unpacked and making themselves at home in the old dojo. In order to keep morale high, Faircastle had given the go ahead for duelling to occur in the middle of the dojo. The waiting fighters cheered on while watching their entertainment begin. Jesse was sat next to Diachi watching the skirmish unfold. Rodrigo was currently beating another member of his dojo. His opponent was not impressed he was losing to such a young fighter. The older fighter huffed and bellowed at the effort he had to exert just to keep up. Rodrigo was toying with him a bit, allowing his opponent to gain a slight upper hand before countering perfectly.

While deflecting the incoming attack, Rodrigo caught Faircastle's eye line and finished the duel. Faircastle did not look very impressed; the smile was gone and only a smouldering look remained. His eyes betrayed his feeling towards playing with an opponent. Two other warriors from the Falchion dojo had to jump in to calm the loser down. He was not best pleased at the situation. Faircastle wandered around the room and sat next to Diachi.

"Did you hear anything?" asked Faircastle. "This morning," he added.

"Morale is pretty low around the city but that is the standard attitude around here," stated Diachi.

Faircastle nodded, scratching his chin, thinking.

"Apparently last week they had an envoy from the Southern Jungles," said Diachi.

Faircastle reacted to this information a little more.

The Southern Jungle was a large competitor for lumber supplies. They would often undercut in order to beat the competition.

"Interesting, so they are making a bid to the dear Baron," Faircastle remarked.

He said no more, preferring to keep his thoughts to himself. The ruler of Rugged stayed put; next to his fellow warriors; watching the next duel happen in the middle of the dojo.

Eventually he said, "Jesse, make sure you have your armour on. They will be making a move soon."

Jesse nodded, he was already wearing most of it, but he stood up so he could put on the arm and leg guards. Just as he had finished strapping it on there was a knock on the door.

Jude stood up from his position at the entrance to answer it. He waited until Faircastle nodded to him to proceed. The door swung open to reveal Locke and several warriors. Jesse was surprised she was not wearing her usual travelling clothes he was used to. She was wearing a long red dress as if she was going to a banquet. Woven in to her black hair was a cascade of red ribbon to go with the dress. Locke bowed low to Lord Faircastle and Jesse could see her favoured weapon was in her left hand behind her. The horsehair tassel on the head of the spear was still blue and moving slightly in the breeze.

"The Baron Jackson has invited you to attend a ball in honour of his son's birthday," she reported.

Faircastle smirked at this.

"My robes," he demanded.

A few warriors produced his usual regal furs from one of their bundles and within a few moments Lord Faircastle was wearing his normal attire. Jesse thought he definitely looked more comfortable in his usual clothing.

"How could I miss out on a party?" asked Lord Faircastle, a broad smile appearing across his face.

Faircastle gestured for a few warriors to join him including his protection detail and Master Raúl with a few of his most favoured fighters.

Locke turned and moved through the waiting warriors behind. They split in two to allow the visitors to pass through them; the gap only just being wide enough to let Faircastle walk comfortably forwards. His large shoulders brushed slightly against their long spears. Jesse could not keep his eyes off Locke, he was enamoured with her look. She had a split in her dress to allow extra mobility for her legs. She looked every inch a skilled warrior and the other fighters around her treated her with a great deal of respect. This was Locke in her element.

The female fighter led them further into the city; Jesse looked back and saw a multitude of lights from the houses behind him. They had only seen a fraction of the dwellings in the city earlier. The sky had darkened quickly and Jesse realised the mountain's shadow had seen to that. The sun had disappeared behind the mountainous landscape an hour ago and while it had not yet hit the horizon it could not be seen from the city. The sky was full of red and orange and the sunset spilled out across the tapestry of the landscape.

The palace loomed ahead and Jesse could see that the entire building was constructed from stone. There were even decorations attached to the side of the building. These included sculptures of weird and strange animals that Jesse had never heard about. There was a jackal looking creature with large canines protruding from its mouth. He could even make out a large phantom sea creature that Jesse assumed had died many thousands of years ago.

Weaver nudged Jesse to bring him back to earth. Jesse looked across and could see that the protection team were analysing potential threats all around them. Enemy warriors were oozing out of every alleyway; some of them were dressed as if to head to the party, while others were just coming back from being on watch. Every now and again merchants made their way through as well, hurriedly looking around for danger.

They seem as nervous as us, thought Jesse.

There was a drawbridge made of heavy oak at the front of the stone palace. It had been lowered to allow visitors inside. Locke went straight through without hesitating. Jesse spotted Diachi and Hesutu were eyeing the drawbridge as if worried if it would be closed behind them after they passed through. Jesse marvelled at Jude who did not seem to be fazed at all by the situation. The experienced warrior was looking around as if he was unimpressed by everything he was witnessing. Raúl also seemed quite relaxed as well. He followed behind Faircastle with a handful of his warriors.

The entrance hall was decorated with portraits of various rulers. Numerous ancient faces stared down on the visitors as if guarding the entrance to the magnificent palace. Dotted around the edges of the room were palace guards each armed with a trident. They gave no reaction to the entering fighters standing to attention stock still.

"Look!" said one of the warriors with Raúl. "It's Jeroboam himself."

The warrior pointed to a painting hanging above the oncoming door they were heading towards. Jesse could see the venerable past ruler. He was sitting on a golden throne with a thick white beard blanketing his magnificent robes. While everyone else was ogling the fine treasure that was lying around the historical figure, Jesse was staring at the weapon the long dead king had in his hand. It appeared to be a long staff. It was hard to tell but Jesse reckoned it was not a quarterstaff like the wooden one he had left back at the quarters. It was too long for that, it had to be a long stave. Why hadn't Thatcher told him he was using the chosen weapon of the previous king of all the supercontinent? But the painting disappeared from view as they made their way through the doorway and Jesse had something else to look at.

The awe-inspiring banquet hall was the most impressive manmade sight Jesse had ever seen. Large chandeliers hung from the intricately painted ceiling casting large quantities of light around the colossal room. Mirrors lined most of the walls reflecting the light all over again. It created the effect of the room feeling even larger than it already was as it reflected the inhabitants of the room as they moved around. At the far end were several thrones that lay empty of occupants. The room was awash with brightly dressed people many of them carrying weapons of various descriptions. Locke stopped and so did Faircastle who was now standing right behind her; the young warrior being dwarfed by the larger fighter. Faircastle's clothes helped create the illusion of him being even taller than he already was.

A thin, well-dressed man stood to the side and with a loud pompous voice announced them to the room.

"Entering now, the Ruler of Rugged, Lord Faircastle," declared the thin man.

Most of the people in the room turned to witness Faircastle and his entourage make their way down the short flight of stairs to get to the ballroom floor. A few people carried on with their drinks, ignoring him. As Faircastle descended the staircase, Jesse was careful not to tread on the hem of his fur cloak.

"Give me a wide berth," Faircastle whispered.

Jude nodded in reply. Diachi disappeared into the crowd almost immediately. Jesse followed Faircastle who was walking through the mass of brightly coloured people making sure to stay a few metres behind him. Jesse lost sight of the other warriors within the crowd. Helpfully, Faircastle was easy to identify as he was standing over the majority of them. The leader's fur robes stuck out against the fine silk and woven clothing around him.

Jesse hoped he could speak to Locke and catch up with her. It appeared she had joined her master; a formidable female warrior who was eyeing up these intruders to the party. The female lieutenant wore a severe look on her face which was accentuated by her sharp cheek bones. She wore a pale blue dress and she was clutching her weapon tightly in her hand.

Lord Faircastle seemed to have found the alcohol very quickly and had already drained his first flagon by the time Jesse caught up with him. A hurried waiter was bustled away to retrieve more for the thirsty warrior.

Jesse noticed that a lot of people were eying him cautiously. They seemed to be staring at his long staff apparently unsure how to react to it. A few people muttered to each other about how 'it was an insult'. Jesse was unsure what they were referring to but he thought it was smarter to stay near to Lord Faircastle and focus on the task at hand. To survive the night while surrounded by potential enemies was the most important thing at the moment. One of the Baron's warriors barged into him as he passed, Jesse chose to ignore it. He stood within a metre or two of Faircastle while leaning against a wall.

The well dressed and haughty man, at the entrance to the ballroom, made another announcement.

"Entering, now, the right honourable, Lieutenant Marx, wielder of the titanic blade, Cataclysm."

The conversation around the room dulled to a quiet whisper as the majority of people in the room turned to witness the warrior entering the chamber. Jesse looked as well to glimpse the legendary weapon. Standing at the top of the short flight of stairs leading down to the ballroom floor was a magnificently dressed fighter. Dressed in the finest white livery was a tall handsomely built man with a heavy-set jaw. Set into his face were brilliant blue eyes but they were hard to distinguish because of the cascade of brilliant blonde hair that flowed down to surround his head. The warrior gave the man announcing him a small nod before descending the staircase effortlessly. His retinue followed suit; large hulking specimens also dressed elegantly. Over their shoulders was slung their almighty weapons, Zweihänders to a man. The massive weapons dwarfed all others around it. They even made Jesse's long staff appear to shrink in size.

Lieutenant Marx led the group onto the ballroom floor and the crowd gave way to let them through. Jesse eagerly eyed the weapon Marx carried in his gloved hand. The blade was named; exceedingly rare among warriors it must have had a rich history of conflict before it even made it into Marx's hands. The revered warrior was still quite young himself. The blade was cunningly brutal in its design, the blade was so large that many fighters needed to use it with two hands and as such there was a handgrip built into it a third of the way up as well as the usual one at the bottom. Both sides had been sharpened so each edge was lethal to the touch.

The conversation rose once again back to normal and Marx slunk off to the side of the room surrounded by his fighters no one daring to approach.

"My dear, Baron," announced Faircastle clearly over the polite conversation and cutting through the music being played at the other end of the room.

Jesse spotted a fairly well aged man who was surrounded by large warriors with grim faces. The ruler of Pretoria had a thin beard and suspicious black eyes which he used to analyse the large fighter approaching him.

"Lord Faircastle. I'm glad you were able to join us this evening," said the ruler.

He said this with an air of grace but it was clear he was not very impressed with the interruption.

"Children are so important, don't you think?" exclaimed Faircastle.

He clutched a fresh flagon of ale in his hand.

"Congratulations for you and your son."

The Baron sniffed at this comment.

"He's not much of a son of mine. I'm afraid."

The Baron shot a look of disgust at a younger man who was showing off for some females in beautiful gowns at the other end of the room.

"I shudder to think what will happen to the capital when he takes over."

The future rulers of Pretoria were decided by birth. This was the way they had done it for centuries and it ensured the city's survival down the years. Having a familiar face inherit the role meant that there was less squabbling and rebellions.

Faircastle said nothing choosing to not comment. The Baron noticed this and changed the subject.

"Now to our usual competition," he said. "Who has the best young fighter? I do so love to beat you every year." Jackson said this with a smile on his face.

Faircastle seemed to find this less funny.

"I do have a new competitor for you," replied Faircastle.

"Do you?" said the Baron. "By any chance is it that long-stave wielding child you have in the corner?"

The Baron finished the question by pointing right at Jesse.

"Perceptive as always," answered Lord Faircastle, his eyes twinkling at the anticipation of the oncoming duel.

"Well, I have my chosen champion," Jackson said. "But be warned he is lethal; he doesn't do practice duels; he goes for the throat."

The Baron smirked at this with an evil look in his eye.

A young warrior emerged from the crowd. Jesse stepped forward as well sensing the right time to approach. The mysterious fighter appeared to be armed with a brace of knives attached to his waist. He was spinning one in his hand absentmindedly barely paying attention to the conversation.

"Well shall we start?" asked Baron Jackson, before signalling the warriors surrounding him. The escort moved into the crowd, getting them to disperse and move to the edge of the room. As they waited for the more drunken guests to get out of the way, Faircastle and Jesse gathered with a few friendly warriors. Hesutu gave Jesse a reassuring smile before patting him on the shoulder. Jesse could not see Weaver or Diachi for that matter. *They must be standing in the crowd somewhere*, Jesse thought.

"I'm sorry about this," muttered Jude under his breath.

"Every now and again, Jesse, me and the Baron have a competition to see who has the finest young warrior. It is common to pick the fighter with the most unique fighting style," stated Faircastle.

His large hand was now clapping Jesse on the back in an apparent attempt to reassure him.

"Fight your own game," stated Faircastle. "Don't fall to his rhythm, command it to yours."

For Jesse these words seemed less than useful. He was about to fight an opponent he had never seen before and judging from the massive pool of fighters the Baron had working for him, his choice was going to be a skilled fighter. Jesse thought back to what Thatcher might have said. But all he could think of was what Locke had said weeks ago. 'Make his dojo proud.' The thought echoed in his mind repeatedly over and over again.

She was staring at him from across the room. Everyone else was taking bets on who would win but was she looking at him with concern or coldness? Jesse could not make it out.

Chapter 27

The spectators moved back to allow a circle to form in the centre of the hall. Many of the partygoers were loudly discussing who they thought would be victorious. The majority seemed to agree that the strange fighter with the long weapon would have no chance of winning.

The crowd fell silent as Jesse's opponent entered the makeshift duelling arena. The young warrior had a cocky swagger as he strode to the centre, clearly feeling that the win was already in the bag. He chose a curved Karambit knife from his belt. The blade was as black as night. The young fighter felt its weight in his hand before clutching it in his left and taking a crouching pose; lowering himself down. Jesse stood away from him at the edge of the circle.

Jesse felt a hand push him forward and he took the hint. He moved slowly towards his opponent. The warrior was younger than he was. His opponent had barely just had his teenage growth spurt but the Baron was clearly no fool. His chosen champion would be a skilled fighter; either equal or greater than Locke's skills.

Jesse took his place on the battlefield; the floor was made of smooth stone. This would assist in greater mobility with less friction than grass or dirt. The crowd held their breath waiting for the signal. Then a flash of crimson, the Baron had thrown in a red lace handkerchief.

Apparently, this was the signal because Jesse's opponent took the opportunity to launch a knife from his belt at Jesse's head. The young fighter accomplished this feat with a sudden flick of his wrist. Jesse's instincts kicked in and he dodged the blade. As it flew past, Jesse also caught a flicker of movement. He turned and swung out with the edge of his long staff. His opponent had used the distraction of the knife to attack from the side.

Jesse's attack forced his opponent to pull back and he held his knife out in front of his face in defence. There was a pause in the combat where both fighters acknowledged the ability of their opponent. *This guy is extremely light on his feet,* thought Jesse. *He will want to get past my guard and nullify my range advantage.*

"Gut him, Giuseppe!" someone yelled from the crowd.

The young fighter gave a sly smirk before attacking again. He slid forward suddenly forcing Jesse to sweep low to push back the attacker. Giuseppe leapt over the attack and swung sideways at Jesse's chest. The attack only scratched the leather armour as Jesse had read the move at the last possible moment. The warrior from the stave dojo stepped backwards spinning his weapon around him. This forced Giuseppe back for a second time. There was another pause as the two fighters planned their next move.

Jesse decided to get off the back foot and stepped forward. He launched several attacking jabs with the end of his weapon. Giuseppe stepped back to avoid them and then ducked underneath. He drove forward once more to get under his opponent. However, Jesse was ready for it and brought the other end of his staff through catching his opponent in the face. Giuseppe flew back, somehow landing on his feet in a crouched position. He spat out a selection of blood and teeth onto the floor. The knife fighter looked at the crowd around him and then snarled.

Grabbing two knives from his belt he flung them at Jesse one at his head and one at his lower body. Jesse was forced to deflect one of the blades and dodge the other one. When he looked up; his opponent had disappeared. Jesse spun to catch sight of him but too late he realised his opponent was under his eye line. Without looking to check, Jesse threw himself forward and flipped over him on the floor. He got to his feet swiftly and realised that Giuseppe had cut his leg quite badly. Jesse felt the hot blood seep down his leg. Luckily, his opponent had not cut too deep. The slash had missed any major leg muscles and sinews.

Giuseppe was kneeling in the centre looking very pleased with himself. Then with a spin, he turned to start forward again. Jesse fell back on his years of experience and went with a defensive technique that he had learnt when Thatcher had spent a month attacking him with a knife. Giuseppe's attack came again and Jesse blocked it. Another knife flew past Jesse's head just missing the spectators behind him.

The knife wielder now had a blade in each hand and was deathly close to him. Jesse had nowhere to go; the crowd was just behind him. The next few moments became something of a blur for Jesse. As Giuseppe attacked several times, Jesse blocked them all somehow. The attacker seemed confused as his opponent seemed to know exactly where the attack was coming from. He attacked again, this time changing up the attack pattern, but to no avail. The knife strokes seemed to either find thin air or the cold steel of the long staff. Jesse caught sight of Locke from across the arena, she had pushed her way forwards to the edge of the crowd. Jesse could see a look of concern on her face. And he wondered why was she worried? He had his opponent right where he wanted.

Giuseppe launched more attacks but his strokes were getting sloppier out of frustration. Jesse struck at the end of the last attack. Instead of deflecting the attack as usual, the long staff met the blade head on. Giuseppe was ill prepared for it. The knife blade was not built for a head on attack like this and as Jesse put his full strength into the blow, the knife shattered under the pressure. Giuseppe fell back under the effort and Jesse followed through. Launching an attack from on high, Jesse stepped forward. The unfortunate opponent had nowhere to go and was forced to block the blow with his Karambit knife and the last blade on his belt.

Giuseppe was now lying on the floor attempting to block the incoming blows from Jesse. The strikes rained in forcing the knife warrior to deflect the attacks. Giuseppe waited for the attacks to slow down and the pace paused for a moment. Quickly, Giuseppe struck again, throwing one of his knives at Jesse's face. Sadly, he did not find his opponent.

Jesse had moved. With a swift side stroke Jesse disarmed the final knife from his opponent. Too late, Giuseppe saw the error; his opponent had intentionally slowed down. Jesse stood back waiting for the immediate surrender. Giuseppe had other ideas; he launched himself forward for a sudden attack. Jesse quickly sidestepped catching the unfortunate warrior in the stomach winding him. With one final attack, Jesse brought his weapon down on the back of his opponent's head knocking him out cold.

Silence ruled the room, nothing could be heard. The crowd's champion laid out flat on the cold stone floor. Lord Faircastle was the only person to enter the arena. He slapped Jesse on the back in congratulations. He did not announce anything to the room but he did lean in and whispered to Jesse.

"Well fought, young one. I had a good feeling about you."

He brought Jesse over to one of the sides of the room allowing the young fighter to collapse on one of the beautifully designed chairs. Weaver rushed over to bandage Jesse's wound. On the Baron's command, the music started up again and everyone carried on as if nothing had happened. The guests of the party continued with their conversations ignoring the last ten minutes.

The dejected form of Giuseppe was still lying on the floor. No one had gone over to check on his condition. People were just stepping over him to get to where they needed to go. Apparently, after you lose, you have no worth in Pretoria.

Chapter 28

Faircastle ordered that they leave the party a few hours later and the visiting warriors trudged out, exhausted by the night's frivolities, none more so than Jesse. He could still feel the gash in his leg burning being pierced by the cool night air. They were escorted back to their creaking quarters by the usual guards; apparently, they had been waiting outside the entire evening. Jesse collapsed onto his belongings that were stacked into a corner and within a few minutes he was fast asleep attempting to cleanse his fatigue.

A few hours later, Jesse was woken by rolling over in his sleep and lying on the cool metal of his long staff. The sudden change in temperature on his side woke him suddenly. He wearily rose to get a drink. On his way, Jesse had a look around. He saw Lord Faircastle resting silently sat up against the wall. The weary leader seemed always prepared for a fight. His weapon was clasped tightly in one of his hands.

Jesse spotted the two warriors who were on watch, it was Weaver and Hesutu. His two teammates nodded to him as he got to the refreshments table. Pouring himself a drink, Jesse took a moment to revel in his earlier victory. Perhaps this would be the opportunity Faircastle would take to make him lieutenant. Nobody had mentioned the title of lieutenant to him.

Jesse also had not brought it up with anybody. To do so for him would have been disrespectful to his former master, nevertheless the thought still burned in the back of his mind. Talking to Jude about it would be a touchy subject with the older warrior, since he had been passed over by Faircastle in favour of Raúl. Every now and again the veteran warrior, despite his obsession to following the rules, would break protocol and be very short with Raúl when conversing with him. Speaking of Jude, where was he?

Jesse could not find the warrior anywhere; he scanned the dojo looking for the sleeping fighter. He made his way over to Weaver and Hesutu. Jesse continued to check as he approached them. They spotted him looking and guessed his thought process by the time he got to them.

"He's outside relieving himself," answered Weaver, before Jesse could ask the question.

Jesse nodded, of course that made sense. He made his way back to the belongings, before falling asleep, still weary from his arduous duel. The younger fighter missed the other important warrior absent from the room.

The following morning the warriors were allowed outside into the general square by Baron Jackson. Some of the fighters, like Rodrigo, had been house bound for most of the day, so they were very grateful to get outside. Again, they split up to duel and train with each other. This time Jesse stayed back, preferring to watch and allow his wound time to heal. Diachi sat with him for most of the time, keen on not drawing too much attention to himself. The mysterious warrior sat there with hat pulled down low hiding from the morning sun. His mood seemed to have improved from the last time Jesse had spoken to him.

"I'm sorry," began Jesse.

Diachi waved the apology away.

"Don't worry, I was just venting," the older fighter said.

"You've been put in a difficult position. Me and Jude have never really got on. He distrusts me because of my past allegiances and I dislike him because I hate authority. Maybe it's my years of being on the road."

The Dao swordsman wore a wolfish grin as he thought back to past memories.

Jesse smiled back grateful to not have to pick a side in the argument.

"Great job on dispatching that sneaky bastard last night."

"Thanks. I don't think I've had to fight anyone that tough before, except of course Sensei and Faircastle."

At the mention of Thatcher, the conversation took an awkward turn. The two fighters looked away from each other.

"My condolences," muttered Diachi.

He looked awkward saying it. He was about to address his lack of attendance at the funeral. But Jesse jumped in.

"What was your Sensei like?" asked Jesse.

Daichi smiled for a moment before answering thinking through his response.

"She was the most patient warrior I've ever met. The crap I put her through and she still trained me and looked over me. There are no words. I missed having someone to trust and to guide me; I guess that's why I joined back up."

Jesse nodded. He understood the feeling. More and more he was realising Thatcher had been a parental role in his life. He thought back to better moments with Thatcher. The first time the old fighter had let him pick up a quarter staff, the moment the older fighter had allowed him to become his pupil. The two fighters sat quietly reminiscing their past to themselves.

The usual stationed guards were circled around them keeping an eye on the ongoing proceedings. A few of the Baron's warriors joined the visitors at lunchtime. Most of them sat watching in their own groups, chatting away and sometimes laughing at an unfortunate loser.

Even Locke made an appearance and sat with Jesse and Diachi. Jesse noticed she was wearing standard duelling armour that had been altered for her. She took a look at Jesse's wound and called him a 'wimp' for making a big deal of it. Jesse shared her smile grateful for the old Locke he had grown up with.

Diachi leaned over and said, "My condolences for the loss of your father."

Locke fell silent at this and focused her attention on the ongoing duel. Rodrigo was schooling a warrior twice his size. The younger warrior was more skilled and aided by the difference of speed because of his youth. He was clearly going to win.

The three warriors sat together watching the duel conclude with Rodrigo finishing triumphantly. *At least he didn't make his opponent wait,* thought Jesse.

A few moments passed and then Locke stiffened suddenly. Her head swivelled quickly to eye some warriors that had appeared in the square. Jesse turned to look as well. Three confident fighters had appeared each clutching their Zweihänder blades. They wore a look of contempt at the visiting warriors lounging around the open area. One of them muttered something to the other two. They all had a chuckle while watching a duel that was going on. Jesse noticed that other warriors from the Baron's dojos kept a wary eye on them as well.

"They seem very cocky," said Diachi and he threw the warriors a look of disgust.

"There is a reason for it," said Locke and she clearly looked very uncomfortable.

Her hands lay cautiously on her spear lying on the floor next to her. Jesse followed suit mirroring her. A few of the warriors from the Falchion dojo stood, they had noticed the intruders. The Zweihänder fighters were now openly mocking the fighting that was going on and were doing so loudly for everyone to hear.

Then the three enemy warriors turned and left and the tense atmosphere was broken. Jesse was grateful they did not need a skirmish breaking out in the middle of an enemy city. Locke still looked a little perturbed and she still kept her weapon close at hand.

After a few more minutes, in which no one said anything, Locke made her excuses and disappeared quickly from view in between two dojos. Diachi made a snide remark about Rodrigo's lack of humility and left as well.

About lunchtime, the warriors were bundled back into the dojo and after they had eaten Lord Faircastle was summoned again.

Faircastle chose his usual protection team except Jude, he stayed behind. Lord Faircastle wanted his troops ready to leave when they got back; he expected the meeting to be quick. Master Raúl stayed as well and he whispered a few words to Faircastle before he left. The reigning lord nodded in agreement with his lieutenant.

A man in well-tailored robes met them outside the dojo. He bowed low before leading them back to the stone fortress. Jesse walked ahead of Faircastle with Diachi behind. Weaver and Hesutu stood either side. While Jesse was concerned, Faircastle seemed quite carefree. The large warrior strolled along, whistling a careless tune, allowing his protection team to get on with their job.

They were taken back into the giant hall of mirrors which was even larger and more impressive with all the people gone. The well-dressed man took them into a smaller room with a large table situated in it. There were heavy oak chairs lined up along either side of the table. The room was vacant before they arrived and they were instructed to take the seats which faced the doorway.

Lord Faircastle took the middle chair and ordered Jesse and Diachi to take the seats next to him. Hesutu and Weaver stood behind them. The five of them waited in silence.

Eventually, the door opposite them opened and several guards appeared. They stood facing Faircastle with their backs to the wall. A minute later, Baron Jackson appeared with four other warriors in his wake. The baron was wearing robes of pure white woven with silk. He looked every inch the ruler of one of the greatest cities of Pangaea Ultima. On his hands were several gold encrusted rings and around his neck was a heavy gold chain with the Sigil of his dojo (a trident). His long-forked weapon was left leaning on his chair. The other warriors who sat down either side of him were all armed with different weapons.

Jesse saw the female Sensei who had stood with Locke at the party. She had switched her dress out for leather armour and she had paired it with a pale blue cape behind her. The formidable fighter left her spear lying on the table in front of her. One of the lieutenants was armed with a trident and sat with it clutched in his hand. The tallest warrior was armed with a short sword but Jesse noticed he had left his large shield resting on the back wall. The final lieutenant was Marx and he was armed with his Zweihänder. The warrior had entered the room carrying the blade on his shoulder. He sat in his chair holding the blade next to him leering at the visitors across from him.

Despite the imposing presence of the Baron with his lieutenants, Lord Faircastle seemed to shrug them off.

"My dear, Baron, I have a copy of the suggested contract that we discussed in our communications."

Faircastle leaned across and attempted to pass the piece of paper to the Baron. Marx leaned over and snatched it. He read it first and then passed it to the Baron. The Baron did not even read it. He chose to pass it along the row to his lieutenants.

"This is not what we expected, when it comes to the price," replied the warrior with the Zweihänder.

"Marx is correct," stated the tall, sharp female warrior. "This is not a competitive price."

Faircastle said nothing for a moment almost as if he was working out how to word the next sentence correctly.

"We are aware that you have been in communication with other potential businesses. You do have other options when it comes to lumber services. We both know that the jungle colonies are not a reliable company to sign a contract with. If you even get the lumber you ordered with them then it will arrive in the incorrect size or even several weeks late. My lumber services are on time, appear regularly and are exact to specification."

Faircastle sat back.

"Baron, we do not need to take this contract," stated Marx shortly.

The Baron held up his hand to signal his associate to stop talking. He knew he had no choice but to accept the contract. The jungle colonies were significantly cheaper but it would be unreliable and it could take weeks to make sure the lumber was to specifications.

"What kind of guarantees can you give us?" asked the Baron.

Jesse saw a small smile emerge from behind the beard.

"I can guarantee that your order will go to the front of the list. I plan on returning, travelling back tonight. Therefore, the first of the order will be arriving by the end of the week," replied Faircastle.

The Baron nodded; this was as good as the offer was going to get. He had no other options.

"The payments will commence on receipt of the first lumber," he stated.

Lord Faircastle nodded in agreement.

"May I have a list of your prescribed lumber? Just bear in mind that you have the list in the right order," he asked.

One of the other lieutenants slid a piece of paper across the table and Lord Faircastle took it. He looked at it and then a look of confusion flashed across his face.

"Other specifications will follow," stated the female lieutenant with the long spear.

Faircastle nodded. He stood up from the table and Jesse and Diachi followed. Faircastle bowed sharply as an act of common courtesy. Then he turned and left the room. Jesse made to turn to follow him and it was then that he realised that the Baron was looking directly at him. The old fighter was fixing him with a steely gaze. Jesse gave a curt bow himself before following on behind glad to escape the room filled with fierce warriors. He missed the small smile on Marx's face.

Lord Faircastle took the lead as they left the palace. He was travelling at quite a pace and the guards that were following had to jog to keep up with the giant warrior's massive strides.

"Let's get out of this wretched city," said Lord Faircastle under his breath.

The mask had slipped now. The leader wore a look of anxiety; he glanced a few times down alleyways as if expecting an ambush at any moment. As the small group hurried to leave the city the heat of the afternoon rose to meet them.

Chapter 29

With the sky darkening, the warriors left Pretoria with the sun setting on their left. Faircastle had hurried them out of the city preferring to not wait a minute longer than necessary. The large fighter set the pace fairly high to begin with. The city quickly disappeared over the grassy knoll of a hill but it was another two hours until the mountain behind disappeared. Jesse was stationed towards the front of the troop caravan and he found himself marching next to Rodrigo till they got to the evening camp.

The two young fighters spent a few dark hours discussing footwork and the merits of different attack positions. Jesse favoured on the side of defence whereas Rodrigo preferred a good solid offensive position. They both agreed that the long-staff was the best weapon for defence.

"You can punish any opening in the attacker's defence so quickly," stated Rodrigo.

Jesse agreed with him but he did think that the long-staff had its own draw backs. While you could punish any errors rapidly, the staff did not have any sharp edges to make sure the fight ended. The amount of damage he could do was handicapped. On the other hand, a weapon like a sword was capable of finishing a fight immediately.

The warriors slept that night in a woodland thicket preferring it to the open plain for its protection from the elements. The sky had opened and it was pouring thick and fast. After a few hours of restless sleep, the order was given to get back on their feet. The camp was flooded and no one was getting any rest. For Jesse, he was already miserable but his wound was now aching something fierce.

The soldiers carried on walking through the sopping wet night, only focusing on the road ahead of them. The pace had slowed to allow safe passage around the quickly forming muddy pools and progress was slow. Conversation was now at a minimum. Everyone preferred to focus on the long journey ahead of them.

Weary from lack of sleep, the mournful procession continued throughout the night.

As the dawning of the sun broke over the hill, the rain eased up. Daybreak revealed a miserable group of soldiers exhausted by the night's journey. In the distance was the outline of a dilapidated barn. Faircastle ordered them towards it and the tired warriors were only too happy to comply. The barn was dirty, dusty but more importantly still had a fairly competent roof. The exhausted fighters collapsed to the floor and many of them fell asleep immediately.

Jesse, Diachi and another warrior were put on watch as the rest of the force slept. Jesse took the main door and Diachi stationed himself at the back watching the road.

The early morning hours slipped by and Jesse had to keep himself awake. He started running drills outside the barn now the rain had finished. He made sure to keep out of sight of the road. Lost in a mind of his own, Jesse ran through Thatcher's training regimen. The wound lessened in pain as the rest of his body ached instead. After finishing the gruelling drills, Jesse was about to go through his own personal regiment of tasks before he spotted someone standing in the shadow of the barn doors.

Faircastle was up and about and had heard the faint splashing of someone moving outside. His face broke into a smile when he saw his one of his best fighters training outside. He paused for a moment, thinking how much the kid was similar to Thatcher. Jesse stopped drilling himself.

"Go wake everyone!" Faircastle shouted to his fighter. "I want to get back home before nightfall."

Jesse nodded and ran inside to go and rouse everyone.

The pace for the rest of the day was slow going. As soon as they caught sight of Rugged, the pace increased. The fighters were excited about sleeping in their own beds tonight. Jesse noticed towards the end of the march that Faircastle and Raúl were arguing about something. The two veterans were fervently disagreeing with each other. Eventually, the discussion ended with Raúl disappearing off with a scowl on his face. Faircastle turned and caught Jesse's eye as he looked back. The mighty lord gave him a wink before speaking to Jude about something. Rodrigo made Jesse discuss his fight in the palace forcing Jesse to go over every single detail.

"You were lucky that the knife was not poisoned," said Rodrigo. "In an actual battle it could have been. I mean if the guy was a cutthroat."

Jesse considered this for a moment.

"Yeah, you're right. I think the guy was from the streets. By the way he was handling the knives, I don't think he was taught in a dojo," replied Jesse.

"What do you mean?" asked Rodrigo.

"His attacks were not very well calculated, he seemed to move on impulse," answered Jesse.

Rodrigo looked away and nodded.

The returning force made its way back into the town. As they got to the inner town through the wooden palisade, fighters started peeling off to their quarters. By the time they had made it to the palace gate only Faircastle was left with his protection team.

"You guys get off," stated Faircastle as he put his hand on Jesse's shoulder.

"Me and Jesse here have an errand to run."

The other warriors left eager to get home. Jude and Diachi gave Jesse an interested look before leaving themselves.

"Come, young warrior. I have another task for you," said Faircastle.

Jesse at this point was thoroughly shattered; he had barely slept all day and had just finished an arduous trek back home. He needed to dress the wound on his leg. He was starting to worry that the damp may have worsened the condition he was in.

Faircastle led him along the castle wall towards a small hut. Jesse recognised it as they got closer, except this time the inhabitant was not smoking outside.

Lord Faircastle filled the whole doorway as he made his way inside. Jesse followed, afraid to jump to conclusions and disappoint himself. A small voice inside told him there was only one reason that he would be brought here. The old lady was weaving baskets in the corner while humming to herself. She did not even realise that Faircastle had entered and jumped when he spoke to her.

"Good evening, my lady," he said courteously.

The old lady turned to greet them with a wide smile on her face.

"I thought you had forgotten about me," she said.

"You know, I wouldn't dare," said Faircastle, flashing his trademark smile. The two old friends smiled at each other before addressing the younger fighter in the room.

"Are you sure?" asked Mamma Zamora. "It wasn't too long ago that he was here before."

"Indeed," replied Faircastle. "But he has given me no choice."

The bearded ruler said this while looking at Jesse and smiling.

"He is ready to become a lieutenant for my town," he added.

Jesse broke out into a weary smile; all the years of hard work had paid off. He had spent so long working and training for this title. Forevermore he would now be seen as a talented warrior, one who was worthy of such a great title. Now wherever he went on Pangaea Ultima, he would be treated with a great respect. He had joined the upper echelons of society; a feat that many never accomplished.

Jesse collapsed on to the familiar sofa, taking off his travelling cloak to reveal his warrior mark. On his arm emblazoned was the sign of Lord Faircastle, the falchion blade lying diagonal in a circle. Now Jesse's long staff would join it, facing in the other direction, the two weapons crossing in the middle of the circle.

Mamma Zamora set to work completing the lieutenant's mark. Faircastle sat on a stool watching the process take place.

"You have proven your position in my high council, young warrior," said Lord Faircastle.

"You have all the strength and the skill you need. Furthermore, you have the wisdom of when to use either. You have served me faithfully and you have the ability to think for yourself. A trait I always appreciated from your Sensei."

At this, Faircastle looked away, fighting something back. Jesse heard it in his voice. The leader was getting emotional. Jesse had never seen this side of Faircastle before, the ruler was usually fearlessly happy. Faircastle took a moment to compose himself and then grabbed Jesse's free hand.

"Your fealty?" spoke Faircastle.

"Is yours," replied Jesse.

"Your will?" spoke Faircastle.

"Is yours," replied Jesse.

"Your life?" spoke Faircastle.

"Is yours," finished Jesse.

"Make sure you keep your students to this oath," reminded Lord Faircastle.

Then he slipped away outside.

Mamma Zamora was quicker this time as she had less to etch into Jesse's skin. The deed was slightly less painful this time as well. In fact, it helped to deplete the pain in his leg. Jesse thanked her before getting to his feet, a little unsteady. The old woman grabbed his hand tightly and then looked deep into Jesse's eyes.

"Watch his back," she warned.

There was a fire in her eyes that Jesse had never seen before; it gave his heart a shock to see that kind of fortitude. He nodded quickly in response. The old woman turned away; she looked a little shaken. Zamora grabbed her waiting pipe and she inhaled deeply to fight back her nerves.

At this strange interaction, Jesse felt himself remembering Thatcher's words. The elder warrior's voice echoed in his mind.

"If the lord is dead, protect the people."

Jesse turned away, grabbing his equipment to head back to his dojo.

"Perhaps I will see you again," the old woman mused.

Her back turned to Jesse, she appeared to be speaking to herself.

Jesse thought about it for a moment before exiting. He deleted the thought from his mind choosing not to dwell on it anymore. Faircastle had left a few minutes earlier heading back to his castle.

Chapter 30

The physician had been and had instructed Jesse to stay inside resting for three days. The tall thin man had taken a look at Jesse's leg and changed the dressing, applying more pressure.

"You need to do nothing, in order to give your body time to heal," ordered the doctor.

Jesse nodded, happy to be given an opportunity to rest his weary body. The physician glanced quickly at Jesse's upper arm before he left, the recent wound catching his eye. He spotted the freshly forged insignia and then caught Jesse's eyes.

"Will that be all, master?" he asked quite politely.

"Yes. Thank you for your skills," replied Jesse.

The doctor bowed courteously before leaving, allowing Jesse to rest in his dojo.

By the end of the second day though, the young warrior was itching to get out of the building. Ignoring the medical advice, he even did some light upper body training, figuring it would not affect his injured leg.

He was disturbed from his exercises by a visitor. The familiar face of Jude stood at the door when Jesse answered it. The grey-haired warrior sat down with Jesse on the porch of the dojo.

"How've you been?" he asked.

"Oh, not bad," replied Jesse smiling a broad smile.

Jude guessed the source of his happiness. The older fighter glanced at Jesse's arm, the complete brand shining out proud.

"Yeah, Faircastle made a comment yesterday about having four lieutenants. The others thought he made a mistake but I guessed as much. The lord does not make many mistakes. I'm really happy for you."

The old warrior smiled.

"I haven't told anyone yet," said Jesse, peeking a glance at it himself.

"How's the wound?" asked Jude glancing down at the dressing on Jesse's leg.

"A lot better, the medic said that I should put my feet up for a week."

"What was that then?" asked Jude gesturing to where Jesse had been exercising.

"I can't help myself sometimes," said Jesse, a smile slipping onto his face.

"Give yourself the time you need to rest," said Jude. "I don't expect to see you at the palace till next week."

He mock wagged his finger at Jesse.

"Of course, you're going to be giving me the orders from now on."

He mused quietly. Jesse did not comment knowing this might have been a touchy subject for Jude.

Eventually, the older warrior shook himself before getting to his feet.

"I need to head back," he said. "I've left Weaver and Diachi in charge. Who knows how long that will last?"

He smiled to himself.

"Thanks for coming," replied Jesse, unsure how Jude felt about his appointment to lieutenant.

"I'm happy for you," said Jude and the elder fighter turned away making his way back to the high street.

Jesse watched him go, not returning to his exercise.

On the third day Jesse sat outside the dojo watching the main road. He could make out the muddy highway from in between two buildings. He saw Master Manish arrive and then leave an hour later, travelling back to his stationed post at Bat's Anchorage. The leader of the dojo wore a look of extreme frustration as he headed back.

Jesse flagged down a street urchin who was scrabbling around the back of one of the buildings. The child had long blond hair coated with mud and dirt. The urchin was only too happy to go and run errands for him, in return for a small amount of change. And as the unkempt boy disappeared around the building on his way to the baker with an order, it dawned on Jesse that he was in a similar place when he was the boy's age. He thought back on the training and the regime he had followed in order to just have a chance of escaping the pattern of poverty he had been born into.

Eventually, the child returned with some thick bread rolls. Jesse caught him eyeing the rolls hungrily. The Lieutenant sent him on his way with a roll and the rest of the change. That would make the child's week.

Jesse spent a quiet evening eating some thin stew with his bread rolls. He got an early night, eager to go and assume the new responsibilities for his rank. He didn't need to be fighting fit to complete all tasks. The first thing he would do is get permission to order refurbishments on his dojo.

Jesse rose in the late morning and as he made his way up the hill, he realised that everyone he was passing was staring at him. Apparently, word had got out about his new appointment. A rich merchant passed him in the road and whipped his hat off as Jesse passed. The portly man bowed low as the Lieutenant passed. It all felt quite alien to Jesse.

At the palace gate the warriors from the Khopesh clan saluted him as he entered after confirming Jesse's mark. Jesse automatically headed for Faircastle's quarters but he found Weaver and Hesutu blocking the door.

"No entry," said Hesutu.

"What?" questioned Jesse, incredulously, assuming it was a joke.

Jude came out of the room ready to answer the question.

"I'm afraid you are not allowed access to Lord Faircastle's quarters anymore," he said.

"Congratulations," said Hesutu, grabbing Jesse's hand and shaking it furiously. The tall fighter was beaming with delight at his comrade's good fortune. Weaver nodded at Jesse with a small smile on his face.

"We can't give you access anymore, now you are a lieutenant," said Jude, explaining the situation.

"Oh!" said Jesse.

He had not considered that his new title would hinder him, but as a lieutenant he was a leader in the city and also a potential threat to Faircastle. Rebellions nearly always started from a lieutenant wanting a change in leadership. While lieutenants were critical for a leader to show their strength, they were also a potential threat to their authority.

Jesse knew where Faircastle would be at this time and headed towards the dining hall. Waiting on the table was a wonderful selection of food, ready for Lord Faircastle, his usual breakfast.

While the mighty lord made sure he was always fighting fit, he also enjoyed his food. Soon enough, the side door to the chamber burst open and Lord

Faircastle entered. Jude, Hesutu and Weaver followed. Faircastle was happy to see his new lieutenant and he sat down at his usual seat at the end of the table. Jesse smiled at him back.

"Good morning to you," said Lord Faircastle. "Are you feeling better?"

"I am, thank you, my lord," Jesse replied.

Lord Faircastle grabbed a turkey leg and started eating. He gestured for Jesse to join him. Jesse took his time selecting something to eat. The sugared bread looked magnificent and after all the years Jesse spent delivering the treats, he had developed a real fondness for the food.

Jesse selected a bread roll with caramelised sugar on the top. He did not notice the glances Jude and Weaver were giving each other. The young lieutenant was about to tuck in when something happened.

Lord Faircastle's head hit the table with a dull thud. His whole body went limp and he slid off his chair, hitting the floor hard.

A few things happened instantaneously. Jude and Hesutu drew their swords immediately and started forward towards Faircastle. Jesse leapt up, initially reacting to Faircastle but he caught sight of the two warriors moving. Weaver was reacting slowly to the situation. The warrior was standing by the door; his hand fell down to grab his weapon.

Jude spun and drove his blade into the side of Hesutu. The tall silent warrior fell to the floor bleeding. He lifted his hand to block the next attack from his leader. His overly large hand held the hilt of the blade tightly, halting Jude's second attack, but allowing the blade to cut into the palm. He did not see the second traitor. Weaver leapt forward and delivered a cruel blow to his exposed back. Jesse leapt over the table, unsure as to what was going on; but his lord was in danger.

Jesse heard the warning bell tolling down the hill. The bell was signalled at the presence of a hostile force. This was no coincidence.

Jude started forward towards Faircastle lying on the floor; the large warrior was completely unconscious, unaware of what was happening to his beloved town. Jesse flashed the end of his staff at Jude to keep him back. Weaver took a step back instinctively, giving Jesse the opportunity to block their access to Lord Faircastle. Jesse stood between the two traitors and Faircastle. The body of Hesutu lay discarded and bleeding on the floor.

"Give me Faircastle now!" ordered Jude.

He walked in front of Weaver, striding forward menacingly.

"No!" replied Jesse.

He was now looking for potential exits; he did not fancy having to fight both of them on his own.

"Guards!" Jesse shouted; hopeful the usual guards would come bursting through to their lord's defence. No one came. Hesutu gave a cough before more blood spewed out of mouth. Then he moved no more, Jesse was on his own.

"He has had this coming for years!"

Jude sneered. He was now moving round Jesse and Weaver moved around his slain comrade, both with their swords drawn.

"Is this because he picked you over Raúl?" questioned Jesse; trying to buy time before they attacked.

His mind thought through several different plans of attack.

Jude's face broke into a look of disgust.

"You think like a child, how could he have made you a lieutenant before me?"

At that moment, Jude attacked. Jesse blocked the initial stroke, his metal staff making the blade spin away. Jesse had to step back to avoid Weaver's attack. He found himself backing into Lord Faircastle who was still out cold. There was nowhere else to move. He had to go on the offensive.

He launched a low attack moving into an uppercut aimed at Weaver. The warrior blocked the attack with both hands on his blade. Jesse moved his head forward, dodging Jude's slice by an inch. The young lieutenant brought his staff through and caught Weaver's right hand. The warrior retracted his appendage, crying out as one of his fingers broke. Jesse brought the other side of his staff backwards forcing Jude to duck underneath.

Jesse stepped forward with his staff, avoiding the incoming attack from Jude and focussed on Weaver. Jesse sent out two attacks. The first his opponent blocked but the second broke through. Jesse had altered the angle of the second attack so it was off kilter to the other one. Weaver predicted incorrectly and the staff met the side of his face. The warrior fell back, cracking his head on the table as he fell. Jesse spun away to avoid Jude following up. One threat was dealt with; but he had given up control of Faircastle.

Jude leered over Faircastle before moving to stab the sleeping giant. Jesse flicked his staff and it caught the edge of a plate lying on the table, causing it to soar through the air right at Jude. The experienced warrior saw the movement from the corner of his eye and he turned his head to meet the projectile. The heavy pottery plate hit him in the forehead. Jesse followed the trajectory of the object and attacked forward, catching Jude in the stomach. The warrior fell backwards but stayed on his feet.

Jesse stood over Faircastle triumphantly; he had regained possession of the high value target. Blood poured down Jude's face from the open wound on his forehead. It slid down into the warriors snarling mouth. Jude spat out the blood onto the floor. The experienced warrior was no fool; he could not beat the long staff fighter on his own.

"You will not get out of the city alive!"

He spat before turning and disappearing through one of the doors. As the door closed, Jesse spotted that there were no guards for some reason. They were meant to be Falchion warriors on detail today, did that mean that the entire dojo was in on the rebellion? He needed more information.

Turning quickly, Jesse raced over to Lord Faircastle. He could still hear the warning bell sounding; at least someone was putting up a fight. Jesse grabbed the fallen lord and sat him up in his chair. The large bearded man was sound asleep but at least he was still breathing. Jesse tried wetting his face but the giant man was not reacting.

Hesutu's body was leaking blood and the pool forming around him was starting to encroach across the room. Jesse grabbed Weaver by the scruff of the neck and sat him on another chair. The warrior was still out cold.

Not for much longer, thought Jesse, bringing the end of his staff down on the traitorous warrior's hand. The man awoke, screaming and clutching his shattered wrist.

"What is going on?" demanded Jesse.

"A mutiny," replied Weaver, spitting through the pain.

He wore a crooked smile.

"You are going to start making sense or I will start breaking more things!" threatened Jesse.

The injured warrior seemed to reconsider for a moment.

Then Jesse brought his staff down again and the stubborn coward gave up.

"We made a deal with Raúl. He would be lord and Jude would get to lead the dojo".

"Wait. What about the other dojos?" questioned Jesse.

Perhaps there would be some assistance for him.

"What of them? The Dao clan is out of the city and the Khopesh clan is too small," remarked Weaver.

He said this with a pleased smile on his face, while glancing at Hesutu's body on the floor.

"You stupid child, if you hadn't won that duel in Pretoria then Faircastle would have agreed the Baron's initial price."

The smile turned into a hateful look.

"The Baron finally agreed to accept Raúl's offer, with Faircastle giving him no choice on the price. We've been trying to get his assistance for months, but this was finally the tipping point."

Weaver spat blood out of his mouth, aiming it towards the lord.

"He is sending more troops to aid us. This is Faircastle's death day."

Weaver started laughing to himself trying to mask the pain he was in.

Jesse considered his options. Could he manage to get Faircastle out of the city? The warning bell must have been sounded by the town guard spotting the Baron's troops. Lady Emma was in play, she would have probably been sent to defend the city from the invading forces. The real problem was the Falchion dojo that could make their way through the city killing any defending forces. Lady Emma stood very little chance; she had less than half of the force of the Falchion dojo. No reinforcements were coming from Master Manish; all his warriors were stationed most of a day away.

The young lieutenant stood there considering his options. One thing was for sure he didn't need this traitorous coward. Weaver was still laughing to himself, a little delirious. Jesse spun, catching the warrior in the face and causing the chair to fall over backwards. Weaver was lying on the floor, silent. Jesse did not care to check if he was still breathing or not. He was going to have to do something drastic to wake up Lord Faircastle. He needed his lord to be awake. The large man was too heavy for him to carry all the way down the hill.

"Apologies, my lord," he said, before hitting Faircastle in the stomach, winding him and trying to shock him awake. The large man's eyes filtered open.

"Drink," he said sleepily.

Jesse looked around the table; he was not sure whether they had laced the drinks with the sleeping agent. Faircastle was well known to favour the alcoholic beverages, so Jesse guessed the water had probably been left. Jesse tasted the translucent liquid. It seemed fine; he was going to have to chance it. He poured Faircastle a drink and then helped him with it. The drugged man was struggling to grip the flagon. Lord Faircastle drank the whole thing down greedily, as if his throat was parched from the desert. He seemed to regain some of his senses.

"What's going on?" he asked.

He looked around the room and heard the warning bell tolling in the background.

"We're under attack," he declared.

Faircastle attempted to get to his feet but collapsed back into his chair; his legs unable to support his giant frame.

"Just take a moment, my lord," replied Jesse and he passed Faircastle another drink of water.

Faircastle sniffed it before it draining it on his own.

"Jude and Raúl have betrayed us. Weaver as well," reported Jesse. "Apparently they made a deal with the Baron."

Lord Faircastle did not react much to this news. Jesse was unsure whether he may have suspected it happening or whether it was the narcotics in his system that caused him to underreact.

"Who is with us?" asked Faircastle, taking it all in.

"Apparently Lady Emma and presumably the town guard. I think Manish is too far away to help us."

Faircastle nodded, taking it all in. He looked to the body of Hesutu on the floor.

"He was loyal," stated Jesse. Lord Faircastle nodded.

"I knew him a good many years," he replied.

They waited together in stony silence for a few minutes while Faircastle gained more control over his body. Jesse wondered what on earth they were going to do. He was glad that he had Lord Faircastle to get through it with.

Eventually, Lord Faircastle staggered to his feet and started moving to leave the room. On the way out he asked, "Is he still breathing?"

Jesse shrugged. Lord Faircastle leaned over Weaver's body, examining the traitorous warrior. With one quick move, he drove his blade into the body.

"Not anymore," he stated.

Jesse caught a glimpse of his lord's face as he led them out of the room. His visage was set in a vengeance seeking snarl, the face of retribution.

Chapter 31

As the two fighters made their way through the castle, Faircastle leaned heavily against Jesse. The palace was completely desolate; all the guards seemed to have disappeared. The first warrior they found was lying by the main door; they were from the Khopesh clan.

"Apparently, Lady Emma has stayed loyal," stated Faircastle, matter-of-factly.

Jesse imagined the mighty warrior was still trying to comprehend the situation they were in. As they opened the main palace door, the defence bell stopped ringing.

Jesse took in the sight before him. The main plaza was a scene of spent chaos. Several soldiers lay slain on the floor. Most of them were from the Khopesh clan; however, Jesse spotted a few fighters from the Falchion dojo. Standing over the slain warriors were five panting traitors with their blades out, slick with blood.

Faircastle leapt forward swiftly, snarling with rage. Jesse followed behind, trying to keep up with the half-doped warrior. The fighters had turned when they had heard the heavy palace door opening. Clearly the warriors that were guarding the palace had been ordered outside and had been slaughtered by a greater force. The first few probably fell before they realised they were being betrayed.

The closest traitor made a move back before seeing Faircastle was hobbling. He smirked smugly and charged forward; confident he could beat an injured fighter. Lord Faircastle stumbled forward, appearing to trip on the sandy floor. It was a ploy. Jesse spotted that the mighty warrior was grasping his weapon tightly. Faircastle reared up and attacked the traitor with one upward swing. The fighter was too slow to block the incoming attack. His face turned to shock as the blade hit him hard. The traitorous man fell, never to rise again.

Jesse leapt forward and dealt with two of the encroaching warriors. The opposing fighters seemed slow and dull-witted compared to Jesse's former opponents. Jesse laid one out flat before turning to realise Faircastle had gutted the other. The ruling lord's forehead and beard was speckled with the blood of his enemies. The remaining warriors turned and fled through the palace gate, heading for apparent safety.

"Apparently the rest of them are down the hill," stated Faircastle, drawing himself to his full height.

"Let's go and purge the city of this scum."

Jesse was starting to feel very worried for Faircastle. He had seen the lord get angry before but never like this. Faircastle had shown flashes of this anger but never all at once and not for this long. Maybe this was the fighter who had been forged on the incalculable battlefields over the years. The lord's eyes were starting to turn red from the rage coursing through him.

"My lord, maybe we should look for allies to help us?" questioned Jesse.

Faircastle met his eye line, saying nothing. Jesse realised the stupidity of the question. If anyone was still living in the city, they would almost certainly be fleeing the town. Jesse realised the suggestion of retreating would not go down well.

"I'm sure we will meet them on the way down," said Faircastle.

They both knew it was a fallacy but agreed upon it regardless. Honour dictated they fight to defend the city.

At least, thought Jesse, *I'm with the strongest fighter in the city.*

A crow called out across the vacant courtyard as the birds started to descend for their feast.

Faircastle was starting to move akin to his old self. The large warrior was tensing his arm muscles, warming them up for their inevitable use.

As the two fighters got to the palace wall; to make their way through the beautiful wooden gate; they smelled the first taste of the next few hours. The town was burning. The fire was roaring through the outer sections of the town. Several buildings in the upper town were also burning. The buildings were sporadically spread out; implying the lighting of the fires was deliberate.

Faircastle took it all into his stride as he carried down the street walking toward the blazing inferno. Random townspeople were running around screaming, trying to save all their worldly possessions. Jesse saw several wagons piled high with goods but no one to pull them. Scattered on the main road were many corpses. Some were warriors, but they were mainly recruits from the dojos and townspeople. The trainees from the Dao clan lay next to trainees from the

Khopesh clan. The fallen fighters lay next to the duelling wooden weapons they had used to defend themselves.

Every slain fighter Lord Faircastle found darkened his mood. The large fighter was now actively swinging his sword round and round, eager for vengeance. Jesse paced next to him, trying to match his stride.

Suddenly, Faircastle turned and took off towards the sounds of combat. There was fighting going on within the houses to the left of the road. Jesse followed the large fighter as he raced towards the skirmish; all thoughts of drowsiness banished forever. Jesse saw some town guards fighting three traitors from the enemy dojo. Faircastle gave a bellow of rage before crashing right into them. The warriors were forced back, two of them falling to the floor.

"He's supposed to be slain," blurted out one of the traitorous warriors.

"Sorry to disappoint," said Faircastle curtly, before slaying all three of them with two swings of his mighty weapon. Jesse recognised the two people being attacked as guards from the town. He had spoken to them a few times. He stooped to help the two town guards up out of the muck.

"My, lord," announced one of them.

The man was desperately happy to see his lord. His eyes shone with hope.

"We feared you were dead, my lord. That is what they have been announcing in the streets."

"What is happening in my city, Reep?" asked Lord Faircastle, wiping the bloody dirt off the hem of his cloak.

"They attacked a few hours earlier," stated the other town guard.

His eyes shone with the excitement that he had been recognised by this valiant warrior.

"We had been sent reports that Falchion warriors were starting fires in random places in the lower town. We sent guards to find out what was going on and then we saw an enemy force incoming. Word was sent to the Khopesh dojo and the emergency bell. We saw Lady Emma disappear down the hill with her fighters following. But the bell stopped ringing."

The exhausted warrior gestured to his partner.

"We were sent with ten others to go and ring the bell. We found that the traitors had taken control of it. We waited for them to move on while hiding in the shadows. Then we saw Master Raúl making his way through the town, but instead of ordering his fighters to stand down he ordered them to burn the town to the floor."

Jesse looked at Faircastle's reaction to this. The large fighter was listening intently but staring away, down an alley. Jesse saw the experienced fighter tensing the muscles in his broad shoulders tighter and tighter as the report continued.

"After we recaptured the bell, we managed to keep it ringing for as long as possible. We hoped that the wood cutters in the forest may come to aid our defence. More guards and warriors returned and we defended as long as we could. We ran for here, looking for Master Jesse, my lord."

The guard gestured to the building behind Jesse and Faircastle. Jesse realised it was the back of his dojo.

"We hoped that the Master could assist us and we came looking for him. We realised these fighters were about to start burning it down and we stepped in."

The guard finished his report and stood still, wearily.

Jesse realised that there was a slow fire burning its way through the front of his dojo. He raced around the building and shoved his way through the smouldering doorway. Lord Faircastle stood at the entrance watching his young lieutenant run around looking for something. Eventually, Jesse realised where he had left it and ran into the communal quarters. A few of the bunks were burning and Jesse ran past them having only eyes for the wooden quarterstaff lying at the end of the room. The ornate shaft had somehow avoided the majority of the creeping flames.

Jesse hurried his way out of the burning wreck of a building. He coughed loudly several times outside. Faircastle patted him on the back to help the young warrior expel the toxic air from his lungs.

Jesse stood to his feet and slung his master's quarterstaff over his shoulders. He needed to retrieve that for his master's sake. Jesse chose to still carry his metal long-staff as his primary weapon. He looked back at the burning dojo; the dilapidated building had been his home for most of his life. Thatcher had started training him at the age of nine. Jesse could barely imagine what his life would have been like without it. It seemed all of Jesse's life was turning to ash before him.

"Come," commanded Lord Faircastle.

Jesse followed, clueless to how they were going to survive this blazing inferno. They all got back onto the main high street, the two town guards following on behind. They seemed to have armed themselves with two of the training staves from the now ruined Stave dojo. Jesse was not sure but he thought that he had trained both of them at some point. So at least they had some idea of the basics.

The fire was now burning in most of the building; it was being aided by the dry wind blowing in from the south. The embers were travelling from rooftop to rooftop freely with no one attempting to stop them. They passed more bodies of valiant defenders and even a body of a Khopesh warrior recruit. Faircastle knelt by him momentarily in memoriam.

"You did not betray me, friend," he muttered, before getting to his feet.

The squad of defenders continued down the hill and came upon the blacksmith's forge. The blacksmiths were packing up carefully, clearly at ease. Two of the blacksmiths were standing at the entrance keeping guard. They had their forge tattoos clearly displayed, the mark of their trade on show for anyone to see. It clearly identified them as smiths and therefore made them untouchable to anyone. Lord Faircastle nodded at them and they nodded back, both of the parties acknowledging each other. The smiths were getting ready to leave the city and head back to their capital headquarters before being sent somewhere else they were needed.

As they passed the smiths there was a yell as several fighters emerged from one of the vacant dojos. Drawing their weapons, the lead fighter licked his lips, eyeing up his potential prey.

"Come, Likan," declared Faircastle to one of the enemy fighters. "I will teach you the ways of the sword."

The fighter considered the situation for a moment and he seemed to take a small step back.

"You shirk from the opportunity!" Faircastle goaded with a sneer on his face.

Jesse stood next to him, analysing the enemies. They were a mixture of fighters he recognised from the trek to Pretoria and recruits from the dojo he barely knew, although one of the opponents looked familiar to him. The young fighter was eying him up, hungry for the fight.

"Stay back and cover us from behind," Jesse ordered the town guard.

They both nodded, feeling slightly more confident with these two experienced fighters next to them.

The confident attacking warriors surrounded their prey, eager for the taste of fresh blood. All of them were armed with cold steel. Jesse was confused, some of these fighters were without warrior tattoos. How could they all have steel? Maybe Raúl had broken common law and armed uninitiated fighters? Jesse felt a roar of anger swell up into him at this insult. He had earned his steel the right way; how dare these uninitiated dare to try and use them.

Jesse attacked first, lashing out at the closest fighter. The warrior blocked the attack, smiling at the ease of it. Jesse used his enemy's overconfidence to his advantage and attacked from below his opponent's blade. The long-staff flew upwards, aiming for the stomach of the opponent. It caught the unfortunate individual and Jesse finished the contest with an attack to the head. Spinning back, Jesse blocked two attacks from either side. The young warrior caught a view of the fighting going on around him. Faircastle had already bested two fighters disarming one literally. The unfortunate individual was screaming at the stump where his forehand used to be. He collapsed from sudden blood loss seconds later. The screaming only seemed to feed Faircastle's rage and he laughed loudly over it, drinking it in.

Jesse focussed on the two fighters in front of him. The first attacker swung his blade forward; Jesse deflected it back into his second attacker. The fighter had to duck to avoid the attack and Jesse capitalised on that. The traitorous man was caught in the face by the long-stave. He fell to the floor, clutching his broken nose in abject pain. Jesse finished off his other opponent in three moves, forcing him to block a heavy attack and defeating him while he tried to recover his guard. The enemy blade was built for speed not blocking and Jesse exploited it heavily.

Jesse and Faircastle turned to fight the final opponents who were attacking the town guards. Jesse dealt with one swiftly, echoing Faircastle who had dispatched the other a second earlier. Jesse spotted one of the enemy fighters fleeing at full pace down the hill. He finally recognised him as Tareq. He was meant to have been expelled from the town.

"Where have they got all those blades from?" asked Jesse.

"They must have been stockpiling them for such a time as this," replied Faircastle. "Now I see why Raúl wanted more resources for his dojo, and I thought it was because he had the greatest number of students. Apparently, he had been buying more blades on the side."

The fighters carried on down the hill, making their way through the outer gate, heading towards their final fight.

Chapter 32

The four fighters entered the lower town and the familiar sight of shops and businesses appeared. Many of them were a skeleton of their former selves; the fire had been even more wide spread here than in the upper town. Several structures had collapsed into their own foundations and the bodies of numerous townspeople lay all around the ruined town. A few warriors from the traitor dojo appeared from behind one of the buildings. They stared aghast at the weary soot-covered fighters descending the hill. Then one of them led the retreat back down the high street.

"I imagine that they are gathered just outside the lower town," said Lord Faircastle.

His face had morphed once again, this time into a solid slab of fury. He gave little reaction physically to the sight of the massacre in front of him. Jesse saw him eye a slain child lying in the street and the large man picked up the pace. He started uttering curses under his breath as well.

As they made their way through the burnt-out town, more defenders emerged from the ruined houses. They had apparently been hiding in fear of their lives. The sight of their lord and one of his lieutenants flanked by town guard, stirred a new fighting spirit in their hearts. Jesse saw injured town guard and villagers emerge from their wreckage of their ruined town, each clutching whatever weapons they could muster. There were even two warriors from the Khopesh clan who were clutching their precious sickle-swords. One of them was Vulcan. They pushed through the gathering crowd of fighters and marched directly behind Jesse and Faircastle. Jesse looked back at them and they both nodded at him.

Apparently, this was the time he had earned their respect. Jesse found a small irony in that. They were almost certainly walking to their doom. They were up against most of the Falchion Dojo and potentially a foreign invading force, which they were yet to identify.

The crowd of defenders filled with men, women and elders as they strode down the road. A few of them had even begun chanting war songs. The thick ashy smoke fell aside for them, as they marched with only one thought in their hearts, vengeance for their destroyed town and for the destruction of its people.

After a few minutes, the market district opened up to the residential district. The houses here were also torched. The fires that were burning were almost spent. The blaze must have started here first. Jesse noticed that none of the fighting force was made up of woodcutters. Perhaps they had been captured separately; maybe there were two invading forces. The other force may have headed off the woodcutters as they went to the forest in the morning, similar to them capturing the boats at Bat's Anchorage. His thoughts were interrupted when they caught sight of their quarry.

Most of the Falchion dojo was lined up along the main high street. Standing there were experienced warriors with trainee recruits. In the middle of the fighters was Raúl and alongside him Jude. Jesse only had eyes for the traitorous bodyguard who had fled from them an hour ago. Jude was staring at him straight back.

Lord Faircastle halted the lead and his defence force spread out to fill out the whole high street on either side of him. The war chants persisted, starting to drown out the choking smell of the burned wood and ash. The two forces stood opposite each other for a minute. Apparently, Faircastle was happy to psyche out his opponent as much as possible so he allowed the uneasy pause to continue without saying anything. Jesse caught sight of a familiar face.

Sloth was standing on the front row of the defenders; he was armed with a quarter-stave and ready for war. He caught Jesse looking at him and gave him a nod of acknowledgement before fixing his eyes on the enemies in front of him. Jesse felt slightly guilty; he had completely forgotten about the baker's assistant for several weeks. Sloth had stopped coming to the weekly training sessions and Jesse had been too busy to find out why. Regardless, he was happy his friend was here at the end of it all. Aman swam into his mind, his other great friend, he would not hear of this for several weeks probably. Maybe he would achieve his dream of becoming a master blacksmith.

The war chants continued to ring through the air and it seemed to heal Jesse's fatigue. He felt new strength flowing through his arms. The songs were cut short, however.

Raúl, with a sneer on his face, produced someone from behind him. A large figure was shoved to the floor in front of him. Jude stooped down and ripped the bag off the figure's head. It revealed Lady Emma.

"Cowards, fight me yourself!" she screamed.

Her hands and feet were bound, forcing her to stay on the floor in the ashy dirt.

"Surrender and you can have her," demanded Raúl.

Ignoring the Lieutenant's offer, Faircastle said nothing. He only wore the now-familiar look of anger and vengeance. It seemed etched in, right to the bone.

Raúl seemed frustrated from the lack of reply. Emma did answer him though. She laughed out loud and long.

"He wouldn't surrender to you, pathetic little man!"

She spat at him. Raúl looked down at her; a look of sheer hatred on his face. He drew his blade suddenly and with a quick move laid it against her throat.

"Do you not have the balls to kill me yourself?" Emma announced loudly.

"You can't kill me, you, filthy traitor," she now spoke to Raúl.

"You couldn't best me when I was facing you and you can't best me now!"

She spat again. Raúl raised his blade to attack before a thicker, much longer blade appeared from behind him.

A tall, thin warrior with long blonde hair, dressed in fine battle armour, appeared. He was armed with a ridiculously long blade. The weapon dwarfed Raúl's sword. It was more the length of Jesse's long staff; a Zweihänder. Despite the obvious weight of the weapon, the tall lieutenant acted as if it was nothing. He carried the monumental blade in one hand, pointing it down towards Lady Emma.

The female lieutenant knelt up, looking dead ahead at Lieutenant Marx, her eyes meeting the eyes of the warrior who had bested her. The warrior lifted his Zweihänder above her head. As the blade fell towards its victim, she shouted something.

"Kill them all, to the last man."

Her final order was followed by her two warriors armed with Khopesh blades. Faircastle walked with them. The defending force moved forward. They outnumbered their opposition but they lacked experience and weapons.

Raúl's eyes lit up as the corpse of Lady Emma fell to the floor. He raised his blade up and announced.

"Forward men, wipe them out."

The traitorous lieutenant led the charge himself. Marx fell back, happy to watch the massacre.

The defending force hit the traitors with a sickening crunch. Several townspeople fell at the first contact. The Falchion blades flashed out and found un-armoured opponents. Jesse deftly threw out several fast attacks. His long-staff was aimed at opponent's faces forcing them to fall back with injures. Faircastle was in his element; everywhere his blade went sowed pain and death. Jesse was forced away from his lord. The traitorous force was starting to show their superior fighting technique. Jesse floored two opponents before finding three more stepping over their fallen comrades. The untrained townspeople were falling all over the battlefield.

The traitorous attacking force was starting to envelop the defending force. The slaying of many townspeople was forcing them to fall back slowly. No one fled; they stood to the last man. After another several minutes the problem was becoming more and more dire. Jesse and a handful of defenders were fighting with their back to burnt-out houses. They had been split up from the rest of the force. More fighters poured forward.

Jesse led the group, attacking the first warrior while the three townspeople stood behind him, blocking incoming attacks. Jesse noticed all three of them were armed with quarter staves. Lord Faircastle was fighting with a handful of town guard and one of the Khopesh warriors. The other had fallen earlier to Raúl's blade. Faircastle carried on meting out death amongst his opponents; the giant man slashing and blocking, seemingly at the same time. His beard was now a mixture of red and the familiar brown; his eyes a terror to behold. They were drowned in red and fury.

Jesse was starting to lose ground again when a fighter broke through the attacking troop; it was Sloth. The small fighter had attacked from behind, braining two opponents to battle through to his friend. Apparently, he was talented with a long-staff. His small stature disguised the speed he could attack at. Jesse saw him defeat one of the bullies at the training lesson. The unfortunate opponent fell to the floor with a severe head wound. There was a small pause as Jude appeared from the line of attackers. He wore a look of anger as he eyed up Jesse. The traitorous man moved forward but found himself defending off Sloth. Jesse tried to jump forward to help his friend, but found himself trapped by two enemy warriors, eager to draw some of his blood.

Sloth and Jude's fight was short and brief. The vastly more experienced fighter defended until Sloth's footwork invariably let him down. Then Jude struck. Sloth fell to the floor, bleeding severely from the arm, his staff falling. Jude kicked it away, out of reach.

Jesse charged forward, launching his metallic weapon through the air at his opponent's face. The fighter did not expect it and it struck his face hard, flooring him. Jesse swung Thatcher's wooden weapon off his back and charged forward to burst through to protect his friend.

Aman's word ringing in his ears, 'Just remember to keep an eye out for our friend.' Jude turned and saw Jesse's desperation. He smirked before striking swiftly to slay his inexperienced opponent.

A foul smile emerged on Jude's face. He had got one over his opponent. Jesse collapsed on the floor next to his friend. He had known Sloth since his time on the street. He had been looking out for him for years. His guilt for ignoring his friend for the last two months mixed with the great feeling of loss in his soul. The other three defenders behind him had retrieved his metallic weapon. The traitorous attackers had paused their onslaught briefly on Jude's orders. Faircastle was still fighting in the background with an ever-dwindling force.

But for Jesse, he no longer cared. He only had eyes or thoughts for his opponent. The malicious smile was still plastered on Jude's face. Jesse rose to his feet, saying nothing. He took his long staff back but hung it behind him, preferring to use his Sensei's wooden weapon. Jude stood still, watching his opponent with a mocking smile on his face and in his eyes.

"Are you ready for me, Jesse?" he asked.

Jesse said nothing, preferring to not give him the satisfaction. He spun his staff around himself and then positioned, ready for the incoming attack, his staff behind him at an angle.

Jude passed his weapon to one hand and then to the other, before launching forward. The attacks came in thick and fast and Jesse had to react quickly. The skirmish forced Jesse back between two of the houses. The other fighters carried on their slaughter. Without Jesse, the defenders fell to the last man.

Lord Faircastle continued on his reign of terror aiming for one individual. Finally, he had found himself the traitor he had once trusted with so much. Raúl seemed unsure of himself as the larger fighter approached. The Lieutenant had skirted the edge of the combat following his troops as they spilled over the left flank. Now the traitor found himself with his back to the left side of the houses.

Faircastle forced another attack forward, slaying the final opposition to his revenge. The unfortunate opponent fell into the now thick mud oozing along the ground.

Raúl blocked the first attack confidently as the incoming strike was not as fast or as strong as he expected. The next attack increased in power and speed. Raúl barely blocked that one and then he had to dodge the next. He ducked underneath and attacked. His blade penetrated his lord's chest. Faircastle made no attempt to block the blade; he wanted this scum closer. With a large fist he caught his lieutenant in the face. Raúl tasted the blood and ash in his mouth as he hit the floor hard; his weapon spinning away from the force of the impact.

Lord Faircastle stepped over his quarry ready to complete the kill. As the blow rained down, a large blade slipped out once again to block the attack. Raúl covered his head with his hands, expecting the blow to hit. He looked up when nothing happened. Lord Faircastle was struggling to force his blade down; his sword was fighting against a confident Marx. The younger fighter slid into the combat replacing the cowed Raúl.

"Sorry. I can't have you kill him I'm afraid. I have my orders you see and apparently this fool needs to live. The Baron has plans with him," said Marx.

The words slid off his tongue with the air of superiority. Lord Faircastle ignored him and attacked straight at Raúl again, this time with a sweep of both arms. Calamity deflected the stroke and Marx now stood directly in the way. His well-tailored armour was completely untouched by the mass of mud, ash and blood flying everywhere else. The rest of his dojo surrounded them both. Thirty warriors each armed with a lethal Zweihänder. They carried their blades slung over their shoulders, many of them leering over the casualties. Their blades were clean, having chosen to not get involved with the conflict. Each of them wore their leather armour confidently and a few wore flowing capes as well.

Lord Faircastle heaved a massive sigh; he was going to have to deal with this annoyance before he could dispatch justice.

Jesse meanwhile was completely unattached from the fight he was in. While his body was fighting in the deadly duel, his mind was full of thoughts of loss and regret; memories of Sloth and Thatcher. The traitors face swam through his mind. One memory would end and another would replace it. He remembered the good times and the bad times he spent with both of them. What a waste of time his life had been. All his hard work and training and he would die here. On this muddy battlefield surrounded by dead comrades and all of his friends and family gone or deceased.

Jude was starting to get angrier and angrier. As well as his weapon failing to find his opponent, he was also failing to damage the wooden weapon that Jesse was using. How could the wooden weapon withstand so much damage? Unbeknownst to him, Jesse was blocking all of the attacks in such a way that the force of the attack was being deflected away back at Jude or was negated by Jesse's blocking style; his well-trained arms buffering all the blows; allowing the wooden weapon to take little to no damage.

"Die already!"

He spat at the young lieutenant.

Jesse awoke from his stupor; at least defeating this scum would achieve justice for some of the wrongs rained down today. Almost as if moving in slow motion, Jesse stepped underneath. Jude reacted too slowly as the end of the wooden weapon flashed from below him. The quarter-stave found its mark and Jude spat out a tooth. Jesse then launched forward driving his opponent into one of the destroyed houses. One enemy warrior followed on behind, watching the duel but another shadowy figure loitered as well. The invading force surged forward to deal with the final ebbs of the defence.

Jesse blocked the incoming defensive attack easily and stepped forward, catching Jude in the jaw. There was a cracking noise as Jude collapsed to the floor; his hand clutching at his mouth. Jesse stepped forward again launching another attack mercilessly. Jude attempted to block but Jesse caught the blade perfectly forcing it to fly off into a pile of smouldering wood. Jude's eye glared furiously at his opponent.

"He was never going to make me a lieutenant!" he whined out loud through gritted teeth.

"Maybe you weren't ready for it," replied Jesse, before finishing the traitor with a swift blow. Jude fell to the floor, shattered never to rise again. Jesse collapsed from the effort as the two spectators moved forward. The cutlass warrior got there first.

"Get up quick," the warrior stated urgently.

Jesse looked up to see Rodrigo standing over him. The young fighter was looking desperately around for anyone else watching. All Jesse could see was the neatness of Rodrigo's clothes; apparently the young fighter had not been involved in the day's events much. There was no trace of errant blood or of the tell-tale sign of black smoke lingering on his clothes.

"Get up," Rodrigo said again, attempting to pull his compatriot to his feet. The other spectator slid in to help.

"I'll get him out," muttered Daichi. The mysterious warrior had appeared from nowhere.

"You have to get him away from here fast," urged Rodrigo.

"I will, pass me his staff," said Daichi, impatiently.

The Falchion warrior passed the long weapon over to Daichi who used it to steady himself and Jesse, who was now leaning on his shoulder. Jesse was clearly out of it, his mind collapsed from the effort. His body carried on moving forward as Daichi hurried them through a collapsed wall and into the remnants of the shattered housing district.

Rodrigo cast his eyes around, looking for something and found what he was looking for; an errant staff that was lying in between the two ruined dwellings. He grabbed one end and stuffed it into a fiery mound that was burning brightly. The fire burst into life again with the adage of fresh wood. Rodrigo tore it out before all the staff had burned away and then he traipsed back to the massacre in the street. At least he had something to try to prove Jesse's demise.

Faircastle, for the first time in a few decades, was being forced to work hard. His much younger opponent was barely breaking a sweat. Somehow Marx was fighting as if his weapon was a fifth of its actual weight. The young fighter was keeping pace with the lord and even surpassing him. Faircastle began to feel the strain of reducing stamina and the ebbs of the drug agent he had drank before. His arms were slowing and his technique was beginning to dull. Marx sensed the opportunity but was smart enough to wait for the odds to be more in his favour. He waited patiently for the opportune time to strike.

A few minutes later it came, Faircastle blocked an attack poorly leaving him open to a swift attack. Marx moved so fast it was as if the very laws of physics were oblivious to him. He brought the handle of his monstrous blade up and hit Faircastle in the face. The mighty warrior collapsed, bested. Faircastle knew the end was near. He drove his blade into the dirt and leaned on it. He looked up at the next generation of warrior and spoke.

"You will kill him if you have the opportunity, right?"

Marx paused for a moment, a whisper of a smile on his face before replying. "Baron willing."

Lord Faircastle smirked at the retort and a smile once more lit up on his face through the smear of blood and mud. Just in time for the Zweihänder to come sweeping down.

Epilogue

Jesse woke to find the rain hitting his face. He was resting in a wooden chair facing a ruined fireplace. The walls of the building were broken down and two of them were missing entirely. Jesse started for a moment, realising he was missing his fighting staves, but he quickly spotted them resting on the wall opposite him.

Daichi entered the room from the doorway that was teetering precariously. He dumped several bags on the floor in front of Jesse. One fell open and several apples fell out and rolled onto the floor. Diachi tutted at this and stooped to grab them. He spotted Jesse was conscious and looked up at him.

"Eat quickly; we've got a long journey ahead of us."

As he said this, he tossed Jesse one of the apples. Jesse bit into it; he was famished.

"What are you talking about?" replied Jesse, still feeling quite light-headed.

"We need to get out of here, they will be back to strip this town of everything it is worth," warned Daichi.

His face wore a look of confirmation and acceptance as if he had lived through this situation before.

"Where were you?" asked Jesse.

"I was delivering a message to Manish on Jude's orders," replied Daichi. "I think we can both work out why that was."

"Are we going to meet up with the survivors?" asked Jesse.

Diachi had turned to sort out the travelling bags but looked in astonishment at Jesse.

"If anyone survived, they will be running for the hills. Which is what we should be doing right about now," the warrior replied.

"We have a duty…" began Jesse.

"Faircastle is dead," replied Diachi interrupting. "I found his body a few hours ago, your oath is completed. We are alone."

Jesse considered the situation for a moment while chewing a large piece of apple. With the reigning lord dead, he now had but one choice.

"You mean we are…" he replied.

He did not finish the sentence, tailing off.

Diachi nodded before grabbing the metal long stave and attaching it to the backpack Jesse would be carrying.

Jesse took a moment to recognise the situation he was in before rising to his feet.

At first, he was a little unsteady, but with the aid of Thatcher's wooden staff he drew himself up to his full height. Diachi turned to leave the ruined building and Jesse followed. He tossed the apple core to the other end of the room and swung his backpack over his shoulders. The two warriors walked through the town. At first, Jesse looked around for any potential ambush or any errant enemies hanging around. The sun was rising in the sky so he must have slept through the night; giving his enemies plenty of time to have left.

Diachi walked south, clearly intent on going the opposite way of any opposition. As they left the town of Rugged, Jesse looked back at the huge forest at the other side of the town. Diachi caught him looking.

"They led the woodcutters away in chains, last night," he said.

Jesse nodded. They would be a valuable asset for any ambitious town. He tore his eyes away from the only home he had known, the town of Rugged. He fixed his eyes forward and followed Diachi heading south.

With the fires of their burnt home pouring smoke behind them, the two Ronin made their way south to an uncertain future.

Tales From the Super Continent – Ronin